FORGED
IN
Flames

FORGED IN *Flames*

MADE OF STEEL SERIES - BOOK 2

IVY SMOAK

This book is a work of fiction. Names, characters, places, and incidents are fictitious. Any resemblance to actual persons, living or dead, events, or locales is purely coincidental.

ISBN: 978-1547214310

Cover art copyright © 2020 by Ivy Smoak

2020 Edition

To not getting swallowed in the darkness. We're all stronger than we realize.

CHAPTER 1
16 Years Old
Flashback

This can't be happening. I tried to take a deep breath as I paced back and forth in the small restroom. My feet stopped when I caught my reflection in the mirror. I barely recognized the person staring back at me. The newest bruise along my jaw was clearly showing through my foundation. My cheeks were hollow. I brushed away my tears with my fingertips and turned away from the mirror.

No matter how much I delayed looking, I knew it was inevitable. I could feel the change. I swallowed hard and closed my eyes tight. For years I had thought my life couldn't get any worse. But this was worse. I wanted to crumple down onto the tiled floor. I'd rather my life end right now than face this alone. I was terrified to handle this on my own. It felt like I was hyperventilating. All I needed to do was open my eyes and look down. Then I'd know. I could plan what to do next. But I really didn't need to see the results. I could feel it.

Please, please, please let me be imagining this. I opened up my eyes and looked at the ceiling. Part of me wanted to pray. But I knew no one would hear my pleas. Even when I screamed no one could hear me. I took a deep breath and turned back toward the bathroom sink. Nothing could get worse, could it? If anything, maybe Don would be nicer to me. Maybe this would be a good thing. He wouldn't hurt me once he found out. Would he?

Someone knocked on the restroom door. "Are you almost done in there?"

I didn't answer. Instead, I slowly looked down. The little plus sign staring back at me felt like a stab in the heart. *No. No, no, no.* I tried to wipe my tears away again. I couldn't even protect myself from him. How was I supposed to protect a baby?

All I could hear was my own heartbeat. I felt sick. But for the first time in a few days, it wasn't because I needed to throw up. I put my hand on my stomach. This baby was going to be half me. That should have felt like a blessing. But all I could think about was that it felt like a curse. Because it was half him too. It felt like a demon was growing inside of me.

"Is anyone even in there?" the lady on the other side of the door said as she jiggled the doorknob.

It felt like my life had just come to a halt. But no one gave a shit about me. I couldn't even remember the last time someone asked me if I was okay. Nobody cared. I had no one. I grabbed the pregnancy test and tossed it in the trash before pushing the bathroom door open.

"Finally," the stranger grumbled as she walked past me.

She didn't see the tears streaming down my face. She didn't see the pain in my eyes. I was invisible. I kept my head down as I walked through the public library. The afternoons I had off after school, I usually came here. It was where I felt safest, surrounded by people, far away from Don. Now it felt like I had tarnished it somehow.

Like I had brought a darkness here. That's how I always felt. It seemed like darkness seeped into the ground every place I stepped. I pushed through the glass doors and quickly walked down the stairs.

Snow was starting to fall. The wind made it dance across my path. I remembered a time when I loved the snow. Now it just reminded me that I had nothing to protect myself against the cold. I wrapped my arms around myself. My winter jacket felt threadbare against the gusts of wind. A bus was pulling to a stop in front of the library. It wasn't the route home. It would wind around the city, making aimless stops for a few hours, before stopping back at the library. Before I could overthink it, I climbed up the bus stairs. Staring out the window of a moving bus had always been calming. It was like the possibility of escape was right at my fingertips. Not that I'd ever try that again.

As I made my way down the aisle, I told myself that I could think it all through on the ride. I could figure out what I needed to do. I shook my head as I sat down in the back of the bus. I didn't need time to think. I knew exactly why I had gotten onto this bus. I knew exactly what stops it made. Yes, this baby was half mine. But it was half monster too. The doors closed and the bus pulled back onto the street.

I knew what I had to do.

***

The doctor pulled up a chair and sat down beside the examination table. "Are you sure that's the route you want to take?" She stared at me like she detested me. Like I was the sinner in this situation. Like it was my fault. "There are so many couples out there that would love to adopt a baby."

It's a demon inside of me. "I'm sure." But I wasn't sure. I had sat in the waiting room for over an hour, with the question rolling around in my head. *It's half me.* My whole family was dead. This baby was a piece of me. How could I do this? How could I get rid of it?

She nodded. "You are early enough to get medication instead of surgery, which minimizes the risks involved. But it is expensive." She was no longer looking at me, just staring down at her clipboard. But I could still see the look of disgust on her face. She loathed me. And she should. I loathed myself.

I can't do this. It's half me. "How expensive?" I said, instead of voicing my concerns.

"It would be about $600 without complications."

How the hell was I supposed to get $600? Did I even want to?

"And you're only 16, correct?"

I nodded my head. I was trying to do the calculations in my mind. I barely made enough money for food. I was biting my lip so hard that I started to taste blood.

"So you'll need to have parental consent in order to terminate the pregnancy."

The calculations in my mind came to a halt. *Terminate the pregnancy.* The words sounded harsh to my ears. I put my hand on my stomach. "My parents are dead." What was I doing here? How could I even consider abandoning this baby the way my parents abandoned me? I loved them. I missed them every day. But I fucking hated them for leaving me to face this all alone. They left me. Just like my grandmother had left me. Just like Miles had left me. *Miles.* Why the hell was I thinking about Miles? I hadn't heard from him in years.

She pressed her lips together. "I'm sorry to hear that, Summer. But that means you'll need consent from your guardian then. Anyone under 18 needs written consent."

I shook my head. "I can't get consent from my guardian." *No matter what choice I make, he can't know.* If I kept the baby, I needed to get the hell out of Colorado. And if I decided to get rid of it, he'd kill me, or at least try. The last time he had put his hands around my neck, I had gone to the police. I had shown them the bruises. No one listened to me. They sent me back home to the monster himself. A doctor who clearly despised me wouldn't listen to me. She had already written me off. I hated the look in her eyes. I hated that she was judging me when she knew nothing.

"I know that situations like this may seem hard at first," the doctor said. "But I'm sure your guardian will learn to accept this. You just need to give it time."

Time. I knew why I had been thinking about Miles. Because I had pictured starting a life with him. I had pictured our kids and a house in the suburbs with a white picket fence. Time had robbed me of that life. God, I was so naive. But still, I found myself placing my hand on the center of my chest where the pendant he had given me rested. I loved the smallest constellations. I couldn't give up on the tiny baby inside of me. I wasn't going to become a monster like Don. I wouldn't let him turn me into one.

I quickly stood up. "I'm sorry, this was a mistake."

The doctor looked relieved. "Does that mean you'll consider adoption? You're only 6 weeks along. You have time to decide."

Time. My heartbeat quickened. I wouldn't let anyone rob me of anything else in my life. But I was running out of time.

"Summer?" she called after me.

I walked out of the clinic without looking back.

CHAPTER 2

I had tried to leave once before. But Don had found me. Weeks of planning and he had found me before I even left the state. He had nearly killed me that night. After that, I never tried again.

I threw my worn copy of Harry Potter and the Sorcerer's Stone down on top of my clothes and zipped my backpack shut. It was one of the last things my father had given me. And one day I'd give it to my baby.

This time there was no planning. I just had to get as far away from Don as possible. For once in my life, I needed to be strong. The next bus was leaving in 20 minutes. Then I'd be free.

We'd be free. "We're going to be okay," I whispered and placed my hand on my stomach. "Everything's going to be okay." Suddenly, he didn't feel like a monster anymore. *He.* Was it a little boy? Maybe he'd have my dad's smile. Maybe he'd have my nose that I got from my mother. He was going to be good. He was going to be so good. I'd make sure of it. But first I had to save him from this life.

"I'm sorry," I whispered as I slung my backpack over my shoulder. "I'm sorry that I doubted you." I wasn't sure how it happened, but this baby had suddenly gone from one of the worst things in my life to one of the best. He was a blessing in disguise. And I'd never let anything happen to him.

David. Thinking of my father's name gave me a sense of peace. If it was a boy, I'd name him David. And if it was a girl, I'd name her Jennifer after my mom. This baby was a piece of me, but it would be a piece of them too. I'd have a family again. Maybe I'd feel whole again too.

I ran down the stairs two at a time. Don would be home any minute. It was now or never. For the first time in years, I had hope. That's what this baby was. Hope. This baby was exactly what I needed. I suddenly had a purpose again. I opened up the back door and froze.

Don was standing there with a cigarette in his hand. His breath puffed out in a cloud in front of his face. He smiled. "Where do you think you're going?" He took another long draw from his cigarette. I could barely see his face with all the smoke. He put the cigarette out against the railing and flicked it at me.

The act made me flinch. I had felt the butt of his cigarette being put out on my skin before. Everything he did terrified me.

My reaction made his smile grow. "I'll ask again, doll. Where do you think you're going?"

"The library. I have a test tomorrow and I need to study." The snow had started to pick up, and all I could hear was silence. There were no cars going by or dogs barking. It was like a quiet blanket had settled around us. There was nothing scarier than silence. It meant no one was around to hear my screams.

"Get back inside." He put his hand on my forearm.

I cringed under his touch. His skin always felt like fire. Everything about him burned with flames, threatening to end my life at any moment. He was unpredictable. Deadly.

Uncontrollable. And I could see it in his eyes tonight. The flames were dancing everywhere.

"I..."

"Now. Don't make me ask again."

"I have to study. I'll be back in a few hours."

He smiled again. "Why? So you can get a scholarship and leave? It's not happening, Summer. We've already talked about this. You're staying right here. Who else will protect you, anyway, huh? I'm all you have. Now get inside." His voice had dropped an octave. Threatening. Demanding. Terrifying.

Protect me? I needed protection because of him. God, I hated him. I hated everything about him. I could go to whatever damn college I pleased. I'd save enough money and provide a good life for my baby. And I'd never see his smug face again. His flames were catching on to me. It was like I had no control over it. But I had never been good at playing with fire.

The snowy night was completely silent as we both stared at each other. His eyes wandered over my body, stopping on my stomach. I swallowed hard. It only took me a moment to figure out that he knew. *How the fuck does he know?*

I tried to step around him but he put his hand on the center of my chest, pushing my back against the brick wall of the house. "You think I wouldn't find out? You know better than that, doll."

I could smell the alcohol on his breath. I wasn't sure there was anything he liked doing more than hurting me. But when he was drunk, he seemed to lose all control. He was worse than any villain I had read about. A hundred times worse. He wasn't even human when he drank. And I could see it in his eyes tonight. The devil himself was staring back at me. He wanted me dead.

"Please, Don." My voice sounded pathetic. I was pleading with someone who could never hear me.

"Please what?"

"Don't hurt me." *Don't hurt us.*

"Maybe you should have thought about that before you got rid of my baby."

What? "I didn't."

He smiled. "There's no point in lying. You know better. That'll just make this worse for you." He put his hand on the side of my face.

"Don't touch me!" I screamed into the silence. *Fire.* I knew better than to let his flames catch on to me. I shouldn't have said anything at all.

He put his hand over my mouth. He looked surprised by my words, but it just added to the force of his hand. "Or what? You'll fight back?" The smile had returned to his face. "You know that I love when you fight back."

Everything about him was twisted.

"You're staying here. And if you don't want my kids, fine. Let's just make it easier on you, shall we?" He pulled a knife out of his pocket.

Get off of me!

Pure evil. There were no other words to describe the look on his face.

"I would never want someone like you to bear my children anyway."

I clawed at the hand over my mouth.

"You're worthless."

He slid his hand up higher, blocking the air from entering my nose too.

"You're weak."

I couldn't breathe. I kicked his shin, but it just made him press his body more firmly against me. He was hard. He got off on hurting me. I was suffocating. I wrapped my legs around his waist and tried to kick the back of his knees.

He smiled, not moving an inch. "You're pathetic."

I reached my hand out and tried to grab his throat. But I was worthless. I was weak. I was pathetic. He didn't even flinch at my touch.

"You're just lucky that you're attractive, because it's the only thing you've got going, doll."

I felt the knife slice into my stomach. The pain was blinding. *My hope. My purpose.* I could feel the life slipping out of me. I was suffocating. But I wasn't worried about myself. He was killing my baby. I couldn't breathe. The pain in my lungs was worse than the pain in my stomach. I tried to scream, but the sounds were muffled.

"Now we don't have to worry about any more accidents."

I bit down on his hand with the remaining strength I had. And I tasted blood. I smelled blood. I just didn't know if it was his or mine.

"Fucking bitch!" He shoved me off the wall.

I caught the railing as I took a huge gulp of air. I had to get away from him. This was my only chance. I started to run down the stairs, but his hands gripped my hair, pulling my face back until my eyes met his. The flames in his eyes burned even brighter.

"I'll give you a five second head start." He shoved me hard down the stairs.

"Help me!" I screamed into the silent night as I fell to my knees, my hands landing in the snow. "Someone help me!" I cried. The fog from my breath curled up in front of me. No one was coming to my rescue. No one could hear my screams. *Get up.* My body wouldn't listen to me. I moved my right hand to touch my stomach. I felt the warmth of blood. I felt the life seeping out of me. *Get up!* I placed my hand back on the ground.

"It's okay," I whispered into the still night. "I'll take care of you. I'll always take care of you."

My legs shook as I got back to my feet. I placed my hand back on my stomach. The front of my jacket was completely soaked in blood. *We're okay.* But I felt dizzy. I tried to run, but instead I stumbled forward.

"Five," Don said somewhere behind me.

"Stay away from me," I choked. I was so dizzy.

"Or what?" He grabbed my arm and turned me to face him.

My hand slid back to my bloody stomach. I could barely keep my eyes open. Every ounce of life had been drained out of me. *We're not okay. I couldn't protect you.* I knew the baby was gone, just like I knew it had been there in the first place. I could feel it. *No.* That was the problem. I couldn't feel it anymore.

"Or what?!" Don spat.

I saw my bloody handprint in the freshly fallen snow as Don shoved me back to the ground. I was everything he had said. Worthless. Weak. Pathetic. I watched the snow slowly fall on top of my bloody handprint. All I could hear in the silent night was the sound of his zipper. My familiar sob as he grabbed my hips. And his grunting.

Or what? My tears seemed to freeze on my cheeks. *I'm going to fucking kill you. I'm going to take everything from you, just like you did to me. And then I'm going to end your life.*

I watched the snow fall until my bloody handprint was no longer visible. I thought I'd feel cold in the snow. But all I could feel were the flames swallowing me whole before everything turned black.

CHAPTER 3
18 Years Old
Present Day - Friday

I took a huge gulp of air as I sat up. *Blood.* I touched my stomach and felt the jagged scar. *It was just a dream.* I tried to catch my breath as the tears welled in my eyes. It felt like I couldn't breathe. Because it wasn't just a dream. I remembered it happening like it was yesterday.

I felt dizzy, as though I was still losing blood. Everything was blurry. I squeezed my eyes shut. *I'm okay.* I tried to steady my breathing as relief washed over me. The memory was painful, but it couldn't hurt me now. Not physically, at least. But God it hurt to remember. I put my hand back on my stomach. Just a scar. No blood. I was safe. Just me. Alone. Always alone.

Fire. It still felt like there were flames inside of me. I wanted to scream. I wanted everything back that was taken from me. I tried to tell myself again that I was okay. But the truth was, I wasn't. I wasn't sure I'd ever be again. *He stole my life.*

I opened my eyes, but everything was still blurry. My head seared with pain. I touched the back of my head where the pain was emanating. There was a huge welt at the base of my skull. My dorm room slowly came into focus.

How did I get here? It felt like I had been sleeping for a long time. All the details seemed to come back in a rush. Don. The twisted game. Joan. I looked down at the inside of my forearm to stare at the bloody message, but it was gone. My arm was wiped clean.

I was disoriented. I put my fingers on my temples. Had I dreamt all of that too? What was happening? I shoved the blankets off of me and climbed out of my bed. I didn't come back here. How the hell did I get back into my room? I spun around.

I couldn't have dreamt all of it. I touched the back of my head again. There was definitely a bruise there from being hit in the back of the head with a gun. It felt like my heart was beating out of my chest. But I had also fallen. I had been in the hospital. Could the bump be from that? Had that even happened? I felt like I was hyperventilating.

"Hey, Sadie. Are you feeling better? I brought you some lunch." Kins walked into the room and set down a dining hall takeout bag on my desk.

It was her. She had to be involved in this. She was the only one with a key to our dorm. I backed away from her until my butt hit my mattress.

"Are you okay?" She frowned.

"I have to go."

"But you just got back."

"How?"

"What do you mean how?" She took a step toward me.

"I didn't fall asleep here." I looked around the room. "I don't know how I got here. How did I get here?" My voice seemed to screech.

"Sadie. I know you're hurting. But screw Eli. Everything is going to be okay." She wrapped her arms around me.

I winced at her touch. I wanted to shove her off of me. I wanted to scream. But instead, I let her hug me. What if I had imagined everything? What if I really was losing my mind?

"I'm really glad you decided not to leave," she said as she released me from her hug. "We're going to get through this together, I promise."

Her words meant nothing to me. No one I had ever met was capable of keeping a promise. "I never left?"

Kins frowned again. "No. You came back a few hours after you stormed out of here. Don't you remember?"

I put my hand on my forehead again. I didn't remember anything after talking to Joan. It all seemed foggy. I had this sinking feeling that I had imagined all of it. There was no box with slippers. There was no message on my arm. Nothing pointed to the fact that it had actually happened. I had been kidnapped and there was no evidence. And it didn't even make any sense. Why would Don kidnap me and not kill me?

"Really, you should eat something. You don't look so good."

Of course I don't look good! I'm losing my mind! I had to find someone from the witness protection program to help me. Anyone. "I'll be back later." I pulled the vigilante's hoodie on and put my cell phone in my pocket.

"Where are you going? I skipped my last class because you said you wanted to hang out. I thought we could talk about what happened with Miles a little more."

When did I tell you all of this? Everything in my gut was screaming that she couldn't be trusted. If I came home last night, I would have remembered talking to her, right? She was making this up. She had to be.

"I'm sorry," I said as I laced my Converses. "I forgot that I had plans."

"Sadie..."

Her words died away as the door closed behind me. I ran down the hall and the stairs until I burst through the front doors of the dorm building. The fresh air helped clear my head. I wasn't crazy. I had been kidnapped. My new identity was compromised. I'd been made. I pulled out my phone and tried Mr. Crawford again. The mocking tone of the woman saying, "this number is no longer in service," echoed in my ears. *Shit.* I typed in "witness protection program New York City" into Google on my phone.

There were a bunch of articles about what it was like to live in the witness protection program from The New Yorker and The New York Times. I didn't need to know what it was like. I was fucking living it. I clicked on a link to the U.S. Marshals Service and scrolled through the contact names. How was the equal employment opportunity contact going to help me? Finally I found a link for local contacts and found the section for New York City. I shouldn't have been surprised that Mr. Crawford's name wasn't on the list. But I was surprised. Was he involved in this too? I didn't think so. He had always tried to help me. What the hell was happening?

I wanted to throw my phone. Instead, I went back to my contacts list, clicked on Mr. Crawford's name, and put my phone to my ear. *Please pickup. Please let him be okay. Please.*

The screeching noise blasted into my ear again. "This number is no longer in service. This number is no longer in service."

Damn it! I turned around in a circle. What was I supposed to do? *God.* I put my hand on the side of my neck. It felt like someone was strangling me again. It felt like I was suffocating. All I wanted to do was find the vigilante's number in my phone. I wanted him to take away my worries and fears. I wanted him to protect me. I wanted him to fix everything I had broken.

But I didn't know him. I looked back at my dorm. I didn't know anyone here. I was in a strange city with a bunch of strangers who I couldn't trust. I didn't have a choice. I had to go to the police. They were the only ones that could help me. They had to.

I started running as fast as I could. I knew where one of their departments was. I had passed it the first day I had met Liza. Maybe I should have looked one up in a less sketchy part of town, but I didn't have time to analyze my decision. I needed answers. I needed help.

By the time I reached the precinct, I was completely out of breath. I pushed through the doors. Part of me expected it to be like a TV show with someone rushing toward me to help. But I knew better than that. I stared at the most likely bullet proof glass separating me from the officers on the other side. No one even looked up at me. I was done being invisible. I was done not being heard. It was their job to serve and protect. I needed protection.

With a deep breath, I stormed up to the glass divider and slammed my fist against it.

An officer on the other side looked up from his computer. "I'll be right with you, ma'am." He looked back down at his screen.

I pounded on the glass again. "It's an emergency!"

He sighed and slowly got up from his desk. And he walked away from me. He fucking walked away from me.

I slammed my fist against the glass again. "Someone is after me. I need help!"

A door opened to the left of the glass. The officer that had walked away was standing there with his arms folded. "This way, then."

I most likely had approached this all wrong. Being demanding and angry wasn't how to get results. They were just going to hate me. I tried to calm down as I followed the officer through the door.

"Wait here." He gestured to a row of chairs. There was a guy with his hands handcuffed to the chair at the end of the row. I wasn't a criminal. I sat down in a chair as far away from the criminal as possible.

Cops bustled around with files, no one glancing at me. A police officer slamming down his desk phone made me turn my head. He looked pissed. Hopefully I wouldn't get him. I needed someone calm and understanding. My stomach dropped when he stood up and approached me.

"I'm Detective Lewis." He put his hand out to me.

I didn't want to touch him. I knew I'd feel flames. Instead of being normal, I tucked my hands under my thighs on the chair. "I'm Sadie Davis."

He lowered his eyebrows slightly as he shoved his hands into his pockets. "What's your emergency?"

"I...I was kidnapped." I knew it sounded crazy. If I was truly kidnapped, I wouldn't be sitting here. He wasn't going to believe me.

He lowered both his eyebrows. "Were you assaulted?"

"Yes. I was hit in the back of the head with a gun. And then I woke up in my dorm room."

He shook his head like my story was unbelievable. "Follow me."

I got up from the chair and followed him to his desk. He gestured to the chair on the other side of the desk from him. I sat down.

"Sadie Davis," he said as he touched the mouse for his computer. "Do you have some ID?"

"Yes, but actually, that's part of the reason that I'm here. My real name is Summer Brooks. I'm in the witness protection program. But my cover's been compromised. And my contact isn't answering his phone. It's been disconnected."

Detective Lewis just stared at me.

"I'm in the program because of my foster father. There's a no contact order between me and him. But he left Colorado and he's in New York. He followed me here even though he wasn't supposed to leave the state. He's awaiting trial."

"Okay, Summer Brooks." He typed something into his computer. "What's your date of birth?"

"I was born on August 15th, 2000."

He typed it into his computer and then leaned back in his chair, like he was waiting for the results to appear. He crossed his arms in front of his chest and just stared at me.

I felt like I needed to fill in some of the blanks. "My foster father kidnapped me last night, with the help of the owner of the Corner Diner, Joan...I don't even know her last name. But she said she had my friends."

He cleared his throat and looked back at the computer screen.

"Alright, Summer Brooks. Born August 15th, 2000 in Sheridan, Wyoming to David and Jennifer Brooks. Is that you?"

"Yes."

He clicked on his mouse and lowered his eyebrows slightly. "She died on October 12th, 2009."

"What?"

"Summer Brooks died of carbon monoxide poisoning the night of October 12th along with her grandmother, Bethany Wagner. Both were dead upon arrival of paramedics."

"My grandmother died of a heart attack on October 12th, 2009. Not carbon monoxide poisoning."

He turned his computer screen to me. "There were blood tests. Both tests detected the poison."

"That's not possible. I'm still alive. I'm sitting right here."

"Look, I get it, okay? Thirsty Thursday? I was in college once. You got drunk, maybe you woke up a little disoriented this morning. You should get back home and get some rest."

I put my hand on my forehead. I couldn't explain what was happening. How could I make him believe me? "I was most recently enrolled in Hanover High School in Telluride, Colorado. Under the name Summer Brooks. You can look it up."

He sighed and typed something else into his computer. "There was no student by that name in the last four years."

"That's not possible."

"Sadie Davis. That's what you said your real name was right?"

"No, that's not..."

"Sadie, I have a caseload full of real problems in this city that actually need my attention. I don't have time to look into whatever bullshit you've been dared to come in here and spill. I need to get back to work."

"But I was kidnapped."

"And did they steal anything from you? Did they threaten you? Did they ask for ransom?"

"I...I don't remember. I can't remember."

"Well, come back if you do. In the meantime..." he gestured to his computer, "I'm busy."

My legs seemed to shake as I stood up. He thought I was making it up. No one was going to believe me. "Don Roberts," I quickly said.

Detective Lewis looked up at me.

"He's the leader or whatever you call it of the mafia." *Shit, what had Liza called it?* Hell something? It didn't matter. That wasn't the point. "He was my foster father. And he was the one that kidnapped me. He's being prosecuted for violating the foster care system and for attempted murder. Against me. Look up the case."

He sighed again as he typed something into his computer. "Don Roberts." His eyes scanned the screen. "He is not enrolled in the foster program of Colorado or any other state. He doesn't even have a rap sheet."

"That's not possible."

"And there is no open case against him. Especially for attempted murder. We'd be aware of such allegations. He's clean."

I couldn't breathe. I took a step back from the desk and hit the chair that I had been sitting in. It squeaked against the linoleum floor.

Detective Lewis looked a little more sympathetic. "Call me if you can remember anything, alright?" He handed me his card. "And get some sleep. I'm sure you'll feel better by tomorrow."

I had lost my mind. It felt like I was dreaming as I turned away from the detective. Summer Brooks was dead. In my heart, I already knew that. A part of me died when my parents' car crashed. Another piece of me died when my grandmother had a heart attack. But I took my last breath the first time Don had touched me.

But that wasn't in 2009. And it wasn't because of carbon monoxide poisoning. I stepped out onto the busy city streets. There were people everywhere. I felt claustrophobic. I needed to be alone. I needed to figure out what was real.

Again, I found myself wanting to call the vigilante. I shook my head. Don was trying to kill him. I couldn't risk leading Don right to him. Besides, I didn't know if I could trust him. How could I trust a man who was hiding behind a mask? He couldn't give me any answers.

I glanced behind me as I walked down the sidewalk. I could feel someone watching me. I could feel my sanity slipping away.

CHAPTER 4
Friday

I clenched my hand in a fist as I stared at the door. I didn't know what else to do. It really felt like I was losing my mind. He was the only one who could tell me what was real. I looked over my shoulder once more. Would being here really make things any worse? Joan already knew he was my friend. I had already put him in harm's way.

Before I could talk myself out of it, I knocked on the door.

Miles opened the door at the same time he was pulling his shirt on. I saw a quick glimpse of his abs. He was just wearing boxers and a t-shirt. No, he definitely wasn't the same boy I used to know. There was nothing at all boyish about him now.

"Hey, Sadie." He looked surprised to see me. "I was looking for you today..."

"Can I come in?" I walked past him before he had a chance to answer. His sheets and comforter were pushed back. I had clearly just disrupted his sleep. I knew I was fidgeting. I knew how crazy I looked. How could I explain why I was here without him thinking I was presumptuous? *God.* I turned back around to face him. He looked truly exhausted. What was I doing here? I couldn't keep harassing him like this. "I'm sorry, I woke you. I should just come back in the morning." I tried to step back around him, but he put his hand on my arm.

"It's okay. You can stay."

I swallowed hard. He had invited me in the other night. If I had taken him up on that offer, nothing bad would have happened. I would have been safely in his arms all night. My memory would be intact. And I was scared to go back to my room. I didn't trust Kins. This was the only place I truly felt safe.

"I want you to stay," he added, when I didn't respond to him.

I quickly turned back to him. *He wants me to stay?* I didn't want to overthink everything. I didn't want to make this something it wasn't. I was here to get answers, not to drag him into a past that no longer made sense. But I needed him to hold me too. For years I had needed him and he was nowhere to be found. Just this one night, I wanted his arms around me. I wanted him to tell me it was going to be okay. I kicked off my shoes and pulled off my hoodie. *So much for not being presumptuous.*

He pushed his hair off his forehead as he watched me.

What was he thinking? I really never had been good at reading him. "Last night when I asked you to hold me, you invited me in. I thought maybe...that we could do that tonight."

A smile was toying at the edge of his lips. "If that's what you want to do."

I nodded my head. My heart stammered as he turned around and locked the door. And it nearly beat out of my chest as he walked toward the bed.

I could have easily gotten lost in this moment. But I came here for answers. I still needed to know the truth. I tried to control my breathing as he climbed back into bed. And I tried not to read into my racing heart as I lay down beside him. Or when he shifted closer and wrapped his arms around me.

He smelled like home. Tears welled in my eyes. I fit perfectly in his arms. And once, that was where I belonged. When I was still whole. Before my life was taken away from me. I closed my eyes tight, trying to prevent the tears from falling.

His thumb was making a small circle under my shoulder blade, somehow reminding me of my injured shoulder and at the same time numbing the pain. He calmed me. He grounded me. And he abandoned me.

Stop. I didn't know his side of the story. That's why I was here. I needed to know why he really stopped writing. "Can you tell me about Summer?"

His fingers stopped on my skin. "I'd rather not talk about the past."

"It's not the past if it still haunts you." I knew that better than anyone. If I couldn't let go of my pain, maybe I could help him let go of his. Maybe I could help him move on.

He shifted his hand and ran his fingers through my hair. It seemed absentminded, and it made me wonder how many girls had been in this same position with him before.

I bit the inside of my cheek. I needed this. And I'm pretty sure he needed it too. "Please."

"What do you want to know exactly?"

I just needed to know about my grandmother passing and what he remembered after that. Instead, "The whole story," slipped out of my mouth.

"It's a long story."

I rested my head against his strong chest and breathed him in. "I have all night."

He shifted so that his chin was resting on the top of my head. His hand slid down my back, stopping at the base of my spine. I was so comfortable in his arms. It was like time had stopped. We were still kids, falling asleep in his tree house. There was no fire. There was no pain. My eyelids suddenly felt heavy. I was home again.

"When I was eight, she moved in next door," he finally said, breaking the spell.

I forced myself to keep my eyes open. I needed to hear this. I had always wondered what our relationship meant to him. For the past several years, I had convinced myself that he had never cared about me. I had told myself that I had made it up in my head. That my love for him was completely one sided. I realized I was holding my breath, and slowly exhaled.

"She was so full of life, I don't really know how else to explain it. The first time I saw her, she was running across the yard, chasing after a bunny. To clarify, she was younger than me. She was only six. Still, I don't know why she thought she could catch it."

I smiled against his chest.

"But that wasn't really the point. What I remember was how her hair caught in the sun. It was this really beau- tiful shade of red. When you looked at it in the sun, it seemed like it was made up of hundreds of different colors. You'll probably make fun of me, but that first moment I saw her, I was completely consumed. I mean, I was just a kid, I didn't really know what love was. But it kind of felt like love at first sight. Summer was the perfect name for her. She had so much warmth. So much joy. So much optimism." His voice seemed to falter.

I didn't say a word. I had never known that. I thought he hated me at first. It reminded me of my babysitter, Julie, claiming that love at first sight didn't exist. Maybe it didn't for her. But it sure as hell did for us. Because I had been in love with Miles Young ever since the first moment I laid eyes on him too.

"And since I was a stupid kid, I just did what stupid kids do. I was horribly mean to her for the first year I knew her. I wouldn't let her into my tree house. I called her names. For a whole month I pretended she was invisible. Every time she got near me I told her how annoying she was. And then one day, I found her crying by the stream in this little park in our neighborhood. She had slipped on the mossy rocks and cut her knee. There was blood everywhere because the cut had gotten wet. It tore me apart to see her like that. I remember thinking that I'd never let anything bad happen to her ever again. That I'd keep her safe."

I closed my eyes tight. I remembered him threatening to come visit me when I was in foster care. How upset he was when he thought someone was hurting me. Why did I turn him away? Why didn't I let him protect me?

"We were inseparable since that day. She was my best friend. We did everything together. But it was more than that. We were young, but, I mean...does that really matter?

I try to look back at it and tell myself it wasn't more than that, but it felt real. I loved her. I truly did love her."

He loved me. He loved me and I pushed him away.

He cleared his throat. "When I was ten, her parents were in a car crash and died. I was there the night when the police officers came. It looked like all the life was sucked out of her. I mean, she was just a kid. We both were. It killed me to see her like that. I promised myself I'd protect her, but I couldn't take that pain away from her."

No one could take that pain away. It was supposed to get better with time. But that was a fucking lie. Everyone who said that didn't understand. It was like there was a hole in my heart. Maybe I just didn't have enough love in my life to come close to filling the vacancy.

"She moved in with her grandmother in another state. The distance was hard. We wrote to each other all the time, but we didn't really get to see each other anymore. She always put on such a brave face. I hated that. I hated that she'd erase things and write over them, like I couldn't see her previous thoughts. Like I couldn't see her pain. I hated that my mom wouldn't let me call her because it was long distance. I hated that I couldn't be there for her." He sighed. "I was a pretty angry kid."

I hadn't known that either. I thought his life was perfect. Star soccer player. Living, loving parents. Popular. I didn't know I had kept him down a notch. And I was angry too. I was angry for letting that have happened without even realizing it. I had ruined his life. I bit the inside of my lip. How could I have let that happen?

"But then her grandmother died too."

Just my grandmother.

"She went into foster care."

I'm not crazy.

"All that warmth and joy and optimism. It just disappeared as she went from family to family. We still wrote to each other all the time. But her letters got less and less detailed. I knew she was hurting. Or maybe someone was hurting her. I don't know. I tried to go see her and she told me no. I pressed it. I blame myself for..."

"Stop." I knew the rest of our story. I blamed Don for everything bad in the past few years. But this was on me. This was my fault. I should have let Miles come. I should have let him help me. I should have let him in. "You can't blame yourself if she didn't want your help."

He leaned back slightly so he could put his hand under my chin. He lifted my face to his. "I made a promise to myself that I'd protect her."

"When you were just a kid." I wasn't sure why, but I was suddenly angry. Angry about the situation. Angry at myself.

"Does that matter?"

"Yes." My anger had bubbled over into tears. I was hysterical. God, I was crazy.

He tried to wipe away my tears but I pushed his hand away.

"Of course it matters!" my voice cracked. He was too good. Way too good for me. I would bring him down. I'd pull him into the darkness. I climbed out of bed.

He ran his hand through his hair in that sexy way of his. "You're mad at me because I'm mad at myself for failing to keep a promise?" He looked exhausted.

"I'm mad at you for still caring." God, that sounded stupid. "I'm mad at you for not living your life. You have to move on."

"I'm trying to live it." He gestured back and forth between us. "Sadie, I'm trying to move on." He climbed out of bed and reached for my hand.

"Well, you can't move on with me."

"Why? I can see it in your eyes. You want to be here. So why are you running away? What are you so scared of?"

"You!" I wasn't sure why I was so mad, but I was furious at him. How dare he give up on his life because of me? How dare he stop living when he still had a choice? I already had enough on my shoulders. I couldn't live with that too. I couldn't. It felt like there were hands around my neck.

"Sadie." He took a step closer to me. "Please just talk to me. You know the doctors told me about the physical abuse. I saw the x-rays. I know..."

"I shouldn't have come here."

"It's the middle of the night. Just stay. Sadie, please."

Time seemed to freeze in my mind and turn over. It really did feel like we were back in his tree house. And he was calling after me as I ran through his backyard, away from my hopes and dreams, away from everything that had ever made sense. "You have to forget about her."

"I'm not upset about her. You brought her up. You wanted to hear the story." He pushed his hair off his forehead. "I'm upset about you, Sadie." He looked pissed. And he probably deserved to be. I was the one that had shown up in the middle of the night. I was the one that had invited myself inside. Yet, I was the one freaking out.

"Then forget about me too." Apparently I had transported back in time and was acting just like an eight year old as well. What was wrong with me? I opened up the door and slammed it shut in his face. I knew exactly why I was angry. Because I made a promise to myself when I was still technically a child too. I promised myself that I'd kill Don Roberts. And no matter how much time passed, that promise was never going to go away. I was going to kill him. And I'd watch the life drain out of him just like he watched mine drain out of me.

Once that was done, there was no going back. If there was any piece of Summer Brooks left inside of me, that would kill her. And Miles couldn't love a person like that. I couldn't let him keep his promise to a monster. He deserved the brightest star in the sky. Not the darkness in between.

CHAPTER 5
Friday

I had no one to turn to. My last bridge had just been burnt. Last night I had made the decision to leave New York City, to try to lure Don out. But this city was the big leagues. Don wasn't going to leave. He had just sunken his claws in. He'd just send someone after me to kill me. He'd still ruin this city.

I waved my key in front of the scanner and the door clicked open. I stepped into the hotel room. At least I had the money my parents left me. At the rate I was going, I'd never graduate. I'd probably never step foot back on campus. I'd need this money. I sat down on the edge of the bed and collapsed backwards.

For once in my life, I wasn't going to run. I was going to stay and fight. I just had to figure out what was going on. Miles had helped with that. It was everything I thought I knew. Minus the part about him being in love with me too. That had felt like news.

I closed my eyes. I was not going to think about him. I took a deep breath and exhaled. The question was, why would Don make it seem like I died? I knew it was him. Especially since his criminal record had changed too. I bit my lip. Joan had mentioned that their leverage was Eli, Miles, and Kins. But what if she had just thrown some of those names in to get me off their tracks? I knew Eli was bad news. Liza had said that Eli's technology was next level. So if Eli was working for Don, then that meant Don had that technology. Which probably would have allowed him to alter files. Right?

I touched my forehead. That was a leap. Eli might not even be working for him. So who was he working for? Because despite Joan putting him on her list of my friends, there was something seriously wrong with him. The anger in his face. The fire in his touch. I shivered at the thought.

And what about Mr. Crawford? Was he hurt? I had this awful feeling that the blood on my bunny slippers was his. There was no way Mr. Crawford could have been bad. He had gotten me away from Don. He gave me all this money. I sat up in bed.

The money. Couldn't people track that? They could certainly track transactions. *Shit.* I wasn't safe here. They could find me. I ran to the door and was just about to throw it open when my cell phone bleeped in my pocket. I pulled it out and looked down at the screen.

"Not that way."

It was from V. How could he see me?

"There's a fire escape outside your window. Get to the roof. Now."

This was ridiculous. All of this was completely insane. If I couldn't trust Mr. Crawford, I certainly couldn't trust the vigilante.

A knock on the door made me jump. I looked out the peephole. There were two huge men in suits standing on the other side. Their arms were folding across their chests, making their muscles bulge. They did not look friendly.

I quietly backed away from the door and opened the window. There was a possibility that they were good guys. Maybe the police had decided to listen to me after all. But Detective Lewis hadn't dressed anything like these men. His suit pants were worn whereas these men were sporting suits with crisply ironed lines. And all I could think was that Don wore suits like that.

One of the men banged on the door a little louder.

I closed the window as silently as possible and started sprinting up the rickety fire escape. I tried not to look down. The warm wind made my hair flutter around my face. I heard a clanging noise, but I kept my eyes on the steps in front of me, refusing to look down.

I jumped onto the roof of the building.

The vigilante was standing there, his gloved hands on the ledge. "Shit." He was staring down the fire escape. "They're following you."

"Who is *they*?"

"We have to go." He turned around and starting sprinting across the roof.

Where the hell was he going? The only way down was the fire escape. I ran after him and watched him leap off the edge of the building. *No. No way in hell am I doing that.* I stopped at the edge and stared down at him. He was on the top of another building. But it was at last five feet away. I looked down. *Shit, I shouldn't have looked down!*

"Sadie, you have to jump!"

I shook my head.

"You have to!"

Damn it. I knew I had to. There was no other way. I backed up and started running again. I ran all the way to the edge and skidded to a stop once again. *Shit!*

"Jump, Sadie!"

"I can't!" I wasn't ready to die. My heart was beating out of my chest. I wasn't him. I couldn't make that jump.

"You can. Remember what I told you? You can do this. You're made of steel."

I was pretty sure I had proven that I wasn't made of steel last night. But his believing in me gave me a surge of confidence.

"I'm right here to catch you if you fall." His voice seemed to echo across the expanse.

I locked eyes with him. He'd catch me. How could I argue with that? I backed up from the ledge again and looked down at my Converses.

I held my breath for one second. If he could do this, so could I.

For two seconds. I was fucking made of steel, damn it!

For three seconds. I ran as fast as I could.

For four seconds. And I jumped into the air. It felt like I was flying. It felt like I was finally living again.

For five seconds. Until I realized I wasn't going to make it. My body slammed again the wall below the rooftop, several feet beneath the ledge. I took in a huge gulp of air as my hands made contact with sleek brick. I screamed at the top of my lungs as I slid down the building, searching for any crevice to lodge my fingertips in.

He promised he'd catch me. He promised! My life was going to end in a blink of an eye.

I felt something hit my back and I ducked my head as I went crashing through an open window in the side of the building.

It felt like all the wind was knocked out of me when something heavy landed on top of me. The familiar sweet scent of his cologne filled my nose. He caught me. Kind of. Barely.

"Were you trying to get me killed?!" I yelled.

"I'm not the one trying to kill you."

"You're fucking crazy!"

He put his hand over my mouth. "Jesus, just be quiet for one second," he hissed. He sat up but he was still on top of me, straddling me, holding me in place. He looked around the apartment.

Get off me! My heart was beating out of my chest. Tears started to prickle in my eyes. I couldn't move. *Stop touching me!* I tried to scream against his hand, but it came out as a muffled sob.

He immediately looked down at me when he heard the noise. There was concern in those eyes.

He wasn't Don. He wasn't trying to hurt me. He had just saved me. But I couldn't seem to stop the feeling of my heart beating out of my chest. And I couldn't seem to stop seething. He pulled his hand away from my mouth.

"Don't you ever touch me like that again," I said and shoved him hard.

He stood up and took a step back from me.

"Don't you dare put your hands over my mouth." I stood up and shoved him again.

"Sadie, I just needed to make sure we were alone. I needed to make sure we were safe."

And I slapped him. The sound echoed around the abandoned apartment. And as soon as it seemed to stop reverberating through me, I lunged at him. Like a wild banshee. Only...not. Not at all. Because as soon as my hands made contact with his strong shoulders, I was kissing him. He immediately groaned into my mouth.

I grabbed the front of his hoodie and deepened the kiss.

His lips seemed hungry and carnal. His tongue made my head spin.

"Am I permitted to touch you here?" His breath was hot in my ear as he shoved my workout shorts down my legs.

God, yes. My fingers dug into the back of his hoodie.

"What about here?"

I felt the leather of his gloves brush between my thighs. I whimpered.

"Because I think you love when I touch you. You're soaked."

I hated how cocky he was. But I loved it too. "Tell me your name."

He shook his head.

"Let me see your face."

He silently shook his head again.

God, he was infuriating. "Then just fuck me already."

He grabbed my hips and sunk himself deep inside of me.

Yes. I tilted my head back, exposing my neck to him. I didn't even try to see him this time. I just let him consume me. He trailed light, feathery kisses down my throat. It didn't make it constrict. It made it feel like I could breathe again. *Take away my pain.*

It was like he could inhale my darkness. And with each thrust I felt lighter. I climbed higher.

"Let go, Sadie," he whispered against my ear.

And I did. I fell. Harder than last time. Farther. But the warmth that filled into me felt even better than the fall. And for just one moment, one speck of time, I was completely whole. I was Summer Brooks again. I closed my eyes.

"You're toxic," I whispered against his lips. I didn't mean for it to, but it sounded like a confession. Almost like I hadn't meant to say it out loud. But I had meant it in a good way. He took away everything bad and put it on himself. He was saving me.

"I know." His lips brushed against mine. "Does that scare you?"

I opened my eyes and looked into his brown ones. "I'm not scared of you."

"You should be. I almost got you killed, remember?"

I laughed.

He immediately groaned. "Fuck that feels good." He kissed me again, softly this time, as he pulled out of me and set me down on my feet.

"You caught me."

"I told you that I would. I'm true to my word."

I suddenly felt so exposed. He never let me see him, but he always seemed to get all my clothing off me. I grabbed my shorts and pulled them back up.

"Are you true to yours?"

I looked back up at him. "Yes."

He shook his head and took a step toward me. "You tried to leave." His voice sounded hurt.

"What?"

"You promised me that you wouldn't leave the city. And you got a bus ticket anyway."

"I was trying to protect you."

"No, you were trying to get yourself killed."

"Don't pretend to be in my head when you're not."

"But I am in there." He leaned down until his masked forehead was resting against mine. "Aren't I? You're certainly stuck in mine."

I swallowed hard as he took a step back from me.

"Now, I either need you to go home, or go to Liza's."

Home? "I thought you wanted me to stay."

He stared at me for a moment. "Of course I do."

I wasn't sure why he seemed confused by my statement. "Then I'll go to Liza's."

He slipped a folded piece of paper into my hand. "Her address is on that paper. Tell her I asked for her to help you."

"But can't I stay with you?"

"I already gave you your two options. Liza will help you. And ask her to check your wrist."

"My wrist is fine." It was my side that was sore. I slammed against it pretty hard when I jumped straight into a brick wall.

He ran his thumb along my bottom lip. "Do you trust me?"

Not really. Instead, I found myself nodding my head.

"Good. Now, I have something I need to take care of."

"But I have a million questions. Last night..." I let my voice trail off as he walked over to the window, clearly ignoring me. "Are you at least going to tell me who those guys were?"

"I'm still working on all the answers." He stepped onto the windowsill and leapt out into the night.

I ran to the windowsill and peered down below. But he was gone.

CHAPTER 6
Saturday

It was past one in the morning by the time I was standing outside Liza's apartment building. I lifted my hand to touch the number for her apartment when it beeped at me.

"What are you still doing here?!" Her voice sounded shrill over the intercom.

"I..."

"Jesus, stop talking. Get up here before someone sees you." The door buzzed.

I grabbed the handle and felt a sigh of relief escape me as the door locked behind me. The vigilante said I'd be safe here. And I already felt significantly better than I had when I was walking through the city. The building was nice. The floors were marble on the way toward the elevators. I was expecting something less extravagant. Was this Liza's actual home?

I looked up at the small camera in the corner of the elevator as I stepped on. It seemed to swivel slightly so that it was pointed directly at me. Most likely, it was her. But I still turned away from it. I didn't want anyone to follow me to her apartment like they had followed me to my hotel room.

As soon as the doors dinged open, I walked down the hallway. There were no lights flickering or rats scurrying by. The carpets were clean, the walls freshly painted, and there was a pleasant smell in the hallway.

"This way!" Liza hissed from behind me.

I spun around. If I thought she had looked mad at me the last time I had seen her, then I didn't know what mad was. She had her hand on her hip and her hair was askew. It actually looked like her nostrils were flaring.

"Come on," she said and gestured for me to hurry the hell up.

I stopped a few feet in front of her, almost scared to get closer.

"Why would you come to my home?! How did you even find me? You're supposed to be gone, what are you doing here?" She pushed me into her apartment before I had a chance to answer her assault of questions. "Well?"

"The vigilante told me it was okay."

"Well, he didn't ask me." She pushed her glasses up her nose as she glared at me. "You keep...waking me up!"

"I'm sorry. I tried to leave. I bought the bus ticket out of here and everything, but then..."

She held up her hand for me to stop talking. "Did he at least say something about me?"

"Who? The vigilante?"

"Yes the vigilante! Who else?!"

Whoa, calm down. "He knew your name."

"That's it?" She pursed her lips as she waited for my response.

It only took me a second to realize the look she was giving me. It was the same look Kins had on her face when she talked about Miles. Liza liked the vigilante. As more than just a hero, which is what her blog claimed was the reason for her writing. *Crap*. My realization had just made things incredibly awkward. I couldn't imagine her throwing a fit like Kins did when she saw me almost kiss Miles, but I wasn't going to risk it.

"He said I'd be safe here, so he definitely trusts you."

A small smile spread across her face as she turned away from me. "I need something to drink. Do you need something to drink?"

"Um...no, I'm okay."

"You can't make me drink alone. You're the only reason I'm up." She walked into the kitchen and grabbed two glasses out of the cupboard.

I looked around at the granite counter tops and stainless steel appliances. "Your place is really nice."

"Yes, it is." She slid a glass toward me.

I didn't even know what was in it. But she wasn't looking at me like she wanted to kill me anymore, and I didn't want to upset her again. I took a small sip and it burned my throat.

"You're in a shitload of trouble."

I looked at her over the brim of my glass. *With her?* "I really am sorry that I came..."

"Not with me. Don Roberts has gone dark."

"I don't know what that means."

She rolled her eyes at me and opened up a drawer filled with forks and knives. She shoved the bin holding the utensils to the back of the drawer and pulled out a laptop.

Who keeps a laptop in their utensil drawer?

She set the laptop down on the kitchen counter like what she had just done wasn't weird at all. "I'm talking about this."

I walked around the kitchen island so I could see the screen she was pointing to. It was just the homepage for the Colorado Post. There was nothing wrong with it. "It looks fine."

Her index finger shifted to the line of text that said, "Your search for Don Roberts did not match any results."

I looked back at her. "I know. His record's been cleared. And I guess the case got dropped?"

"No, not dropped. It disappeared. Along with his rap sheet. It all vanished. With him."

"He's gone?" For the first time all day I felt a little hope.

"Yes. I've been watching the feeds all day. He hasn't been spotted on any cameras since last night. I thought he followed you out of the city."

I swallowed hard.

"But then I saw you check into a hotel room like a freaking amateur so I knew you didn't leave." She set her glass down on the counter and stared at me expectantly.

"I'm sorry, Liza. I have no idea what you want me to say."

She pushed her glasses up the bridge of her nose. "A thank you will suffice for starters."

"I am grateful for you letting me stay here..."

"Not that. After you left my place last night, I kept digging because I still wanted to help the vigilante once you were gone."

Harsh.

"And do you know what I found out?"

"Something useful I guess?"

"Obviously." She narrowed her eyes at me. "I found out that your identity was stolen."

What? "I don't get it, who would want to steal my identity?"

"No, you misunderstood me. No one stole your identity. You stole someone else's."

"What are you talking about?"

"Sadie Davis is a real person. And she looks almost exactly like you. Same brown hair and brown eyes. Same height. Same birthday as you, minus the year." She turned her screen toward me.

There was video footage of a woman stepping onto a subway car. It was in black and white and slightly grainy, but I could still make out the similarities. Honestly, if someone had shown me this picture, I might have thought it was me. "I don't..." my voice trailed off. Something seemed to catch in my throat as the woman turned to face the doors as they closed. She looked almost exactly like me. Which meant she looked like my mom. It was like time stopped as I watched the subway car drive away. I knew that my mom had red hair and blue eyes like me. But in this black and white image, the similarities were uncanny. I knew it wasn't her. But it still felt like I had seen a ghost.

"She's one of Don Roberts' associates. I think that maybe they needed a scapegoat if things went south or something. That's probably why he changed your name when he adopted you."

It felt like my veins were filled with ice. "Don never adopted me."

Liza lowered her eyebrows slightly. "Yes he did. In 2012."

"No." I shook my head. "No he didn't."

"I can show you the paperwork..."

"He didn't adopt me!" My voice seemed to echo around the apartment. This wasn't possible. This couldn't be happening.

"I read the articles before they disappeared." For the first time she actually sounded like she felt bad for me. "I know what he did to you." She put her hand on top of mine.

"Don't touch me." I took a step away from her. I had a father. A wonderful, perfect, loving father. How dare Don tarnish that? It's like he had somehow taken that away from me too. Like he had pissed on my father's grave. *He adopted me?* I put my hand on my forehead. That disgusting asshole.

"I can tell that you don't want to talk anymore tonight."

Then why are you still talking? I turned away from her. I didn't want her to see me cry.

Liza cleared her throat. "But as soon as Roberts went dark, the real Sadie Davis appeared. I did some more digging and there was a huge drug bust out west. I think he went to go clean up the mess. And I think she's here to make things run smoothly in the meantime. Which means you need another name."

"No."

"What?"

"I'm done running. Don isn't here. So I'm going to be here waiting for him whenever he gets back. I'm not scared of whoever that woman is. I can handle her."

"Sadie..."

I turned back toward her. "My name is Summer." I needed someone to call me that. I needed someone to know I was still alive. I needed someone to remind me that I wasn't dead.

"Okay, Summer. There's a guest room down the hall. We can talk more about this in the morning."

CHAPTER 7
Saturday

Every time I closed my eyes I saw my mother's smiling face. But she was never looking at me. She was always in my father's arms, staring up at him, laughing. For her, the sun rose and set with him. Maybe that's why I had always believed so strongly in love. Maybe it was why I was still so infatuated with Miles after all these years. It was like my love for him was a part of me. It had seeped into my bones. And I did still love him. But I was so mad at him. How could he throw away his life waiting for a girl who disappeared? How could he have stopped living when he still had a choice?

I watched my father dip my mother low as the two of them danced. Why couldn't I remember her smiling at me? *Look at me.* She smiled back up at my father. They were so happy. They were still so full of life. How could they be gone?

I touched the center of my chest. I wasn't sure I'd ever stop reaching for my pendant that was no longer there. My heart ached. And I knew that I wasn't going to be able to sleep. I pushed the sheets off of me and climbed out of bed.

The cold wood floors made me shiver as I made my way out into the hall. I tiptoed into the kitchen, trying hard not to wake Liza up.

If Don Roberts had adopted me, it meant that he really had never been part of the foster care system.

It meant that Mr. Crawford was a fraud.

Those brief few days where I had felt safe in this city were a lie. Mr. Crawford had sent me here for a reason. He had lied to me for a reason. And it all came back to Don.

I sat down on the stool in front of Liza's computer. She had left it open. I clicked on her blog and read the latest article about the vigilante's good deeds. It was almost like the button to write a new post was calling to me. I clicked on it and started typing feverishly. I wrote about how he had saved me. How he truly was a hero. I ended it with Liza's usual sign off: "Someone in this city is watching us." But I added, "And it's time to unmask him," at the end. I pressed enter and the screen went black.

Static blasted into my ears and then something dark blue appeared on the screen. My eyes focused on a zipper of a hoodie.

It's him.

My heart seemed to knock against my ribcage as the vigilante slowly appeared on the screen. His mask was still on and his hood was still shadowing his face, but the hoodie wasn't zipped all the way up. I could see the very top of his chest. It was almost like he had read what I wrote and was trying to show me more of him.

"Go to sleep. You need your rest," the vigilante's voice rumbled.

"I know why you sent me here. I'm not changing my name. I'm not backing down. I've been weak and cast aside my whole life. I'm done."

"Good. Which is why you need your rest. Goodnight, Sadie."

The name sounded jarring to my ears. He had turned his head slightly away, as if it pained him to hear it too. It almost looked like he was locked behind that screen. Tortured. Tormented. "Tell me your name."

"V."

"And what does that stand for? Vigilante? Something else?"

He lifted his head slightly, but it didn't let me get a better view of him. "Something else."

For some reason his words gave me chills. It was like he thought I should know what it was. But I hadn't the slightest idea. "Thank you for saving me. For catching me when I fell."

He didn't say anything.

"I want to be ready for Don when he comes back. Will you help me?"

"If you delete the article you just wrote."

"Why? It's just the truth. This city deserves to know that you're not the villain."

"I'm not the hero you think I am. And this city isn't ready to see the real me."

"But..."

The screen went black. The article I had written was staring back at me. I had this feeling in the pit of my stomach that I should be scared of the vigilante. Just this small, nagging thought. He tried to tell me to be afraid. But I wasn't. And if I was being honest with myself, I was falling for him. He made me forget about the chaos. When we were together, all I could focus on was him and whatever mystery he was hiding. If he wasn't ready to be exposed for the hero he was, how could I make that decision for him?

I highlighted the article. I couldn't let go of my feelings for Miles. So how was I ever supposed to move on? Did I even want to?

I pressed delete. If only pieces of my own life were so easy to get rid of. Out of the corner of my eye, I saw a glimpse of light coming through the window. I stood up and walked over to the windowsill. The moon was shining bright. Without hesitating, I shoved the window up and climbed out onto the fire escape. I put my hands on the metal railing and stared out at the city street below. The wind blew through my hair and I closed my eyes, relishing the familiar feeling. The air even smelled fresh so far above the city. I let out a sigh I didn't realize I had been holding.

Wyoming wasn't my home. Colorado wasn't my home. But New York could be. I could see a future here. *Miles.* I opened my eyes. He had always been my future. I turned my head up and looked at the few stars visible in the sky.

The problem was that I wasn't the same girl I used to be. He loved Summer. He liked Sadie. But he didn't know either one of them. I didn't know either one of them. Maybe one day I'd be whole again. Maybe one day I'd deserve a bright future. I looked down at my hands. But not any time soon. All I could seem to focus on was putting my hands around Don's throat. I had a darkness in me that I wasn't ready to let go. The vigilante didn't judge that. He wanted to help me embrace it.

I gripped the railing and watched my knuckles turn white. Even if killing Don meant living in pain for the rest of my life, it would be worth it. I had already given up on living after he had taken my last shred of hope. I placed one of my hands on my stomach. I knew there was a fine line between vengeance and justice. The only problem was that I didn't care if I crossed it. I wanted vengeance and justice. I'd go to the ends of the earth to destroy Don.

I let my tears stream down my cheeks. Years ago, I told myself I'd follow Miles to the ends of the earth. Time didn't heal anything. It just changed us. It ruined us. I would never be that carefree girl he had fallen for. I needed to give him up. I needed to learn how to walk down that hall without stopping at his door. I needed to re-imagine a future without him. And I needed to accept the fact that my life didn't necessarily have a happy ending. Because after all was said and done, I might be the one living behind bars for the rest of my life. That's what crossing the line resulted in. But I had already stepped over it and there was no going back.

CHAPTER 8

Saturday

"You really don't think it's possible that Don changed those records too?"

Liza was silent as she sipped her coffee.

Apparently she didn't think my question deserved an answer. And she was right. I had already asked it five times in different ways. Don really had adopted me. It made my skin crawl. It made me feel like he owned me. "Can't I get emancipated or something?"

"I don't really understand why you're so fixated on this. It doesn't really matter."

"It matters to me."

She shook her head. "Well, you can't exactly just call up a lawyer and file a suit. You're legally dead now, remember? And if for some reason that wasn't an issue, the stolen identity would be. What we should be focusing on is why Don found it necessary to turn you into a criminal. He left a very clear cyber footprint on the death certificate. It makes it look like you pretended to die and then stole this Sadie Davis person's identity."

"Why would someone assume I did it?"

"Why would anyone in their right mind assume someone else did? Is there anything else you're not telling me? Think, Sadie."

She had gone back to calling me Sadie. I think she was doing it out of spite since I kept refusing to change my name. She thought sleep would have brought sense to me. But the joke was on her because I hadn't slept at all.

"I've told you everything. I think we need to go back to how Mr. Crawford might be involved in this. He seemed like such a nice guy. I thought he cared."

She gave me a sympathetic smile.

Seeing someone smile at me like that made my skin crawl too. It reminded me of the months following my parents' deaths. Everyone had walked on eggshells around me. And I hated it. *Stop looking at me like I'm damaged.*

"You know I can't do anything without a picture of him. I can't do facial recognition to figure out his real identity if I don't have an image of his face. Are you sure he said he was with the foster care system?"

"I'm positive."

"Well, just because he lied doesn't mean he's necessarily aligned with Don. There could be other reasons."

I stared down into my coffee cup that was still full. I didn't like coffee. It reminded me of being back at the coffee shop with Mr. Crawford. I tried to think of anything that would give me a clue about who he really was. "You know, every time I talked to him, he always said he hoped it would be the last. It was kind of...rude almost."

"Hm." Liza took a sip from her cup. "Maybe he just didn't like you."

"That's not really helpful."

She shrugged. "I doubt you're everyone's cup of tea."

Tea. Now that was something I actually liked. But I didn't say a word. I just kept staring into the coffee cup.

"I think you should talk to that friend of yours and see if you can get him to divulge any information."

I looked back up at Liza. "Who?"

"The one with all the tech."

"Eli? He's bad news. I'm pretty sure he's working for Don too."

"Or maybe he's working with Mr. Crawford," she said.

"We don't know if there's a difference."

"But what if there is?"

"I can't get any information from him. We're...fighting." I almost said we broke up, but we had never technically dated.

"So make up."

"He's not going to tell me anything."

"Then persuade him."

"How?"

She shrugged. "You can start by seducing him."

"I'm not doing that." Just thinking about the way his touch set my skin ablaze made me start to panic.

"Well, figure something out. I did a background check on him and it turned up zilch. No one is that perfect. Whoever created that facade was in a hurry. He'll crack, trust me."

"You act like you've done this before."

"Of course I've never done anything like this! I'm not a crime fighter. And you're the one that's insisting on pretending everything is normal." She pushed her glasses up her nose. "If you're not going to follow any of my advice at least you can go out and get us a new lead. So go be normal and sleep with your boyfriend. I don't have time to babysit you all day. The sun's out. You're safe. Go figure something out that I don't already know. And next time our vigilante friend wants to send you here, tell him to ask me in person."

Her chair squeaked on the wood floor as she stormed off.

What the hell was her problem?

***

I glanced over my shoulder to make sure no one was near me before waving my access card in front of the reader. The sound of the door clicking closed behind me made me relax slightly. Ever since I left Liza's apartment I had been on edge. It was weird staring at other pedestrians, searching for my face. I was hoping whenever I did run into Sadie Davis, I'd be able to see the differences instead of the shocking similarities. I needed to not freeze.

Even though my body ached from slamming into a brick wall, I forced myself to take the stairs. I kept hoping the vigilante would contact me about helping me train. I wasn't going to back down from anything he wanted me to do. So I certainly wasn't going to back down from some stairs.

My motivation didn't stop my thighs from protesting though. I was completely spent by the time I reached my floor. As soon as I opened the door my eyes gravitated toward Miles' room like they were magnetized. He claimed he still wrote to Summer Brooks. Now I didn't have any reason to doubt his word. Don had changed my name probably in part to keep me hidden. Maybe that was why we had moved so much too, so that I would never get

Miles' letters. But why? Why was Don so hell bent on ruining my life?

My feet paused in front of Miles' door. It was selfish, but I wanted to knock. I wanted him to hold me again. We were just kids when we fell in love. He was supposed to move on. I had been angry at him for the past five years for doing just that. And now I was angry at him for not moving on. How could I walk away knowing that what we had was real? That he still loved me too?

I shook away the thought. I needed to be selfless. He had a life that could still be lived. I wasn't Don. I wasn't hell bent on ruining anyone's life. Especially not Miles'. I would not lead him down a path of darkness and destruction. There was nothing to debate. I turned away from his door and walked down the hall to my dorm room.

Kins had sent me about a hundred texts with varying degrees of her freaking out. If I was going to play all of this off and try to be Sadie Davis again, I'd need to spin a web of lies. It shouldn't be hard. I had always been an expert at make-believe. I put my key into the lock and opened the door.

I thought Kins would launch herself at me. I thought I'd spend the afternoon explaining away my crazy. But all my plans went out the window when I saw who was sitting on my bed.

"Eli?"

CHAPTER 9

Saturday

Eli gave me his best boy-next-door smile as he slid off my bed.

A week ago, his smile would have made my stomach flip over. But a lot had happened since then. "How did you get in here?"

He put his hands up, like he wasn't going to hurt me.

I didn't believe it for a second. I took a step backwards and grabbed the handle to my door.

"Kins let me in," he said. "She just went to the bathroom so we only have a minute..."

"Get out."

He lowered his eyebrows slightly. "Sadie, I'm sorry about our fight. I didn't mean what I said, you know that. I was just upset."

I tried to steady my rapid breathing. It felt like my mind was going to explode. He was working for Don. Or for someone else. I could feel his flames from across the room. I gulped. "I asked you to leave. I'm not going to ask you again." He was clearly good at sneaking into my dorm room. Maybe he was the one who had left the box. Maybe it was him who snuck me back in here after I was kidnapped. It felt like my heart was going to beat out of my chest.

"I'm not going anywhere until we talk about this. Kins called me. She's been worried sick about you. She said you didn't come home last night."

Maybe it was anger that flashed across his eyes. Or maybe it was something else. I truly didn't know him. Everything I had learned about him was most likely a lie. But there was a nagging thought in the back of my mind. I needed information from him. I wasn't sure Liza was ever going to speak to me again unless I got her what she wanted. The problem was that I didn't know how dangerous Eli really was.

I took a deep breath. "What I do is none of your business."

His smile faltered. "Look," he said, lowering his voice. "We really need to talk."

"I just...I need some time to think about everything." It wasn't a lie. The room was stifling. I was finding it hard to breathe. I needed to think about what taking Liza's advice would entail. I wasn't sure I knew how to get information from Eli even if I tried.

"Please, Sadie..."

"I asked you to leave." I turned around and opened the door.

"I know that your real name is Summer."

My hand fell to my side and the door closed with a loud bang. I turned around to face him. "What?"

"I know your name isn't really Sadie Davis. I know you're not from North Dakota. I know your parents are dead. And I know you're tied up in something that you don't understand."

"How do you know that?"

"Because I've been watching you."

A chill ran down my spine. It couldn't be him. Could it? I looked down at his hands. His hands had burned me, but the vigilante wore gloves. He hid everything from me. Except his eyes. I looked up into Eli's eyes. He had brown eyes too. The anger was gone. There was just the kindness there that had originally attracted me to him.

"I know that you're scared." He stepped toward me. "But I'm right here, and I'm not going anywhere ever again. I can protect you."

I thought about the late nights he claimed he was boxing. I thought about the bruises on his skin. I thought about the blue hoodie in his drawer. *It's him.* It was obviously him. I had made him the villain in my head because I was scared. But I could see it now.

"I'm sorry that I lied," he said. "I should have told you the truth, but..."

"It's you."

He didn't say anything, but he didn't have to. I knew I had forced him to tell me before he was ready. Last night when we had talked on the computer, I could see that he was fighting with himself. He was tortured, but so was I. Now we didn't have to face any of it alone. There didn't have to be any more secrets. I ran over to him and wrapped my arms around him.

He immediately pulled me even closer.

I exhaled slowly. Everything was going to be okay.

The door creaked open. "God am I glad to see you two made up."

I turned my head to see Kins standing there with a smile on her face.

Eli slowly let his arms fall from my waist.

"Oh, no, don't let me interrupt. I'm sure you have a lot of catching up to do." She winked at me. "I'll be at Patrick's if you need me." She walked back out of the room without another glance.

I had a million questions for Eli. I reached up and touched the side of his face. There was scruff along his jaw line. I had been dying to see what was under that mask and it was right in front of me the whole time. "You're so handsome." Why would he ever hide his perfect face?

He smiled. "And you're beautiful."

I suddenly realized that I was finally allowed to see all of him. My questions could wait a little longer. I undid the top button of his shirt. This time, my hands didn't shake. It was almost like him wearing a mask at first had cured me of my fear somehow. I wasn't scared. I wanted him. I undid another button as I thought about him pressing my back against the rock in Central Park. And the feeling of him taking me right against a wall. I needed him again. He made me feel alive. He made me feel whole.

"I thought you'd have some questions," he said.

I took a step back and pulled my shirt off over my head. I watched his Adam's apple rise and fall as I unclasped my bra. I finally got to see his reaction to my body, and I wasn't disappointed. The want in his eyes was almost palpable.

I swallowed hard. "We can talk later."

He took a step toward me. "That's probably a good idea." He hooked his finger between the cups of my bra and slowly pulled it down, exposing my breasts. His throat made this sexy, guttural noise. It reminded me of how his voice rumbled when he was dressed like the vigilante. Just the thought turned me on even more.

He put his hand behind my head and drew me in for a kiss. This was better than any other time I was with him. This was more real. He trusted me with the truth. That meant more to me than I could even express.

"I'll go as slow as you want," he whispered against my lips.

"I think we both know that I like it a little rough."

He groaned into my mouth as he lifted my legs around his waist. He set me down on the edge of the bed and leaned into me. I could feel how hard he was against my thigh. I pushed his shirt off his shoulders and let my fingers explore his biceps. He really could protect me. He really could be everything I needed him to be. My hero.

"It's you," I whispered against his neck. "It's really you."

"It's me."

I closed my eyes and let the sensation of his lips on my skin take over. I let myself feel the fire from his touch. I let myself trust him. Because the truth was, I loved to dance in the flames. It made me feel alive.

The rip of foil made me open my eyes. We hadn't used a condom before. He always just took me like I belonged to him. Before I could say anything, he thrust himself inside of me.

Oh, God. He felt different with a condom. Not bad, just different. It didn't take away from the intimacy of the moment. It still felt like we belonged together. But right now, there was no pain I needed him to take away. I just wanted to enjoy the moment. I wanted to let go.

His fingers dug into my hips as he slammed into me.

"Eli," I moaned.

"You have no idea how long I've been waiting for you to say my name like that." He leaned into me, pushing my back down on the mattress.

I buried my hands in his hair as his lips found my neck. I had never been able to completely give myself to someone. But I found myself slipping there. I found myself believing in him. Trusting him. Falling for him. I was sick of living in fear. I was sick of living alone. I didn't just want him. I needed him.

He shifted his hips, somehow going even deeper inside of me. He groaned, feeling the same pleasure as me.

Jesus. I was glad it was him. I was so happy that I could finally let go. "Eli, I'm so close."

"Say my name again." His breath was hot against my neck.

"Eli!"

"Summer," he whispered in my ear and gently bit down on my earlobe.

I didn't have to hide anymore. He could see me. And he wasn't scared of what I was. "Oh, God, Eli!" I felt myself clench around him.

He pulled me back to a seated position and held me close. I felt his body shudder against mine and he moaned my name. I wanted to hear it over and over again. I loved the sound of it on his lips. For the first time in as a long as I could remember, it felt good to be Summer Brooks. I didn't feel broken anymore.

I leaned back and looked up at him. A bead of sweat fell down his forehead. I reached up and wiped it away. I felt this connection between us. Not built on fear, but on hope. "I'm sorry I pushed you away." I locked eyes with him.

"I'm sorry that I gave you a reason to." He put his hand on the side of my face.

Fire. But I knew I could live in the flames with him.

CHAPTER 10
Saturday

We were a mess of knotted limbs. I couldn't keep my hands off of him. I let my fingers trace the contours of his six pack as I stared into his eyes. There was this peace settled around us, but I still had questions. He probably did too.

"Why didn't you just tell me who you really were?" I finally said, breaking the silence.

"Honestly, I thought you'd be upset. This wasn't the reaction I was expecting at all."

Upset? "I'm definitely not upset. I'm thankful that you trusted me to know the truth."

He reached up and tucked a loose strand of hair behind my ear. "And I'm thankful that you're giving me a second chance."

I moved my hand to the side of his face and let his stubble tickle my palm. "I'm falling for you." It fell out of my mouth before I even knew what I was saying.

He smiled. "Last time we talked about this, I'm pretty sure you had a panic attack."

"Because I knew you were holding something back. But I get it now. I know why you didn't want to tell me. We don't have to hold anything else back now, though."

He smiled.

"You know," I said as I propped my head up on my hand, "this is definitely going to make our psychology project easier."

"Now that we're not fighting?" He smiled. "Absolutely."

I laughed as he rolled onto his back and pulled me against his chest.

"You smell different." I thought about the expensive cologne that his vigilante clothes always carried. "Not in a bad way or anything." I placed a gentle kiss on his chest. "I love the way you smell. It reminds me of sunshine."

"Well, you smell perfectly the same." He touched the bottom of my chin so that my eyes would meet his.

"I do have more questions for you. A ton of questions. But I could seriously just stay like this forever."

"You know, I was thinking." He intertwined his fingers with mine and kissed the back of my hand. "What if we just put a pause on all the questions. What if we just acted like two normal college students for one day."

I smiled. "What do you have in mind?"

"Hmm." A smile formed on his lips. "What do normal college students do on a Saturday afternoon?"

"Study?"

He squeezed my hand. "I said normal, not nerdy."

"Hey!" I lightly swatted his arm.

I laughed as he rolled on top of me, pressing my back against the mattress.

"I was leaning more toward staying in bed all day."

I wrapped my legs around his waist. I'd give up anything to be normal for just one day. And staying in bed with Eli sounded like the best afternoon ever.

***

It was easy to forget my problems when I was with him. I didn't feel like I was out of my mind. I didn't feel like I was in danger. I stabbed at the rice with my chopsticks as I stared at him out of the corner of my eye.

"You're missing the best part." He gestured to the TV screen.

I looked back at the TV. We were watching a rerun of The Office. Jim had just played an epic prank on Dwight. Even though I loved the show, I couldn't pay attention. Not when I could stare at the corners of Eli's lips turning up into a smile. Or hear him laughing. God, I had been so stupid to push him away. I was lucky that he was willing to give me a second chance.

The afternoon had been great. It was just what I needed. I felt calmer and more centered. But now I wanted to sort out the huge mess that was my life. I couldn't just hide in this room forever. He had promised me he'd help me learn how to defend myself. And we needed to sit down with Liza and figure all of this out together. I didn't know when Don would be back, but I had to be prepared. A day off from everything was what I wanted. What I needed was a whole different thing.

I set aside my Chinese takeout container. "How long have you been watching me?" I needed to know exactly how much of my past he knew about.

He tilted his head down toward mine. "We said we weren't going to talk about this today."

"I'm not going to be mad or anything if that's what you're worried about. I just need to know how much I need to fill you in about."

"Seeing something and understanding it are two completely different things."

I nodded. "That doesn't exactly answer my question though."

"I mean, I want you to tell me everything. From the beginning. I want to know." His hand drifted to my thigh as he stared into my eyes. "But I want to talk about it tomorrow. Just one normal day. That's all I'm asking." He lifted his hand and tucked a loose strand of hair behind my ear.

"No matter how much we want to, we can't exactly freeze time." My life was on the line and Eli was acting like it wasn't an emergency.

"I promise that nothing bad is going to happen to you tonight. I'm right here. Just try to relax." He kissed the side of my neck. "Or do you need me to make you relax again?"

"Hey lovebirds," Kins said as she stepped into the room with Patrick. "Who's ready to party?" She threw her arms up in the air.

I would have bet all the money sitting in my bank account that Kins was wasted. "We were just going to hang out here tonight," I said.

"Actually, it might be fun," Eli whispered. "We've been holed up in here all day."

Because I'm scared to leave.

"Actually I just needed to change," Kins said. "But it would be more fun if you two came." She gave me an exaggerated wink.

I wasn't sure what she was winking about. Really, she should have been winking if she left us alone in the room.

"Don't mind me," she said as she turned around and started to take off her shirt.

"Whoa, babe," Patrick said and immediately stepped in front of Kins at the same time I covered Eli's eyes with my hand.

Eli laughed. "I promise I won't look."

I removed my hand from his face and he was smiling at me, not caring at all about Kins' striptease.

He had the cutest smile on his face. "I think we should go."

"I really don't feel comfortable going out tonight."

"And a little alcohol never made anyone feel more comfortable?" He smiled. "You can't stay locked up in here forever." He jumped off the bed and stretched.

"You really want to go?"

"Yeah, it'll be fun."

"Yay!" Kins said. "It's about time we had a proper double date. Tonight is going to be epic. Put this on." She tossed a dress at me.

It was similar to the blue one I had liked when we went shopping together. It was light weight and short, perfect for the weather. Normally I would protest about being forced to take off my sweatshirt. But my bruises were healed. I wanted to look nice for Eli. And wearing something like this would make me blend in better.

"Give me one sec." I slipped out of room and went to the bathroom. I quickly changed into the dress and stared at my reflection in the mirror. It would have matched my blue eyes perfectly if I wasn't wearing colored contact lenses. I pressed my hand in the middle of my chest. It still felt like a part of me was missing. For most of my life, my pendant had almost been an anchor. I wondered if that feeling would ever go away. Trying not to overthink anything, I made my way back into my dorm room.

"And how about these shoes?" Kins said and held up a pair of stilettos. They were the exact kind of heels you'd see some woman in a movie trip in while running down a dark alleyway.

I looked down at the Converses that I was still wearing. "No, that's okay, I'll stick with these."

"But...they don't match."

"I think they look cute." I looked up at Eli.

He shrugged and put his arm around my shoulders.

Apparently I was the only one that thought my shoes looked okay with the dress. But I didn't care. If I needed to run, I wanted to be able to go as fast as possible. Eli should understand that.

My heart seemed to race more the farther and farther we walked away from the dorm. "Where are we going exactly?" I asked.

"A friend from my Econ class invited me to their house party," Patrick said. "It should be fun."

"God my feet hurt," Kins said. "I should have worn ugly sneakers too."

Kins usually didn't have much of a filter. But apparently when she was drunk it was nonexistent.

"Hold on, babe." Patrick leaned over and lifted Kins into his arms.

She squealed with delight. "To the party!" she yelled and pointed down the sidewalk.

Patrick sprinted off with her in his arms.

"Maybe if I get on her level I won't be worried about anything at all."

Eli laughed. "I would probably avoid the blackout level if I were you."

I had never been blackout drunk. I just laughed, pretending I knew it all too well. In a few minutes, I started to feel the ground vibrating. We had reached a row of townhouses. "Their poor neighbors," I said.

"Come on, let's check it out for at least a few minutes." He pulled me inside.

The music seemed to pulse through me. The rhythm echoing in my head. I felt frantic. I wouldn't be able to hear if someone snuck up behind me.

I clung to Eli like he was my lifeline as we wound our way through the crowd.

I drank each shot that was pushed into my hand, trying to stifle the panic rising in my chest.

"Can we go?" I tried to yell over the music.

"Just try to relax."

His hands were on my hips. People kept bumping into me. My whole body felt like it was on fire.

But I had learned how to dance among the flames a long time ago.

CHAPTER 11

Saturday

"Can I steal her?!" Kins yelled over the music. It almost looked like there were two of her in front of me.

I giggled. God, I was probably even drunker than her. Eli was a complete genius. I don't think I had ever been so relaxed.

He seemed to reluctantly let go of my hips. I liked how much he liked me. I was getting caught up in the feeling. I stepped toward Kins and immediately grabbed her arm so that I wouldn't fall over.

"You okay?" Eli said with a smile.

"Peachy!" I toasted my red Solo cup against his bicep and he laughed. "I'll be right back."

Kins started pulling me away from him and he disappeared in the crowd of people.

"Slow down," I said.

"Girl, you are so drunk."

"Me? You're the one that's drunk."

She laughed. "Fine, we're both a little drunk." When we reached the side of the makeshift dance floor, she turned to face me and put both her hands on my shoulders. "I just hope I can remember tonight tomorrow because Patrick just told me that he loved me!" She started jumping up and down.

I had a feeling she wanted me to jump too, but I was almost positive I'd fall over if I tried. "And that's a...good thing, right?"

"Of course it's a good thing! I'm obsessed with him. You know that."

Are you though? "Well, I'm happy for you."

She beamed at me. "How was Eli in bed?"

"Would you keep your voice down?" I took another sip of the beer in my hand.

"No one can hear us over the music. How was the sex?!" she yelled even louder.

I laughed. "It was good."

She gave me an exaggerated frown. "Just good? Not great?"

"I mean...yeah, it was great." I looked over my shoulder to see if he was nearby. Why did I just say good? I smiled to myself. Probably because it was better with the mask. I couldn't explain why, it just was. I tried to stifle my laugh. *What is wrong with me?*

"Do you love him?"

"What? I think it's a little early for that. I barely even know him." We hadn't really gotten a chance to talk today. I still had all my questions for him. I glanced again at the crowd, but I couldn't find him.

"You two will get there eventually, I just know it. Oh my God, we can be each other's maid of honors. Ah! Double wedding!"

I laughed. "You're so drunk."

"You're so drunk! I'm going to go find my hot boyfriend who loves me. Don't do anything I wouldn't do!" She disappeared into the sea of people.

I smiled to myself. It felt like I was having déjà vu. Except Kins sounded just like me when I was little. So much faith in love. And I sounded like my babysitter, Julie. The problem was, I knew the truth. Love didn't really exist. The world was dark and cruel. I would never love Eli the way he deserved to be loved. I wasn't capable of loving him. He knew that, right? Why did he want to be with me when he knew that? And where was he, anyway?

I pushed through the crowd of people as I looked for him. He might as well have been a magician because he was stellar at disappearing acts. I laughed at my own joke as I made my way up the stairs.

Eli was nowhere in sight. If I somehow did miraculously believe in love again, I certainly wouldn't love someone who just abandoned me at a party that he dragged me to. *Asshole.* I made my way outside and let the fresh air hit my face. It probably would have sobered me up if I hadn't taken those last few shots.

Music still swirled around in my head. I took the steps two at a time and started walking back toward my dorm with a skip in my step. Liquid courage was a wonderful thing. This was probably the first time all semester I hadn't even been a little scared. I smiled at the thought. *God, I really am drunk.* I giggled to myself as I walked down the sidewalk.

Barely anyone was around, which was strange for a Saturday night. But I decided to take advantage of the empty sidewalk. I twirled around in a circle and let my dress fly up around my waist. I used to love to do that when I was little. My feet stopped as my eyes locked on the stars above. All day long I was hoping that Eli would teach me how to jump across the rooftops. I wanted to be close to the sky. I felt invincible, like I could suddenly touch the stars. God, I missed the stars.

I twirled around again, dancing to the beat of the music in my head. This was what living was supposed to feel like. My feet seemed to guide me toward the school's observatory. I stopped when I was standing right outside Grenada Hall. It wouldn't still be open this late, right? I reached for the handle of the door and was surprised to find it unlocked.

I knew I was drunk. And underage. And that this was private property that belonged to the school. *But I need to see the stars, damn it.*

I walked inside as quietly as possible. It seemed newer than the other lecture buildings on campus. The tile floors almost glistened in the dim light. There was absolutely no one around. It made me feel like I was trespassing. The thought sent a thrill through me. I pressed the button for the elevator.

It immediately dinged open, echoing through the entranceway. "Shh!" I said out loud as I stepped onto it. My eyes scanned the buttons. *Observation deck.* That sounded good. I clicked the button above the words.

My stomach churned slightly as the elevator rose. I held on to the handrail to steady myself. Maybe this was a bad idea. I didn't want to get in trouble.

But all my worries flew away as soon as the doors opened. "Oh my God." I stepped out of the elevator and stared up at the glass ceiling. It was like I was standing in the stars. I twirled around again. Tears pricked the corners of my eyes. It was absolutely breathtaking. I wanted to live up here. I giggled to myself, remembering thinking the exact same thing about Miles' tree house.

Miles, Miles, Miles. Why did my rambling thoughts always wind up on him? I walked over to the closest telescope. I had no idea how to use it, but I bent down to peer inside.

And my heart seemed to stop. *Sagitta.* It was angled perfectly at my favorite constellation. The arrow was bright in the sky. It was the perfect season for viewing it. Hell, it probably would have been Miles' secret password right now.

"It's pretty amazing, huh?" Miles said.

I jumped, knocking into the telescope. It swiveled and slammed into his stomach. Hard.

He made this quiet gasping noise, like all the wind had just been knocked out of him.

"Oh my God, Miles. I'm so sorry." I put my hands on the front of his t-shirt. "Are you okay?"

"I'm better now."

I realized my palms were pressed firmly against his abs. His perfectly defined abs. *Stop molesting him!* I laughed awkwardly and removed my hands from his shirt. "You scared me half to death." I took a step back from him and tucked a loose strand of hair behind my ear. "This place is amazing. Do you bring all the ladies up here?" *What the hell am I saying?*

He smiled out of the corner of his mouth.

I loved that smile. It still made my heart race after all these years. I swallowed hard.

"Not all the ladies, no."

I laughed. "Well, you should." I looked up at the glass ceiling. I couldn't help but twirl around again. "It feels like I'm dreaming." The music was still swirling around in my head.

"I like your shoes."

"What?" I looked back at him.

He nodded down toward my Converses. They didn't match my dress at all. Everyone else thought I was weird for wearing them. I couldn't hide the smile from my face. I remembered when I had thought Miles would like it if I wore more grownup shoes like Julie. They had been Converses actually. That night, so many years ago, he had complemented my bunny slippers. But tonight we were all grown up. The thought made me stop spinning.

"Thank you," I whispered. My heart started racing as he walked up to me. Time seemed to slow as I smelled a hint of grass lingering on his skin. How could he still smell the same after all these years? "I love the way you smell," I said, before I could stop myself.

He smiled out of the corner of his mouth again.

My eyes gravitated toward his lips. "And your smile. The way it's weighted to one side. It makes my insides melt."

He laughed and pushed his hair off his forehead.

"God, and that too." I mimicked his action, by pushing my bangs out of my face.

"Is that all?" His eyes danced across my face, studying me.

"No. There are a million more reasons why you're making it impossible to stay away from you. And before you give me some line about how you don't want me to stay away, you should know that I'm breaking all sorts of rules right now. And..." I lowered my voice to a whisper..."I'm so drunk."

"Oh yeah, I can tell."

I laughed. "I thought I was hiding it pretty well."

"Not at all."

"Well, aren't you going to report me or something?"

"No."

"But you're my RA. It's your job to turn me in." I put out my wrists.

He looked down at my outstretched hands, and I could have sworn I saw his Adam's apple rise and then fall. *What on earth is he thinking right now?*

"Turn you in? I'm not a cop. And I may be your RA, but I have the biggest crush on you. I think I've made that pretty obvious."

I put my hands back to my sides. "I'm dating someone."

"You're looking at me like you're not."

I blinked away the stars in my eyes. "That's not true, I..."

"Are you two serious?"

Again, Eli and I had somehow avoided the boyfriend/girlfriend conversation. And he had ditched me again. I never seemed to know where his head was at. "I don't know, we haven't really talked about it. I should report you, you know. For not reporting me."

"Maybe wait until the morning. You may reconsider."

"I don't think so. You, sir, are in a whole lot of trouble."

"How about you sleep on it?"

"I'm not sleeping with you. I just told you that I'm seeing someone."

He laughed. "I said sleep on it. Not sleep with me. Now let's get you back to the dorm safely. See, I can be a good RA."

A spark shot through me when he placed his hand on my lower back. I let him escort me toward the elevator. There was this weird tension building in my chest. Suddenly my crazy drunken mind seemed perfectly clear. And my heart was still broken. Miles had broken it. It was still beating, just barely. And it beat for him.

"Was that you who pointed the telescope at Sagitta?" I asked. I had to know if he still looked at that constellation and thought of me the way I thought of him. I needed to know if his heart beat for me too. The girl I used to be. Not this drunken mess in front of him now.

It looked like he was studying my face again. "Do you know a lot about astronomy?" he said.

Why didn't he answer my question? "When I was little, I loved looking at the stars."

"Me too."

"Well, I mean, I still do. But it's different now." *Looking at them without you was never the same.* I put my hand on the railing of the elevator as it started its descent. "Looking at them alone is so..."

"Isolating."

Exactly. "Is that why you come to the observatory alone on a Saturday night? To isolate yourself?"

"Maybe I've just been waiting for someone to want to come with me."

I laughed. "We've had this conversation before, Mr. Popular." I gestured toward him. "Any girl on campus would be thrilled to spend a night under the stars with you." *I know I would.*

"You don't get it, do you?"

"Get what?"

He stuffed his hands into the pockets of his jeans. "People see me a certain way. A jock. Captain of the soccer team. Econ major. A future bright with a boring desk job pushing papers." He shook his head. "But no one ever takes the time to really see me."

I see you. I feel your pain. The elevator doors dinged opened. I didn't want him to be sad. And I didn't want tonight to end. I wanted to dance with him under the moonlight. I wanted him to hold me tight and not let go. I wanted to laugh under the stars with the boy I loved. Maybe it was the alcohol coursing through my blood. Or maybe it was just the fact that it killed me when there wasn't a smile on his lips. But I couldn't let tonight end on a sad note. The night was young, and so were we. I saw him. I had always seen him. This was the only way I could show him, without spilling my secret. "Come with me." I grabbed his hand and pulled him out of the elevator. "Let's show New York who you really are then."

"What does that mean?"

I laughed and pulled him across the street toward Central Park. God, I hadn't felt this alive in years. It was like we were running around in my grandmother's backyard playing tag. *Tag!* That would be perfect. I could always see him clearly because I knew all the things he liked. At least,

I used to know. I let go of his hand and started walking backwards.

"When I was little, I wasn't scared of anything. I loved the feeling of the wind in my hair. And the grass between my toes. God, do you ever miss it?"

"Being a kid?"

"Yeah."

"Sometimes, I guess."

"You guess? I know you miss it." *Because you miss me. You miss the little girl who chased bunnies. The girl who stared at you like you were the brightest star in the sky.* I leaned down and started unlacing my sneakers.

"What are you doing?" he asked.

I kicked off my shoes and socks and stepped into the grass. "Doing what I love." *And I know you love it too.*

He just shook his head.

"You're it," I said and lightly tapped his chest. I took a step back from him.

"You're so drunk."

"That doesn't mean you're not it." I turned away and started running through the grass. "Come and get me!"

"You're going to get us arrested!" he called after me.

But when I turned around, I saw him kicking off his shoes too.

I knew Miles Young. And I knew he wouldn't let me get very far without him.

CHAPTER 12
Saturday

My feet slid in the dew on the grass as I changed direction at the last moment. I landed with a thud on my butt. *Ow.* I quickly pushed myself up and ran behind the huge rock beside me. I stopped to catch my breath. Every time he was it, he tagged me almost immediately. Maybe hiding was a better tactic.

I tiptoed around the edge of the rock. As I peered around the side, he suddenly appeared. I squealed as he grabbed me around the waist. He lifted me up over his shoulder and spun me around. Our laughter was all I could hear. The sound almost brought tears to my eyes.

He slowly lowered me down, keeping my body pressed firmly against his. My buzz was wearing off, but when I was with him, it still felt like my head was spinning. When he set me down on my feet, he kept his arms wrapped around me. I hadn't even realized I was cold. But I knew if I stepped away from him I'd shiver.

Suddenly I wanted to tell him everything. I wanted to tell him the truth about what happened to me. I wanted him to see my scars and love me in spite of them. I wanted him back. But I was scared. Unlike him, I wasn't ready to be seen. I wasn't sure I wanted anyone to see me ever again. Instead of saying anything, I started humming Dancing in the Moonlight. I grabbed his hand and lifted it up in the air, twirling beneath it.

Miles laughed.

"We get it almost every night," I sung. I shook my hips and winked at him.

He grabbed my waist and pulled me against him again. His hands seemed to linger right above my ass. I could feel the heat. It wasn't like I didn't feel our chemistry. Ever since I was little I felt as though we were written in the stars. He swayed with me. We were dancing to a tune that neither of us were singing. It couldn't have been more perfect.

I blinked up at him, staring at his brown eyes. This was now on the list of the best nights of my life. I didn't have many on my list after the deaths of my parents. Really there was just one, when he came to visit me at my grandmother's. Everything else was bathed in darkness.

"I should probably get you back. It's getting late." But it didn't sound like he wanted to take me back to my room at all. It sounded like he wanted me to join him in his.

"You know, you're actually a really good RA. Maybe I won't report you after all." I laughed awkwardly.

"I don't want to be a good RA."

I swallowed hard. "I don't want you to be either." And I meant it. I held my breath for one second.

I don't want to live if I can't live with you. For two seconds.

Maybe I could hide my true self. Maybe I could live my life as Sadie Davis, always hiding. For three seconds.

But the facade wasn't real. Mr. Crawford wasn't real. None of this was real. My stomach seemed to churn. For four seconds.

Miles tilted his head down toward mine.

For five seconds. And I tilted mine down to his chest as all the alcohol I consumed seemed to come back up. I completely emptied the contents of my stomach all over his shirt. And his pants. And ruined my second chance with him in five freaking seconds.

But he didn't curse. Or say I was disgusting. Or even back away from me. He gently helped me kneel to the ground. He held my hair. He rubbed my back. He told me everything was going to be okay.

And I started crying. Because in that one moment, I realized exactly why I had to give him up. His soul was still intact. His future could still be bright. And the realization slowly began to dawn on me. My whole life, it felt like Don was this villain and I was trapped in a nightmare. But if I continued down this path, I'd be the villain. I'd fill Miles' life with darkness. And it killed me. How could something so right be so wrong?

But I let him hold my hair.

I let him whisper soothing words to me.

And I let myself believe that this could be my life. For one night. What could one night hurt?

***

I swallowed hard. It hurt so fucking much. More than I even thought possible. I was completely out of my mind. I couldn't explain it. But the longer he held me, the more it hurt. Because I wasn't falling in love with him again. I was falling more in love with him.

He had walked me back to our dorm. It didn't take much persuading for me to follow him into his room. And snuggle up to him. Now I felt like I was going to be sick again. I couldn't do this to him. My life was a mess.

"I love you, Miles Young," I whispered before slipping out from under his arm.

He groaned as I climbed out of bed.

I laced my shoes and quietly exited his room without looking back. Fortunately for me, my walk of shame was a short one down the hall. Besides, no college student in their right mind was up this early on a Sunday morning.

My dorm room was unsurprisingly empty. I thought about how Patrick had told Kins that he loved her. She had been so happy. Their lives were so normal. The only time I seemed capable of professing my love was to someone sleeping. I collapsed on my bed.

I thought about dancing with Miles in Central Park. I thought about him chasing me through the grass. And the feeling of his hands on my hips. It felt like a dream. A beautiful, impossible dream. The small amount of light filtering through the blinds already seemed too bright. I put my arm over my eyes.

God, I shouldn't have pulled Miles into Central Park. I should have just let him walk me home like he had originally wanted to. Why did I insist on constantly putting myself through this pain? It was as if I loved torturing myself. Drunk me had no self control. I sighed and climbed off my bed. If I was ever going to be able to move forward, I needed to finish what I had started.

I switched on my laptop and started pacing the small floor space. As soon as the browser loaded, I typed Sadie

Davis into Google. There were millions of results. I clicked on the first few to no avail. I slammed the laptop shut. This wasn't going to work. I needed more answers. I needed to talk to Eli.

I grabbed my phone off the nightstand by my bed. I had a few unread texts. The first one was from Eli, apologizing about having to run off last night. "Duty calls?" I mumbled under my breath. He said he was here for me, yet he never seemed to be able to put me first. He knew I was scared to leave the dorm. And he left me alone. *Inebriated.* I could have been killed.

There was another message from last night, from about the same time I had probably stumbled out of the frat house. It was from V. I rolled my eyes. Eli could have just texted me as himself. Maybe he was having an identity crisis. *Kind of like me.* I shook away the thought. My eyes scanned the message. He wanted to know where I was. *What the hell?* He knew exactly where I was, because he left me there. He should have just come back for me.

The last unread message was from Liza. "Did you find anything out from Eli yet? I've got nothing."

I tossed my phone onto my bed. Yesterday had been a complete disaster. Pretending my problems didn't exist wasn't going to fix anything. There was no point in acting like a normal college student. I wasn't normal. I grabbed my shower caddy and stormed out of my room. Everything would be better if I just pretended like last night had never happened. I needed to focus on what really mattered. Vengeance. I swallowed hard. I meant justice. I pulled back the shower curtain, ignoring the screech of the metal rungs. It didn't matter what I called it. Soon enough

I'd be a murderer. I'd have blood on my hands. I'd be guilty. My life would be over.

CHAPTER 13
Sunday

The terrible headache from my hangover was making me act insane. I knew it, but I couldn't seem to stop it from happening. It was like I had a taste for blood in my mouth. But now I wasn't sure if it was Don's or my own that I was about to see. I peered around the lamppost at the Corner Diner.

I knew perfectly well that the lamppost wasn't hiding me. But for some reason it made me feel safer. My eyes were glued on the window. The diner was as busy as any regular Sunday. The only difference was that Joan wasn't posted at the hostess stand. Or talking to customers. Or anywhere in sight. Where was she?

I wanted a fight. I wanted to scream and punch and throw things. There was an electricity coursing through me and I needed to unleash it. I bounced on the balls of my feet and clenched my hands into fists. I could take Joan. She was an old lady. I could get her to tell me what Don was planning.

My phone buzzed in the pocket of my jean shorts. I pulled it out and opened up a text from V.

"Roof. Now."

Fuck you. I wasn't even sure why I was so angry at Eli. I stuffed the phone back in my pocket. But why did he have to be so vague? It was like the mask messed with the circulation to his brain. Couldn't he see that I was busy doing surveillance?

I continued to stare inside the Corner Diner. Seriously, where was she?

My phone buzzed again. I yanked it back out and looked at the new text. "She's gone too. Roof. Now." I looked up at the top of the buildings. He was standing on the ledge of one nearby the diner. Why couldn't he just take off his mask and come talk to me like a normal person? I walked down the street until I came to a rickety emergency escape ladder. The bottom of it was already pulled down, like he had been expecting me to show up here. As if he could read my thoughts. For some reason that just made me even madder, because I couldn't read his thoughts at all.

I climbed up the steps, being careful not to look down. All I could seem to focus on was the pounding in my head anyway. I stepped up onto the roof and stared at him.

"Do you have a death sentence?" His voice rumbled.

"What does it matter if I do?" Tears bit at the inside corners of my eyes. "No one would miss me. I'm already dead."

"Sadie..."

That's not my name! He knew that. Why was he still calling me Sadie? I put my hands over my ears. It was like my name was echoing around me, teasing me. *Stop.*

He took a step toward me and grabbed my wrists, removing my hands from my ears. "I'd miss you."

"Well, you're the only one."

"You said you were ready to train. You don't seem ready."

Was he seriously insulting me for being hung-over? My current state of mind was his fault. "It's your fault that I'm not ready." I put my hand on my forehead. It felt like I was freefalling off the building. My emotions were all over the place. God, I didn't want to burst into tears in front of him.

He put his arms around me, silencing me, and I melted into him. How could he so easily absorb my pain? "All I want to do is turn back time," I mumbled into his chest. "But I can't undo what's already been done. And I can't keep going like this. It hurts too much. Everything hurts. I can't do this. I thought that falling for you would make everything easier, but I can't move on. I can't just keep living like my past means nothing."

His hands tensed on my back. "You're falling for me?"

I wasn't going to repeat myself. We had already talked about this. Besides, the truth was that I was mad at him. Furious, really. "And you know what? You can't just show up whenever it's opportune for you. How do you think that makes me feel?" I unwound his arms from me and took a step back. "And I'm...I'm really mad at you. You completely ditched me last night."

"What? Where were you yesterday?"

He wasn't allowed to be upset about what I did after the party. I would have been perfectly happy spending the night with him but he didn't exactly leave that as an option. My head was pounding. "I'm not even sure you really care."

"Of course I care. I told you to stay with Liza or to go home." He sounded pissed.

"I was with Liza. Until she kicked me out. You didn't exactly ask her if it was okay if I stayed with her. So I went back to my dorm and you were there. Sitting on my bed. With all your apologies and then you just ditched me again."

"What are you talking about?"

"You left me at the party without even saying good-bye."

"What party?"

"The party last night!" God, was he seriously playing innocent? "The one you dragged me to even though I was terrified to leave my room."

His hands clenched into fists. "Who do you think I am?"

I was about to punch him in the face. "Eli, stop messing around."

He shook his head. "I'm not Eli."

"But you're...Eli said..."

"I told you to trust no one."

It felt like my heart stopped beating. "You're not..."

"Your abusive boyfriend?"

"He's not abusive. And he's not technically my boy-friend." *God, what the hell have I done?* I told Eli I was falling for him. I fucking slept with him. And he lied about everything. He let me believe he was the vigilante. I felt like I was going to be sick. My stomach churned.

"You could have fooled me," said the vigilante.

I took a step away from him. "Who are you?"

He just stared back at me.

"Tell me who you are. Or I'm leaving." There was nothing keeping me in New York now. I hadn't gotten on that bus because I wanted to find my pendant, but it was long gone. I had stayed because I at least thought I could trust the vigilante. I shook my head. There was no way I could trust someone who wouldn't even give me a real first name.

His silence was unnerving.

"How do you know about my relationship with Eli? How do you know so much?"

"Because I've been watching you."

Goosebumps rose on my skin. It was the same thing Eli had said to me. Right after he told me he knew my real name. And lied about being the vigilante. "Why are you doing all this? Just tell me who you are."

"I need a little more time." He reached out and gently ran his fingers down my forearm.

"Don't touch me." I took a step back from him. "I don't know what I was thinking staying here. This is insane." *I'm insane.* "I don't know how to fight. I don't know what any of this is about. I'm getting the hell out of this city." I turned around and walked toward the stairs.

"You're not going anywhere," he called after me.

Fuck you.

"I have something that you're looking for. And I know you won't leave without it."

My pendant. I turned around, but he was gone. "V!" I ran to the opposite end of the building. He was nowhere in sight. "Damn it!" Tears started streaming down my cheeks. I was exhausted. And hung-over. But that wasn't why I was crying. I was crying because I was furious. V was blackmailing me into staying. Why would he do that when he kept telling me to go home? What was I missing? What didn't I understand?

I put my hands on the ledge and stared out at the busy city street. A city that I loathed. A city that was making my sanity slip away. And this small part of me wanted the pain to go away. I wanted the memories to stop replaying in my mind. I wanted to see my mom and dad.

I could do it. I could end it all right now. I wiped my tears away with my fingertips. How satisfying would that be for Don. That he was capable of killing me from another state? I wasn't going to give him that.

So instead, I screamed at the top of my lungs. I tried to scream away the pain of losing my parents. The pain that Don put me through. The pain of all the lies I'd been fed. And the pain of having to let Miles go.

Not a single person looked up from the street below. Not a single person heard me. Not a single person cared. I let my knees collapse, put my face in my hands, and cried uncontrollable, ugly tears. It could have been for hours for all I knew. I couldn't seem to stop.

A whooshing noise made my eyelids fly open.

An arrow was sticking out of the concrete in front of me, pierced directly in the middle of a handwritten note.

Have Eli meet you in front of the diner at 8. I'll take care of him. And then I'll give you what you want.

-V

I glanced over my shoulder. There was no one there. And I had this overwhelming feeling that the vigilante didn't exist. That I had made the whole thing up in my head.

It didn't matter either way. I was done playing other people's games. I grabbed the arrow and tried to pull it out of the concrete, but it wouldn't budge. Instead, I gripped the edge of the note, tore it from the arrow, and crumpled it up in my fist. It was about time I was the one calling the shots.

CHAPTER 14
Sunday

It wasn't 8 o'clock, it was only 7. And I wasn't standing outside the Corner Diner, I was standing on the steps of one of the entrances to Central Park. Eli was supposed to be meeting me any minute. The electricity I felt earlier was back running through my body in strides. I wanted to jump up and down. Maybe I should have used some of my pent up energy to go for a run. But it almost seemed like that's what the vigilante wanted. He liked pushing my buttons. He liked making me feel on edge. It was as if anger was the main fuel for being a superhero. I didn't buy it.

I needed to figure out what was happening by myself. I didn't need superpowers for that. And it felt good to defy the vigilante. I looked across the street, trying to see if Eli was coming. Knowing exactly when he'd arrive would give me the upper hand, at least in my chaotic mind. What I didn't expect to see was Sadie Davis. The real one. The one that looked just like me. Standing across the street staring at me.

The similarities really were uncanny. It was like my new appearance was made to mimic hers. My hair was dyed the exact same color and cut to the same length. Our eyes matched. We were the same height. She even had my nose. I couldn't seem to move. It was like I was staring in a mirror, aged slightly with time. How was that possible? It wasn't like I had a relative I just didn't know about. There was a reason I had entered foster care. Yet, she had my face. Or maybe I had hers?

It was as if she knew what I was thinking, and was enjoying my confusion. A thin smile curled over her lips as she lifted her hand in the air. For a second I thought she was waving at me. But her fingers were spread apart, almost as if she was telling me to stop.

I hadn't moved at all. I hadn't done anything. We both stood completely still, staring at each other until my eyes burned. I blinked. And in that fraction of a second, she disappeared. I took a step forward, but I had no idea which way she had gone. The sidewalk was almost completely empty. It wasn't like she could be hiding in a crowd of people. *I'm imagining things.* I put my hand on my forehead. *I'm losing my mind.*

"Hey," Eli said from behind me.

I knew I jumped. Especially because when I turned toward him he had concern written all over his face. Fake concern. Everything about him was fake. It was just like Liza had said, his facade was too perfect. And I was about to find all the holes.

"You okay?" he asked.

I had a whole speech planned. I was going to tell him that I knew he was working with Don. My words were going to be angry, yet composed. I had a million things to throw at him. But as soon as he asked me if I was okay, all I could see was red. Of course I wasn't okay! How dare he lie to me? How dare he pull me out of my dorm and put me in danger? How dare he even show up here tonight, knowing all the shit he put me through? I walked up to him, getting angrier with each step closer to his stupid smile. And when I was just a few feet in front of him, I pulled my arm back. The smile faded from his face one second before my fist made contact with his jaw.

Fuck that hurts! I grabbed my hand, cradling it against my stomach.

"What the hell is wrong with you?" He put his palm flush against his jaw.

"What's wrong with me?!" I cocked my arm back again.

He caught my fist in his hand and yanked my arm to the side. Before I even knew what was happening, he had spun me around so that my back was against the front of his torso and my arm was twisted behind me.

"Do you want to fill me in on what's happened in the few hours since I've last seen you?" he whispered into my ear.

I considered screaming. But there was no one around. Even if there was, no one ever cared about my pain. It would still make a good threat, though. "Let go of me, Eli, before I scream at the top of my lungs."

He put his free hand on the side of my neck.

I closed my eyes tight. *Fire.* There wasn't any air left in my lungs in order to scream.

"If I let you go, can we have a civilized conversation?"

I kept my eyes clamped shut.

"Summer?"

"Go to hell." My voice wasn't as forceful as I wanted it to be. The words barely came out at a whisper.

"I thought we were on the same page. You said your forgave me."

"That was before I realized you were lying." I squirmed in his grip, but it just made him tighten his fingers on my arm. "Seriously, Eli, let me go." I pushed back against his torso with all my might. My action had no effect on him. He stayed completely still.

"I think we need to have that talk that we put off yesterday."

"I have nothing to say to you." That wasn't true. I had a million things I wanted to say to him. But his fingers on my skin made it hard to concentrate on anything but the fire spewing in my chest. *Let go of me.*

"Would you take a breath? I don't know what you think you know, but I'm not trying to hurt you."

"Bullshit." I tried to elbow him in the ribs, but his grip just tightened on me.

He sighed. "Fine, I guess we have to do this the hard way." He pressed his fingertips into the side of my neck.

My vision immediately started to go blurry and my head started to spin. I lifted my foot so I could stomp on his, but my body seemed to collapse forward. I was just...so...tired...

***

Slowly my eyes focused on Eli's face. I tried to stand up, but something dug into my wrists. Did he seriously tie me to this bench in the middle of Central Park? I pulled on my arms. It just made the rope dig into my wrists even more.

"Now, can you please tell me what the hell is going on?" He was crouching in front of me. Pretend concern on his face.

I peered over his shoulder. We were far away from the walking path and the sun had definitely set awhile ago. I didn't exactly have any option but to talk to him. "You made me believe that you were the vigilante, asshole." I glared at him. I tried to move my leg to give him a swift kick in the nuts, but found that my ankles were also tied to the bench. *Damn it!* I clenched my teeth together.

"I said I had been watching you. I never said I was the vigilante."

"Yes you did. I said it was you and you didn't deny it."

"Those words never came out of your mouth. I thought you were saying you understood where I was coming from. And forgave me."

"Eli, untie me." I pulled on the rope again.

"You said you were falling for me..."

"Because I thought you were the vigilante!"

He lowered both eyebrows. "Wow. I guess I misread that." He put his hands on his knees and slowly stood up.

I shouldn't have cared if I had hurt his feelings. He was a fucking traitor. But for some reason, I regretted my words. Maybe it was just a game, but the look in his eyes seemed real. I had clearly upset him. "I was happy when I thought it was you," I said. "I wanted it to be you." And I think it was the truth. I was relieved when it was him. I wasn't even sure why.

He put his hand over his mouth and looked down at me. He nodded his head and then dropped his hand by his side. "So that's the only reason why you slept with me?

You thought I was the masked psycho roaming the city streets at night?"

"He's not a psychopath."

Eli shook his head. "Jesus, Summer, I put my whole career on the line for you."

I twisted my wrist, ignoring the burn from the rope, as I tried to untie the knots. "What do you want from me? It's like you expect an apology when you're the one that should be apologizing to me. I know that you're working for Don."

He shook his head, completely incredulous. "I'm an undercover cop. I've been trying to bust Don Roberts for over two years."

My breathing seemed to slow. "That's not true. I'd recognize you from back home."

"Does the word undercover mean nothing to you?"

"So, you don't really look like that?" He was more like me than I realized. Hiding his true self. But not because he was scared and weak. Not because he was on the run from a monster.

"No, I do. I was incognito in Colorado. I pretty much do look like this. Minus the preppy clothes. I was trying to blend in as a student."

"So...you're not really a student here?"

"I'm 26 years old. I already have me degree. I enrolled here specifically to keep my eyes on you. And you haven't exactly made it easy."

"Is your name even Eli?"

"Yeah. But my last name isn't Hayes. It's Serrano."

I stared at the complete stranger in front of me. "How long were you watching me in Colorado, Eli Serrano?"

He sat down next to me on the bench. "I wasn't watching you. I was watching Don."

"But by default, that means you were watching me too."

Eli nodded. "I was doing surveillance for the past couple of years. Mostly outside the house. We got lucky enough to bug one room in his most recent house, but it was almost as if he knew it. Our audio never picked up on anything suspicious at all. We mostly just watched the house, him going in and out."

I thought about the house back in Colorado. Don rarely ever stepped foot into the living room. It had become almost a safe haven for me in the last few months I was living with him. That couldn't be a coincidence. But if Don had known, why hadn't he bothered to remove the bug? Not talking about the awful things he had done didn't exactly make him innocent.

"I didn't understand it at the time," Eli said, pulling me out of my head. "Why you stayed there instead of at a friend's house or something."

"I didn't have a choice."

"And I'm sorry that I didn't know. I would have stepped in if..."

"If what? You knew that he forced himself on me? That he beat me?" A few tears started to run down my cheeks. "He tried to kill me, Eli. I feared for my life every fucking day."

"Summer, I swear I didn't know. Not until I saw the bruises on your neck here. I thought you just stuck around because you were loyal to your father."

"He's not my father!" There was a sour taste in my mouth.

"I know that now. But I didn't when I was doing surveillance. The adoption paperwork was sound. There was no reason to look into anything. From the outside, everything seemed legal."

"He was hurting me."

"We weren't looking for evidence of something we didn't know existed. And I was close to putting him away on charges so much bigger than domestic violence."

"Bigger than that? Each day you didn't step in, a piece of me died. You dismissed my life as part of some better cause?"

"I swear I didn't know what he was doing."

"Untie me, Eli."

"Summer, I swear I didn't know. All I knew was that I saw a broken girl who deserved more than whatever life her criminal father could give her. But I thought you wanted to be there. I thought you were choosing to be there."

I wanted to punch him in the face all over again. "And did you enjoy it? Watching me? Following me?"

"Jesus, it wasn't like that. It was a job. And if I had ever heard him hurting you, I would have stepped in. You have to believe me, Summer."

"So you...what? Decided to stalk me here? You've been watching me for two years. But I only just met you. You may think you know me, but you don't. You only know the broken part of me."

"Yes, I was kind of infatuated with you. I had to pull a lot of strings to get this gig."

"You're sick."

"I do know you, Summer. You get a wrinkle in the middle of your forehead while you're studying. And you cry when you read novels. Almost 80 percent of the time. Even if it's not supposed to be sad."

"Stop."

"And you don't laugh nearly enough. You do this thing where you smile but it doesn't quite reach your eyes."

"Stop!"

"And I think I fell in love with you over a year ago when I was listening to you practice the lines of a play. A play you never even tried out for. Because you were too scared to let anyone see you."

It was like I was truly seeing him for the first time. Maybe someone else would have been flattered by the attention of a young, undercover cop. But I wasn't. All I could think about were the times I screamed when I thought no one was listening. Couldn't he have heard that from the bug in the living room? Why could no one ever hear me when I was in pain?

He leaned forward and wiped my tears away.

I tilted my face away from him. "You could have saved me from the hell I was living in. And you chose not to." My throat felt dry. I felt like I was going to be sick. "During the blizzard at the end of 2016, did you hear me scream?"

He shook his head. "I'm not even sure I was on surveillance yet."

"Bullshit, it was less than two years ago."

"When I was first put on surveillance, you weren't at the house, Summer. It was that winter but it was definitely after the blizzard. You didn't show up until over a week after I started."

"Because I was sitting in some dingy apartment with a nurse decked out on heroin, recovering from undocumented surgery."

"Summer..."

"He stabbed me." I was choking on my tears. *He killed my baby.*

"I didn't know." He put his hand on my knee.

I swallowed hard. I felt the fire from his touch. It was as if I was back in Don's grip. I couldn't breathe. *He took the last ounce of me. He killed me too.*

"You have to believe me, Summer. I didn't know anything about the abuse. I swear to God. I'm sorry..."

"Get off of me, Eli."

He kept his hand on my knee. "I am so, so sorry."

"Get off of me!"

"If I had known..."

"She asked you not to touch her," a voice rumbled.

Eli spun around, giving me a view of the vigilante. It was probably right around 8 o'clock when he had wanted me to bring Eli to the Corner Diner, to do who knew what. And here he was, saving me once again.

"It's my job to protect her," Eli said.

"No." The vigilante cocked his head to the side and stared at me. "She doesn't want your protection." He almost asked it as if it was a question.

Was he asking me permission to save me because I had acted insane earlier today? Because I pushed him away like I push everyone away? "Please," I mouthed silently.

The vigilante took a step toward me.

Eli put his hands out. "Don't get any closer to her. I'm not going to let some lunatic..." his voice faded out as he grabbed the side of his neck. He teetered to the side and coughed.

In a split second, V was crouching down in front of me.

"You're okay, now," he said as he untied my wrists and ankles. "I've got you." He lifted me into his arms.

It was the same thing he had said when he had lifted me into his arms the last time. I had been drugged before and had fallen asleep against his chest. This time, I just didn't have the energy to move. All the fight in me seemed to be gone. The electricity had evaporated. I just wanted to cling to the one person who always seemed to just show up when I needed him.

I heard a thud and knew it was Eli's body falling into the grass. The vigilante must have used whatever kind of dart he had used against my assailant the first time he had saved me.

Eli claimed he hadn't known about the abuse. I thought about how loudly I screamed when I had the energy to fight Don off. I thought about how Don would cover my mouth with his hand, stifling my voice. In that second that I could be heard, couldn't my screams have reached the living room? I closed my eyes, remembering the feeling of not being able to breathe. Eli had been outside Don's house that whole time. But apparently I hadn't been worth helping. If that was love, I was right to not want it. Love was as evil as hate. I could have died and Eli would have let it happen. He put his career ahead of a life. What kind of person did that? He could take a thousand years trying to explain it to me, but I'd never understand. He was just as bad as Don.

I rested my head against the vigilante's chest. He heard me scream. And he had stepped in immediately. I breathed in his cologne. "Where are you taking me?" I whispered.

"The only place I can keep a proper eye on you."

He's taking me to his secret lair.

CHAPTER 15
Sunday

"How much of that conversation did you hear?" I asked. I wasn't sure what the vigilante knew about my past. Don. The abuse. Any of it.

"Enough."

"What does that mean, exactly?"

"It means your friend squandered his opportunity."

"Of what?"

The vigilante didn't reply.

"Of having me?"

"No, not of having you." His hands seemed to tighten around me. "Of deserving you, maybe. But that wasn't what I meant."

"I can walk, you know. I'm not injured."

He looked down at me. "I know. But you're in shock."

I stared into his eyes. I wasn't really in shock. Honestly, I was used to lies. I was used to being in pain. Maybe he just wanted an excuse because he liked having me close to him. Maybe he was as insane as me. I heard a clanging noise and realized he was walking up a fire escape.

After several minutes of climbing, we stopped outside of a window. The vigilante reached out his hand and pressed some numbers into a keypad. There was a whirling noise as the window began to rise.

I wasn't exactly sure what I was expecting. I had pictured him as a sort of Robin Hood superhero, stealing from the rich and giving to the poor. That would mean he knew what living in poverty was like. His lair would be a rundown building in the slums of the city. But something like that wouldn't have a touchpad that operated a fancy door-like window.

He carried me into a room bathed in total darkness. The sound of his shoes on the floor was the only sound in the room. He slowly lowered me to my feet, in such a way that my arms stayed wrapped around his neck after my feet touched the ground. I breathed in his exhales. They were so much sweeter than oxygen. I was pretty sure I could live off of his breaths.

"Why are you doing all this for me?" I asked.

He pressed his forehead against mine. "I'm only here because of you. You created me."

"But what about the bank robbery? And the random muggings you stopped? That has nothing to do with me."

"Help yourself to anything in the kitchen," he said, ignoring me, as he let go of my waist and stepped back. "Athena. Lights on."

There was a clicking noise and suddenly I could see him again. I squinted my eyes at the blast of illumination.

I was still adjusting to the brightness when he added, "I'll be back soon."

"Where are you going?"

"I have to go back for Eli."

"Why?"

"Because I didn't get to interrogate him yet. Don't break anything while I'm gone."

The window automatically shut behind him before I got to ask him any more questions.

"V, wait!" I looked around the window for a way to open it. I didn't actually want to leave, but I thought it was important to know how. "Open," I eventually whispered when I couldn't find any buttons or knobs that would do the trick.

"Access denied," said a computerized female voice from above me. I looked up to see a speaker above the window. And a camera. Had he seriously locked me in?

I turned around and let my eyes wander over the room. The place looked like it was a combination of a bachelor pad and a high tech computer lab. If he had been poor, he was certainly keeping some of the missing money from his conquests for himself. I walked into the center of the huge room and turned around in a circle.

Glass partitions were the only thing that separated the different areas. There was a section with workout equipment. Several glass desks were decked out with computers and monitors. There was another glass table filled with small vials of a clear liquid. A kitchen that looked like it had never been used was off to one side. And there were three doors that led to who knew where.

Everything was glass or stainless steel. And there wasn't a spot on anything. It was like he had just wiped it all clean like a criminal not wanting to be detected. I wondered if he had a thing about smudges and dirt. I thought about the gloves he always wore when I saw him. Did he wear them all the time?

The other thing that was odd was that there were no decorations. Well, I guess there was one: the five-foot target hanging on the far wall. Not a single arrow was in the bull's-eye. Some arrows were even sunk into the drywall. I walked over to it and I touched the end of one of the arrows on the outer ring of the target. I was lucky he hadn't hit me when he shot that note at me earlier today.

I took a step back and looked at the wall covered in holes. He was practicing, perfecting his technique. But why? Why did he have to get better at what he was doing? All we needed to do was take down one man. Just one. This didn't need to be a whole operation. This couldn't be all about me.

The image of Sadie Davis popped into my head. My mind seemed to focus on her outstretched hand, telling me to stop. Was she warning me somehow? Maybe she was trying to help me.

I glanced over my shoulder, that eerie feeling of being watched suddenly overcoming me. I looked up at the ceiling and saw another camera and speaker. Hell, maybe the vigilante was watching me right now.

I walked over to one of the doors and grabbed the handle.

"Access denied," said the computerized voice before I even had a chance to turn it.

I went to the next door and the same thing happened.

The last door opened without anyone yelling at me. It was a bathroom that was as immaculate as the rest of the house. The shower was incased in glass. There wasn't a single splash of water or stray hair anywhere on the vanity. It was like he never stepped foot in here, yet I knew that wasn't true. I closed my eyes and took a deep breath. I was completely overcome by the enticing smell. It was his cologne. The whole room smelled just like him. I closed my eyes and took a deep breath. It was embarrassing that the smell turned me on.

I stepped out of the bathroom before I did something embarrassing like smell his body wash. I looked around the main room again and bit the inside of my lip. So, there was a bathroom but no bedroom. Which meant he didn't live here. Also, why was there no front door? There was just the window to the emergency escape. There should have been a door entering the main building. I walked around the room, but I didn't see a door anywhere. *He really did lock me in here.*

I walked over to the glass desks with the computers and sat down in the only chair. My feet barely touched the ground. I grabbed the lever on the side and lowered the chair until it was a comfortable height. If I was locked in here, I could at least make myself useful. I pressed the power button on the closest computer monitor.

"Access denied," said the female voice.

I pushed the chair to the side and pressed the power button on the next computer.

"Access denied," she said again.

I thought about when the vigilante had said "lights on," and the room had immediately been illuminated. "Computer on," I said.

"Access denied."

What had V said before the command? Athena? "Athena, computer on."

"Access denied."

"You've got to be kidding me." I sighed and stood up. Out of the corner of my eye I noticed a few papers strewn about at the end of the desk. I picked one of them up. It looked like a sketch for a new mask. He definitely wasn't planning on stopping this any time soon. I pressed my lips together. I didn't want to drag any of this out. As soon as Don was back, all of this had to end once and for all. I wouldn't be the reason that V got himself killed. I placed the sketch back down on the desk and turned around.

What was I supposed to do in here? My stomach rumbled. I was almost pissed off that the vigilante had told me I could help myself to anything in his kitchen. It was like he knew that I'd get hungry. How does he know more about me than I know about myself?

"Am I allowed to open the fridge door?" I asked to the speaker above me.

The computerized voice didn't respond.

My eyes wandered back toward the bathroom. Was it really that weird to smell his body wash? While I was debating whether to make myself a sandwich or just dive right into being a crazy person, a whooshing noise sounded through the apartment.

The vigilante emerged through the window, carrying Eli's unconscious body over his shoulder. V heaved Eli off his shoulder and dropped him unceremoniously on the floor.

"Any ideas?" he said and looked from me to Eli's body.

"Me? I don't know how to interrogate someone."

"You know him better than I do."

I shook my head. The truth was I didn't know Eli at all. "You're not going to hurt him, are you?"

"Good idea. It's probably better if we make it look like I might." He grabbed Eli's limp arm and dragged him across the sparkling clean floors.

"That's not what I meant."

V ignored me as he pushed Eli's body to a seated position underneath the bull's-eye. The one he was still clearly learning how to use. He grabbed the bow and an arrow off a nearby glass table and kicked Eli's thigh.

"Please don't hurt him."

V glanced at me over his shoulder. "He'll be more scared if he doesn't see you." He nodded for me to go into the bathroom.

"Don't hurt him."

"I'm not going to kill your boyfriend if that's what you're worried about."

I couldn't even believe it. He was jealous. How could he be jealous of anything I did when he wouldn't even show me his face? It wasn't like we were in a relationship built on honesty. But it didn't stop me from feeling terrible about it either. I had been a little relieved when I thought the vigilante was Eli instead of some stranger under a mask.

"I thought he was you."

He shook his head and turned back to Eli.

V was right, it would be better if I wasn't watching. And I didn't want to witness this. I flinched when V kicked Eli again. The truth was, I had feelings for both of them. I wouldn't have just slept with Eli because he was the vigilante if I didn't like Eli in the first place. I retreated into the bathroom and let the enchanting smell calm me down.

CHAPTER 16
Sunday

I leaned my head against the doorjamb and pulled my knees into my chest. I tried my best to listen to their exchange while suppressing the need to jump in. If I just listened, maybe I could finally get some answers. No one ever seemed to want to tell me anything when I asked. This was the best way. But so far, I hadn't learned anything new.

"I said how long?" the vigilante's voice rumbled.

"I wasn't on surveillance that whole time."

"How long were you on the case?"

"I was put on it shortly after I joined the force three years ago."

Three years? I shut my eyes. Three years of hell that could have been avoided.

"What do you have on Don Roberts?" the vigilante said.

"Nothing. That's the problem."

"With three years of trying to put him away? I highly doubt that."

"I'd tell you more if..."

A crunching sound made my eyes fly open.

"Jesus! You nearly shot my ear off!"

"Tell me what you know!"

"You're fucking crazy," Eli said.

"Fine, you don't want to talk about Don? Then let's talk about Sadie. How could you not connect the dots? There was a missing persons case for her. It was all laid out for you. All you had to do was look."

Missing persons case? I was in the foster care system. Don Roberts had even gone to the lengths to adopt me. I wasn't missing.

"My job was about breaking Don. It had nothing to do with..."

"It had everything to do with her!"

Another crunching noise, as an arrow landed in the dry wall again.

"Fuck!" Eli yelled.

"What happened to that case?"

"It was dropped almost as soon as it was filed. Kids from foster care run away all the time. No one was looking for her."

"Someone was looking for her. Or else the report wouldn't have been filed."

Crunch.

"I care about her too, okay?" Eli said.

Crunch.

"Jesus Christ stop shooting arrows at my head!"

"Tell me what you know!"

"The only reason I even know about the damn file was because it showed up on my desk a few months ago."

"Who gave you the file?"

"I don't know. Look, would you just untie me and I'll tell you everything that I do know?"

Crunch.

"After you got the file, why didn't you put the pieces together right away?" V said.

"Because it was a case about a little girl named Summer Brooks. She didn't look the same. She had a different name. Honestly, I thought the file landed on my desk by mistake. I didn't think anything of it at first. There was no reason to suspect that anything was amiss. I had looked up Sadie Davis when I was first put on the case. The adoption paperwork was sound. Everything was perfectly legit. There really was no reason for me to think anything was going on."

"What about the bruises on her neck! And the scar on her stomach? And her broken bones!"

I cringed and put my hand on my stomach.

"She did a hell of a job hiding it. What do you want me to say? I didn't know. I thought she was there by choice. And the only reason I knew that the missing persons case was dropped was because I went digging," Eli said. "Because I cared about her. Because I didn't want her to have to keep living with a criminal. I was the one that took the time to figure out what the hell was going on. But by the time I connected the dots, it was too late. She was gone. When she turned up here, I uprooted my whole life to come here and make sure she was okay. So don't you dare fucking act like I don't care about her."

"You think you love her? You don't even know her!"

Crunch.

"I'll know her better than you ever will," Eli said.

Crunch.

"You're shooting at me because you know you can't have her. You're hiding behind a fucking mask. No one in their right mind would want to be with you."

Crunch.

"And you think she's going to choose you?" V said. "You were sitting outside her house while someone was hurting her. You could have stopped it! You could have protected her."

"I didn't know!" Eli said.

"It's written all over her face. I knew it as soon as I saw her. And you couldn't see it in all that time?"

I swallowed hard. *The vigilante pities me.* I hadn't thought about that before. He felt sorry for me. Is that why he started all this? I thought I had become great at pretending I was fine. He had stripped me of my mask as soon as he met me.

"People like you prey on weakness," V said. "You saw hers and you latched on. She's scared of you, you know that right? She thinks you're going to hurt her."

V thinks I'm weak.

"She's not scared of me," said Eli. "She likes me just as much as I like her."

"The only reason she even likes you is because you remind her of what she knows."

I felt like I was going to be sick. Was that true? Did Eli remind me of Don? I thought about the way his fingers seemed to dig into my skin when he was mad.

"You took advantage of her," V said. "You crossed the line. This whole time you should have been protecting her, and you did the fucking opposite. You're just as bad as him."

I couldn't take them talking about me like I couldn't hear every word they were saying. I didn't want to know what else the vigilante thought about me. That was already enough. I stood up and stormed out of the bathroom. At first neither of them noticed me. Eli's head and upper body were outlined with arrows. There was a little blood on the top of his right ear, like an arrow had skimmed it.

"What missing persons report?" I said. I wasn't going to acknowledge what else I had overheard. If V thought I was weak, scared, and pitiful that was fine. Fuck him. And fuck him for thinking I liked Eli because he reminded me of Don. The only reason I hadn't really fallen for Eli was because of the small similarities. They both thought they knew me. Well, neither one of them knew anything about me. Screw both of them.

They both turned to me.

"Thank God," Eli said. "Can you please untie me?"

"What report?" I repeated, ignoring him. If someone had been looking for me, I wanted to know who. It could point to something important.

"Tell her what you did," the vigilante said.

"It wasn't me who buried it. I hadn't even joined the force yet. I..."

Another arrow landed right next to his left arm.

"Okay." Eli was breathing heavily. "Okay, just stop shooting at me. When you were 12 years old, apparently you vanished. Officially, Summer Brooks has been missing for the past six years."

"I was in the foster care system. I was with Don that whole time. Liza said he adopted me," I added and glanced over at the vigilante. "And that he changed my name. But why? Why did he do it?"

"I don't know," Eli said. "But this is deeper than you might think. Don was never enrolled as a foster father. And it wasn't just a normal name change. He altered personal identities and made it look like you stole someone's identity. He wanted you to look like a criminal too. He's up to something big, I just don't know what."

"I already knew all that."

Another arrow sunk into the wall beside his arm.

"Stop!" I glared at V.

"You just said you already knew that. He's being unhelpful."

"Please stop shooting at him before you accidently miss. We're trying to get information, not kill him."

He sighed and lowered his bow.

"Who filed the missing persons report?" I asked.

The vigilante looked over at Eli.

"Someone named Rebecca Young," Eli said.

Miles' mom? God, Miles didn't just think I stopped writing. He was probably worried that I was dead. Or was it possible that he thought I just ran away and never spoke to him again? Just the thought made my chest hurt. The other night when I had asked him to tell me about Summer, I had cut off his story after he said I had entered foster care. I thought that was all there was to validate. But if he had kept going, he would have told me about thinking that I had run away. That I had abandoned him, not the other way around.

I had to tell him the truth. Enough was enough. All of this had escalated beyond anything I had ever imagined. I needed to talk to the one person I could actually trust. "I...I have to go."

"You can't leave," V said.

Oh, yes I can.

"Don't leave me with this maniac," Eli called after me.

"You can't." V's voice seemed to rumble an octave lower than usual. He was mad.

Well, I was mad too. I was mad at him for thinking those thoughts about me. I wasn't weak. I had been in hell, but I was still breathing. Neither one of them knew anything about me. I was almost at the window when I heard V loose another arrow from his bow.

"Fuck!" Eli yelled.

"Shit," V said.

I turned my head and skidded to a stop. An arrow was sticking straight out of Eli's thigh.

"What is wrong with you!" I ran over to them. Maybe V was right. Maybe Eli did take advantage of his position as a cop to be with me. But that didn't make shooting him okay. It also didn't just suddenly evaporate any feelings I had for him.

"It just slipped. I didn't mean to..." V's voice faded away.

I shoved V hard as I ran over to Eli. The fact that my shove didn't make him move an inch pissed me off even more. I crouched down next to Eli. The fabric around the arrowhead was already stained with blood. "It's going to be okay," I said, probably not at all convincingly.

He groaned.

I had no clue what to do. Should I pull it out? Would that make it even worse? God, this was all my fault.

Eli's head drooped forward. The pain must have caused him to pass out.

"V, do something! We're losing him!"

"We're not losing anyone," he said. "The arrow was laced with the same serum I use in the darts. It just knocked him out, that's all." He grabbed the arrow by the shaft and unceremoniously pulled it out. "You should probably stay the night to take care of him, though." He placed a medical kit at my knees and walked away.

"Are you serious? You shot him so that I wouldn't leave?"

He didn't respond. He just walked into the kitchen.

"What is wrong with you?"

"I said it was an accident." He opened up the fridge. "Are you hungry?"

Eli was right. The vigilante was a lunatic. I turned back to Eli, ignoring V's question. I looked down at the gash in Eli's leg and grimaced at the blood. Of course I wasn't hungry. If anything, I thought I might be sick.

CHAPTER 17
Sunday

"I want to go back to my dorm."

V kept his back turned toward me and didn't say a word. He was stirring something on the stove.

"V."

"Dinner will be ready in a minute."

"I'm not hungry. Please, I just want to go back to my dorm and get some sleep. I'm exhausted and I have classes tomorrow." My stomach growled, completely betraying me.

"It's almost ready," he said.

"Really, I just need to get back. My roommate is going to be worried about me."

"Kinsley isn't worried about you. She's spending the night with her boyfriend."

"How do you know that?"

He ignored me as he poured a pot of pasta into a strainer.

"Did you bug my room, V?"

"No. I pinged her phone. Why, are you worried I've been watching you change or something? I've already seen you naked, if you recall." He said it so calmly, as if this conversation was normal.

I glanced over my shoulder at Eli. His head was still slumped forwards. He was definitely still asleep. I had slept with both of them. And I was almost positive they both knew. They had been watching me. The thought sent a chill down my spine. This night wasn't just horribly stressful. It was horribly awkward too. If V thought I was going to spend the night in this studio apartment with both of them, he had lost his damn mind.

He set a plate down in front of me and uncorked a bottle of wine.

"I'm only 18."

"This won't exactly be the first time I've broken the law." He poured us each a glass.

I was still standing by the counter. I crossed my arms in front of my chest. But the dinner did look good. Pasta with tomato sauce, chicken, and green beans. My stomach grumbled again. *Stop betraying me!*

"It's just dinner. You're hungry. Eat."

I didn't like him telling me what to do. And I didn't like him thinking he knew anything about my wants. Especially since he was right. I sighed and sat down in the stool across from him. "Then I can go home?"

His eyes flashed toward mine. There was something there, but I couldn't tell what it was. It was like he was waiting for me to say something.

"I want you to stay the night," he finally said.

The way he said it made my heart rate accelerate. Dinner, wine, and spending the night? Was he trying to make this into some weird date? Eli was passed out twenty feet away from us. "What is this?"

"It's just dinner, Sadie." He picked up his fork and expertly twirled it in the spaghetti.

I wish I was as good at ignoring awkward tension as he was. God, he was infuriating. I took a bite of my pasta. It practically melted in my mouth. He fought bad guys and knew how to cook. But he also had anger issues and was clearly not good at trusting people. I took a huge bite. And he obviously knew my name was Summer. Why was he still calling me Sadie? I shoved another bite in my mouth.

"I knew you were hungry."

I stopped chewing mid-bite. I looked down at my half empty plate. Apparently I ate really fast when I was angry. I finished chewing and swallowed the massive amount of food in my mouth. "You're a good cook. But it's getting late. I should probably go."

He took a sip of his wine and set the glass aside. "Is the idea of spending the night with me really that appalling?"

Seriously? "Spend the night with you?" I whispered. "Eli is right there." I pointed to his passed out body.

"I just meant here. Not sleeping with me. You'll have your own room."

"Don't put words in my mouth. You said spend the night with you. That means sleeping together."

"Okay. Fine." He put his elbows on the counter and leaned forward slightly. "Then why is the thought of sleeping with me suddenly so appalling? And I know it's not because Eli is right there. I know it has nothing to do with Eli, actually. Because you're mad at him. He lied to you. All those years he could have stepped in and he didn't. You couldn't possibly forgive him for turning a blind eye to your pain."

He was making my blood boil. "Yes, I'm furious about all of that. But I'm mad at you too."

"I've only been trying to help."

"You're so full of yourself, you know that, right?"

"I just..."

"You said you could see my weakness!" I said, cutting him off. "As if I have a huge neon sign above my head that says I'm damaged. You pity me. And I feel so stupid." I tried to dismiss the pain in my chest. "I thought you believed in me."

"I said that the abuse was easily detected."

"It's the same thing. I thought I was good at hiding it. I thought..."

"You shouldn't hide from what happened to you. Roberts deserves to pay for what he did. There's no reason..."

"Of course there's a reason!"

"Nothing that he did was your fault, Sadie."

Sadie. The name seemed to echo around in my head. I wanted to scream, but instead, tears just started to pool in my eyes. "I'm ashamed of myself. I couldn't fight him off." I thought about that night when the snow was falling. I couldn't protect myself. How did I ever think I could protect anyone else? I placed my hand on my stomach. "I'm so ashamed."

The next thing I knew, V was wrapping his arms around me. I let his heavenly scent surround me as I pressed the side of my face against his chest. He didn't complain about me getting his hoodie wet with tears. He just held me.

"You're right. I am weak."

"I didn't mean any of that. I was just trying to crawl under his skin so that he'd talk."

"It doesn't mean it's not true. You said I liked Eli because he's..." God, I didn't even want to say it out loud. I swallowed hard. "Abusive. That the way he treats me reminds me of Don. What if you're right? What if I'm so messed up that I can't find myself again?"

"You're perfect just the way you are."

The reason why we worked was because he didn't judge me. And I didn't judge him. The whole premise wasn't stable. Just hearing him say I was weak ignited something inside of me. I wanted to throw a million things at him in retaliation. How dare he judge me when he was so messed up too? So even though we may not have been speaking our judgments, they were still there, waiting just underneath the surface. We were a ticking time bomb, ready to explode at any second.

He leaned down and kissed the side of my neck.

"I'm not perfect."

He pushed the strap of my tank top off my shoulder. "You're perfect to me."

I melted into him. It was easy when his lips felt this good on my skin. But at the same time, it was like I could hear our relationship, or lack thereof, ticking down. "You said you'd give me what I wanted if I brought Eli to you."

"You didn't exactly follow the instructions on my note." He gently kissed my clavicle.

My hips pressed against him, reacting to his lips on their own accord. I couldn't even control it.

"But what is it that you want so badly?" His breath was hot on my skin.

I wanted my pendant. But standing in front of him right now, with his arms wrapped around me, I wasn't sure it was what I wanted most. "I want to see your face."

"That's not what you want."

I swallowed hard. "I want to know your name."

He shook his head and kissed my shoulder. "Tell me what you really want."

I knew what he was getting at. He wanted me to say that he was what I wanted. He was purposely making it hard to think straight. "I want to know what we're doing. What is this thing between us to you?"

"A moment of borrowed time."

"Borrowed time?" His kisses were starting to make me dizzy.

"I think we both know that I'm not the one you end up with," he said.

"Why?"

"Because I can't give you more than this. And it's not nearly enough."

I pulled his face away from my neck. "Why do you get to decide what I deserve? What if I want to be with you?"

He put his forehead against mine and didn't say a word. It was almost as if he was trying to read my thoughts. "You can't choose me." His voice sounded strained and he took a step back from me. "You just can't." It was as if he could hear me asking "why?" again even though I hadn't opened my mouth to speak. "It's late. You need to get some sleep. Tomorrow is going to be a long day." He walked away from me and over to one of the locked doors.

A moment ago he wanted me. And now he was telling me that I couldn't be with him. He was so hot and cold. It was impossible to read him.

I watched as he wrapped his fingers around the doorknob. A moment later there was a clicking noise and the door opened. I stood up and followed him, knowing full well that I didn't really have a choice. I stopped as soon as I stepped into the room and stared at the single king-sized bed. No pictures. No decorations.

He opened up one of the drawers of his dresser and pulled out a t-shirt. He walked over to me and placed it in my hand. "Let me know if there is anything else you need."

"I can sleep on the couch."

He shook his head. "I need to keep an eye on Eli anyway. Goodnight, Sadie."

"Why do you keep calling me that? You know that my real name is Summer."

He turned away from me. "Athena, lights off."

The room turned completely dark as V shut the door behind him.

How could I be so angry at him yet want him so badly? I sat down on the edge of the bed and lay backwards. The sheets smelled like him. I closed my eyes and let his scent waft over me. *Borrowed time.* It was as if he knew who I was going to end up with. And it wasn't him. Why did that thought make me so sad? I didn't know anything about him.

I shook my head. That wasn't true. I knew that he cared about me. There was nothing more important to me than that. I opened my eyes. The room was pitch black. He had left me all alone in my darkness. The thought made my chest hurt.

"Athena, lights on."

"Access denied," said the computerized voice.

I closed my eyes again, trying to block out the room. And I had this overwhelming sense that I understood what V was talking about. What if I didn't end up with him because I didn't end up with anyone? What if I was the one living on borrowed time?

CHAPTER 18
Monday

I slowly opened my eyes. The room was still dark, but there was some light filtering in under the door. I rubbed my eyes as I sat up. No wonder it was pitch black in here last night. I hadn't realized it before, but there wasn't a single window in V's bedroom.

I had slept surprisingly well. Better than I had in weeks. Maybe because I felt truly safe for the first time since moving to New York. No one could get in or out of V's lair. And even if they could, they wouldn't be able to get past him and figure out how to get into this room. I was glad that I stayed. I needed rest. *Just like he said.* He seemed to know everything about me.

Pushing the sheets back, I climbed out of bed. I had changed into the t-shirt he had given me. Part of me didn't want to take it off. The material was soft against my skin and it smelled like him. I could wear it for a few more minutes at least. I desperately needed a shower. I rummaged around the dark bedroom until I found the clothes I had been wearing last night.

Hopefully Eli and V were still sleeping. I balled up my clothes and opened up the door. I tiptoed out and quietly closed the door behind me.

Someone cleared their throat and I dropped my clothes as I turned around.

Eli and V were calmly sitting at the kitchen counter eating bowls of cereal. Staring at me. More specifically, staring at my very exposed legs. The t-shirt was so short that it barely covered my ass.

"Sorry," I mumbled as I bent down and gathered my clothes back up. "Um, is it okay if I take a shower?" I pulled at the hem of the t-shirt so I wouldn't accidentally flash them. *I've already seen you naked, if you recall.* V's words from last night started to echo around in my head.

V pointed to the bathroom that I had already found last night. "Of course. Make yourself at home."

Eli dropped his spoon in his bowl and it made a loud clattering noise. He pushed the bowl away. "I have to get to class. I'll see you in psychology, Summer."

I was glad that someone was referring to me as my real name. "You're still going?"

"My cover hasn't been blown. We need to pretend that everything is normal."

V glared at him.

"How's your leg?" I asked.

"It's been better." He glared back at V. "But I've had worse. I'm fine."

"Okay. Well, I'm just going to..." I pointed to the bathroom over my shoulder. This was probably the most awkward start to a day I'd ever had. I disappeared into the bathroom and closed the door before anyone could say anything else. Neither one of them had even tried to hide the fact that they were staring at me. God, what on earth did they have planned?

Spend my days with Eli and my nights with V. I rolled my eyes. I'm sure that wasn't their plan. What was I even thinking? I pulled the t-shirt off over my head and threw it onto the tiled floor. I turned on the shower. It only took a second for the water to get warm. This was definitely a hell of a lot nicer than my dorm.

I stepped in and immediately opened up the body wash. I was right. It smelled just like him. I quickly washed up, trying not to focus on how arousing V's scent was. Or the fact that I was completely covered in it now. I rinsed off, stepped out of the shower, and wrapped one of the fluffiest towels I had ever touched around me. V clearly lived a life of luxury. So where had his soft spot for the poor come from?

I opened up a drawer in his vanity. It was completely empty. As was the next. And the next. The only thing in the bathroom were one toothbrush, a small tube of toothpaste, and a roll of floss. Luxury on the cheap, I guess.

After running my fingers through my hair, swishing some toothpaste and water around in my mouth, and pulling on my dirty clothes, I was ready to walk back out there. I pressed my ear against the bathroom door. I couldn't hear a thing. If they were both still sitting in the kitchen, they weren't talking. That thought didn't surprise me. But I hoped that Eli had left for class.

I opened up the door and stepped out. V was standing at the sink, still in his disguise, doing dishes. He turned and shut the water off when he spotted me emerging.

"I'll pick up a few things for you," he said, as if reading my thoughts.

"I wasn't planning on spending the night here again."

"You didn't sleep well?"

"Actually, I slept really well. Probably better than I have in years." I walked into the kitchen and sat down at one of the stools. "There wasn't much in your bathroom."

"Then I'll pick up a few things," he repeated.

I shook my head. "You don't have to do that." I looked around the room instead of pouring myself a bowl of cereal. "It doesn't even seem like anyone lives here. You have nothing in your drawers. There isn't a spot on anything." I stared at one of the gleaming glass separators.

"I'm not here all the time. And I rarely ever sleep here."

"Where are you usually?"

He wiped his hands off on the front of his sweatpants and walked over to me. It took me a second to realize he wasn't wearing his gloves. I couldn't seem to look away from his hands. It wasn't that there was anything unusual about them or anything like that. But I wondered if they'd feel like fire if they touched me.

He cleared his throat and I looked back up at his face. "I don't live here is all that I meant."

"So where do you live?"

He sat down next to me.

And I couldn't even control myself. I reached out and grabbed one of his hands. They were warm, but not hot. They didn't burn me at all. Actually, the feeling of his skin on mine felt soothing if anything.

I thought he might pull back, or get upset. Instead, his fingers curled around mine. His hands were rough and I could feel the calluses on his palms. Everything about him emanated strength. He made me feel safe.

He turned my hand over and ran his thumb down my palm.

My breathing hitched.

He looked back up at my face. "I'm sorry about last night."

I swallowed hard. "Which part?"

A smile spread across his face. "About what I said. No, we don't end up together. I can't change that. It doesn't mean we have to stop whatever this is."

"And what do you think this is?" It really felt like my heart was going to explode.

He continued to rub his thumb against my palm. "A way to breathe a little easier."

That wasn't exactly what I thought he'd say, but I wasn't entirely surprised. I didn't expect him to suddenly make any sense. At the same time, though, I completely understood what he meant. He made me feel better. He took away the pain. And I did it for him too.

"Make no mistake, Sadie. Our time may be limited, but I plan on making the most of every second."

He grabbed my waist and pulled me in for a kiss.

I couldn't possibly say no to him when he was holding me like this. I parted my lips and let him make my head spin. And the truth was, I didn't want to say no. This was what living was supposed to be like. Taking leaps. Not wishing on a star that your life would suddenly be less dark.

"I need to get to class," I whispered against his lips.

He kept me firmly in his arms. "We're going to figure all of this out. I promise."

I nodded. As soon as he let go of my waist, this feeling of guilt seeped into me. Last night, if V hadn't accidentally shot Eli, I was going to go tell Miles everything. Nothing had changed. I had found out the truth and it was eating away at me. He had been looking for me. He most likely thought I abandoned him or that something terrible had happened to me. Didn't he deserve to know the truth? God, what would he think of me now? "Can I tell someone else about all this?"

He took a moment to study me. "Who do you want to tell?"

Miles. But I couldn't say that. I saw the way V glared at Eli. I didn't want to upset him. "Kins," I lied.

"Telling anyone would put them in danger. Let's just keep it between the three of us. Well, four actually."

"Four?"

"Liza."

"Oh. Right, of course." I had completely forgotten about Liza. I remembered how weirdly she had acted when I was at her apartment. "She has a crush on you, by the way."

V laughed. "No, she doesn't."

The sound made me smile. "I'm not joking. She does. Although, she thinks your computer skills could use some improvement."

He shook his head. "Well, it just so happens that I'm a little preoccupied by someone else right now."

His words should have made me happy. All I could seem to think about, though, was how our sort of relationship was ticking down. "But if we don't end up together..." I let my voice trail off.

"That doesn't change how I feel."

It should. I didn't want to be talking about this right now. *Borrowed time.* I knew it had to be referring to me. And Don. I tried to shake away the thought. "What am I supposed to tell Kins? She's going to wonder what I'm up to."

"Tell her whatever you need to in order to distance yourself."

"I don't want to distance myself. She's my friend, I..."

"Telling anyone would put them in danger," he repeated.

I bit my lip. "So I can only talk to Liza, Eli, and...you."

"Mostly just me."

I shook my head. "I really do need to get going. I'll see you tonight."

"So you are spending the night again?"

Crap. I hadn't really meant to say see you tonight. It just kind of slipped out. But I did want to see him again. I felt safest here. "Do I really have a choice?"

"No. Athena, unlock the entrance."

I heard a clicking noise and looked over my shoulder. The window slowly rose.

"Why doesn't she let me ask her to do anything?" I asked as I walked over to the window.

"She's probably jealous." He must have seen the look on my face because he laughed. "She's only programmed to answer to my voice."

I nodded. "Why the name Athena?"

"She's the Greek goddess of war."

"And..."

"You've started something here, Sadie. We're going to finish it. Together."

His words sent a chill down my spine. "I guess I'll see you later." I stepped out onto the fire escape, thinking about what Liza had said about the increase in crime. Had I brought a war to this city?

CHAPTER 19
Monday

Kins waved to me from the front row as I entered the lecture hall for our sociology class. As I made my way toward my seat, I couldn't help but realize that everything I had been dreaming of had suddenly vanished. College was supposed to be my escape. It was supposed to be my fresh start. But Don had ruined that too. I couldn't get away from my past no matter how hard I tried.

V wanted me to distance myself from Kins. That would be like giving up the last normal thing I had left in my life. Kins was the first true friend I had made in years. No, she didn't know the real me. It felt like she at least knew glimpses of me, though. That was more than I could say about so many others. I didn't want to have to push her away.

At the same time, I knew I was putting her in danger. The feeling of normalcy wasn't worth hurting anyone. I sat down in the seat next to her. Maybe pretending everything was normal was a mistake. The real Sadie Davis was out there. She might be watching me right now. Just sitting next to Kins might be putting her in peril.

"Hey, are you okay?" she said and lightly touched my arm.

I winced slightly. "Yeah, I'm good."

"I noticed that Eli didn't come back to his dorm last night." She raised both her eyebrows.

"That's because we spent the night together." Technically it wasn't a lie. But Eli had been tied up, and not in some kinky, sexual way.

She lightly slapped my arm. "God, I'm so glad you two worked it out. You make such a cute couple."

I pulled my notebook out of my backpack. "You think?" I thought about him sitting outside Don's house while I was in pain. So close but so far away. I knew in my heart that he would have stepped in if he had known. He wasn't a monster. So why couldn't I forgive him? Would I ever be able to let that go?

"Mhm. You know, you never told me if you still think Eli is the vigilante. What ever happened with our investigation? We should start that back up. I never got to look in Patrick's dresser and I need a good excuse to go snooping."

I looked down at the blank pages in my notebook. "Eli definitely isn't the vigilante."

"How do you know?" She leaned on the armrest between us and lowered her voice. "Did you see him again?"

"No. Actually, I haven't seen him again since our kiss. It was just that one time." I shrugged my shoulders.

"Oh. Well, that's for the best, right? Now you can give Eli your undivided attention."

I bit the inside of my lip. "Mhm."

"So...no more snooping, huh?"

I laughed. "The investigation is officially closed."

"But what if it's someone else we know? We could still try to crack the case together."

I couldn't even figure out who he was when he was standing right in front of me. "I don't think it's anyone we know."

"Well, you never know. I watched a documentary once about how you can never truly know someone. Everyone has secrets. It was about like...criminal neighbors or something. Crap, or was that the show The Americans? You know...the one where the FBI agent's neighbors are working for the KGB?"

I laughed awkwardly. "I don't think that's true." It was absolutely true. I was the perfect example. And I was pretty sure she didn't suspect that I wasn't who I said I was.

She shrugged her shoulders. "Oh, shh, the professor is here."

I shook my head and lifted up my pen. At least if I never got to see Kins again, I'd know I'd impacted her life in some way. When we had first met, she dreaded sitting in the front row. And now she seemed eager to learn. Darkness seemed to follow me everywhere, but it didn't mean I couldn't still make a positive impact.

**

I was one of the first people to my psychology class. Focusing in sociology had been almost impossible. I couldn't stop wondering if vengeance was the right path. Don deserved to die. That wasn't the question. The issue was whether or not it was worth giving up the rest of my life in order to get revenge.

With my mind so preoccupied, there was no reason to sit in the front row. I wound my way through the desks and sat down in the back. I couldn't stop thinking about the concept of borrowed time. My parents had died too young. What if I was about to follow in their footsteps? What if I didn't want to? There had to be another way. Right?

"Hey," Eli said.

I turned my head toward him just as he was going in for a kiss on my cheek, I assume. And his lips brushed against mine. I immediately tilted my head away from his. "What are you doing?"

He sat down and leaned close to me, his lips right against my ear. "We need to pretend everything is normal. This would appear normal for us, right?" He slipped his hand into mine.

I pulled my hand away from his. "It's probably more normal for us to be fighting, don't you think?"

"Sadie." He put his hand on my knee. "You believe me, don't you? I swear I didn't know he was hurting you."

I thought about what Kins had just talked about, how you could never truly know if someone was telling the truth. Was it possible that he'd push my issues aside for the greater good of putting Don away? "I don't know what to believe."

"I had no idea," Eli said. "If I had known, obviously I would have done something."

"How am I supposed to believe anything you say? You've been lying to me since we first met."

"You've been lying to me too."

"That's different. You knew who I really was." People were starting to filter into the room. "We can't have this conversation here."

"Then let's go. We really need to talk about this."

"You waited two years to talk to me. You can wait another hour."

"Sadie, please..."

I pushed his hand off of my leg. Just thinking about him not stepping in made my blood boil. And not just because he could have helped me. But because I needed him to. I had been too fucking weak to be able to help myself.

"How are everyone's projects coming?" Professor Bryant asked.

I hadn't even noticed him come into the classroom. I tried hard to keep my attention on the front of the room instead of on Eli's stupid face. I didn't care how sorry he looked, I still hated him.

"Yes, Mr. Hayes?" the professor said.

My eyes snapped to Eli. He was just lowering his hand.

"Is it too late to change our topic?" Eli asked.

"Eli, what are you doing?" I whispered.

He ignored me, his eyes glued on our professor.

Professor Bryant laughed. "Let me guess. You want to change your topic to James Hunter?"

Eli laughed too and shook his head. "No. But we're having a hard time getting the necessary information about the New York City vigilante. We thought someone would have discovered his true identity by now."

"Eli, stop it," I hissed.

"Any parts of the assignment that can't be answered are fine as long as there is an explanation. But all the topics are locked in. I don't want to spend another half hour sorting out repeats. And I'm really looking forward to your interpretation of his motives."

"That's the problem though," Eli continued. "What if his motives aren't sound? I'm pretty sure we're trying to figure out the interworkings of a complete lunatic."

I swallowed hard.

A few people in the class snickered.

Professor Bryant smiled. "Again, as long as you explain your reasoning, it isn't an issue. But if you're still really having trouble in a few weeks, talk to me after class and we can figure something out." He turned his gaze away from Eli. "Yes, Miss Tucker?"

I blocked out Miss Tucker's question. "What is wrong with you?"

"Recently it seems like all our time is monopolized by the vigilante," Eli said. "I don't want to waste a second of any free time we have together thinking about him. It's already bad enough that he's a part of this."

A part of trying to help me? You had two years and you did nothing! I shook my head and tried to focus on Professor Bryant's words. But again, I couldn't stop my thoughts from wandering. Not only was my mind consumed by the concept of borrowed time, it was preoccupied with the fact that I wanted to punch Eli in the face again.

As soon as class was dismissed, I grabbed Eli's arm and pulled him out of the room. And once I realized he probably wasn't protesting because he liked that I was touching him, I immediately dropped my hand. God, where could we talk about this without anyone hearing? I grabbed the handle to an unmarked door and opened it. A janitorial closet. This would work. I pulled on Eli's arm again and shoved him into the small closet.

The door closed behind us and we were bathed in darkness.

"What is wrong with you?" I shoved his chest. "You're drawing unnecessary attention to us. Are you trying to ruin everything?"

"I can't stand the thought of you with him."

"You're jealous? That's what this is?"

"Yes. Okay?" said Eli. "I am jealous. I'm in love with you. I've been in love with you for a long time."

"You can't love someone you don't know!" I shoved his chest again, but he caught my hand, holding it against him.

"I do know you. And I'm sorry that I missed the most important thing. It kills me that I didn't know he was hurting you. Summer..." his voice cracked.

I stopped trying to pull my hand away. "Well, I don't know you."

"Then give me time to show you who I am." He put his hand on the side of my face.

Maybe if my life was normal, I'd be willing to give him that time. But I was living on borrowed time as it was. "You were right about me."

"What are you talking about?"

"When we had that fight outside my dorm. You said that some people couldn't be saved."

"Summer, I was upset. I didn't mean..."

"No, you were right. I can't be." I took a deep breath. "I'm going to kill him." It was strange hearing those words out loud.

"You may think that's what you want now, but in the moment..."

"He took everything from me. You couldn't possibly understand."

"I will if you let him destroy your life," said Eli. "If you let him take you away from me."

"And that's the difference between you and me. I don't believe in justice the same way you do. You're on the wrong side."

"I'm on your side, Summer."

"The cops were never on my side." I swallowed hard. "He beat me until I couldn't move."

"Summer..."

"He's broken almost every bone in my body."

Eli held me as my body started to shake. Emotion washed over me like a wave. I stepped closer to him and let him wrap his arms around me. He ran his hand up and down my back, trying to soothe me.

"He raped me, Eli."

His hands froze on my back.

"He put his hands around my throat until I couldn't breathe..."

"Okay. We'll do it your way."

I lifted my head. "You could lose your job."

He wiped my tears away with his thumbs. "I know you don't think I care about you, but I do. And if him rotting in a jail cell isn't justice to you...then we'll do it your way."

"You should be arresting me. I just told you I was planning to commit murder."

"And I told you that I was on your side."

I shook my head. "I'm impossibly bad at forgiving people."

"I have time to wait."

I closed my eyes and pressed the side of my face against his chest. He might have all the time in the world. But I was running out of it. I held my breath for five seconds. And I let the feeling seep in that at any moment, those seconds could be my last.

CHAPTER 20
Monday

I stared down at the inscription that my father had written for what seemed like the hundredth time.

Summer,

I hope that I'm beginning to instill in you a joy of reading and a sense of adventure. Just remember that one day, your real life will become an adventure even greater than the stories you've read. When that time comes, I know you'll embrace it. You may not have a scar on your forehead, but I know you're destined for great things. Never stop believing in the impossible.

Love always,
Dad

My eyes pooled with tears. When I had read this just a few weeks ago, I truly felt like my life was starting over. Like I could be anything I wanted to be. But that wasn't true. My adventure was coming to an end, not beginning. I ran my fingers across the words. And the impossible that he was referring to was now my revenge. I had somehow turned the most optimistic inscription into something dark. This wasn't the adventure my parents would have wanted for me. I knew that. But I was going to do it anyway.

I shoved the worn copy of Harry Potter and the Sorcerer's Stone into my backpack. Going against the words almost felt like a weight was on my shoulders. I shook away the thought. It wasn't as if I could disappoint someone who was dead. The thought made me feel numb.

I zipped my duffel bag shut and pulled it and my backpack onto my shoulder. Even though I kept telling myself this was temporary, I had a feeling it wasn't true. I looked around at my dorm. Most of my stuff was still there, but everything that really mattered to me was either in my duffel or backpack. I couldn't stay in this room when I didn't know who else had access to it. And I did feel safe in the vigilante's apartment. I needed to at least stay there for a few days until I got my head straight.

My phone buzzed in my pocket.

I pulled it out and stared at the text from V. "The meeting of The Four starts in half an hour. I picked up a few things in case you'd like to spend the night again."

I slid my phone back into my pocket. I hadn't told him that I was planning on staying awhile yet. From our conversation this morning, I knew it's what he wanted. But I wasn't staying because of the reasons he probably thought. I was pushing any romantic thoughts about both V and Eli to the side. There were more important things in my life than that. And I didn't have enough energy to waste on something that would never pan out anyway. There was no future for me.

The door to my dorm room clicked closed behind me and I walked down the hall. As if we were still kids, Miles seemed to sense my presence, because he stepped out of his dorm at the exact same moment as I was passing by his door.

He smiled out of the corner of his mouth.

It felt like a stab in my heart.

"Going somewhere?" He eyed my backpack and duffel bag.

"I'm staying at a friend's house tonight."

He raised his eyebrow. "Just a friend?"

I shrugged. *Kind of.* "Yeah, just a friend."

The smile returned to his face. For some reason, I couldn't look away. The other night I had been so close to kissing him. It's as if his lips were taunting me, rubbing in the fact that they were something I could never have.

"There's a meteor shower tonight. Watch it with me."

He's asking me on a date. My heart seemed to skip a beat. "I can't tonight." All of this was my fault. I had led him on when I had pulled him into Central Park. And I couldn't even blame it on the fact that I was drunk. I just loved spending time with him. It was like I was addicted to that smile of his. And his laugh. I wanted to hear him laugh again.

"We can't exactly catch it another night," he said. "And the observatory is great even when you're not drunk. I promise."

I laughed. "Yeah, well..." I let my voice trail off. "Thanks for not reporting me by the way."

"Thanks for not reporting me."

God, I had completely forgotten that I had threatened to do that. I pressed my lips together as I stared up at him. "Can I have your number?" I didn't realize what I was saying until it had already slipped out. "I mean, just in case

I end up watching it. I can text you during." *What am I doing?*

He smiled. "Yeah, one sec." He disappeared back into his room and then reemerged with a pen in his hand. "Do you mind..." his voice trailed off as he reached out and ran his fingers down my wrist.

Not in the slightest. I lifted my hand.

He turned my hand over so that my palm was pressed against his. He pulled the cap of the pen off in his mouth and wrote his number on the back of my hand.

I swallowed hard when he didn't let go.

He rubbed his thumb along the numbers, probably making sure they were dry. But it just seemed like he wanted to touch me. In that moment, being with him in the future seemed like it would be believing in the impossible. Maybe a life with him was the adventure I should be embracing. Why was I so actively running away from him?

To keep him safe.

"You know, one day you're going to say yes to me."

I locked eyes with him. "In your dreams."

He laughed and lowered my hand.

The sound made my insides flip over.

It took me a second to realize that we were standing in the middle of our hallway holding hands. For all I knew, this could be the last time I ever saw him. I didn't want to let go of his hand. But I knew my choice had already been made. "Enjoy the meteor shower." I dropped his hand. My whole body instantly felt cold. "I know how much you like watching the stars alone."

The smile seemed to fade from his face.

And I knew why it faded. Because it was a lie. He missed watching them with me too. I could see it in his eyes. He thought I abandoned him. Or that I was dead.

He pushed his hair off his forehead. "Have a good night, Sadie." He walked back into his room and closed the door without another word.

For the first time, I thought maybe I had it all wrong. Maybe avoiding him and pushing him away wasn't the answer. Because it seemed like I was hurting him either way.

I quickly walked away from his room. He was upset because I was leading him on. I pushed through the door to the stairs. Asking him for his number one minute and then reminding him that he likes being alone didn't exactly align. He should be mad at me. I was mad at myself.

I was furious with myself for sleeping with Eli. And I felt cheap for sleeping with the vigilante. The first time we were together, I felt completely heartbroken. I had slept with him to help forget about Miles. But it wasn't exactly easy to dismiss the only person I had ever loved.

My back started to ache before I even exited the stairs. I should have let Eli walk me to the vigilante's lair when he had offered. But a part of me didn't want Eli asking me a million questions about why I was bringing so much stuff with me. I walked outside and took a deep breath. All the thoughts rolling around in my head were just distractions. I needed to stay focused on what truly mattered.

For some reason I found myself taking the route that allowed me to pass by the Corner Diner. I stood outside again and peered in. No Joan. She had completely disappeared, just like Don. None of it made any sense. I was missing some important link.

When I turned away from the window of the diner, I froze. About a block ahead of me on the path was the real Sadie Davis. She was standing in the middle of the sidewalk, obstructing the normal flow of the other pedestrians.

A smile curled onto her lips.

I stepped forward and she immediately put her hand up again. Just like she had the last time. Her five fingers were spread out, signaling me to stop.

Why did she never try to hurt me? Was she just watching me? I certainly had enough people watching me already. If she really was working for Don, maybe she didn't know everything he had done. Maybe she would flip sides. I could talk to her. I could try to make her understand. We didn't have to be enemies.

But then she lowered her thumb.

My thoughts about peace completely evaporated. Four. *She's counting down.* Yesterday she hadn't been telling me to stop. She had been telling me that I had five days. And now I only had four. I was in some new twisted game.

Someone bumped into me on the sidewalk, knocking me slightly to the side. When I regained my balance and looked ahead of me, Sadie Davis was gone.

Four days. It was like my pulse was pounding in my ears. The normal sounds of the city seemed to fade away. *What the fuck is going to happen in four days?!*

CHAPTER 21
Monday

By the time I reached the top of the fire escape, I was completely out of breath. I hadn't stopped running since I had seen the real Sadie Davis. *Four days.* I swallowed hard and pounded on the strange window-like door of V's lair. There was no answer.

"V!" I banged on the window again. God, where was he? Was I early? I was about to pull my phone out of my pocket when I heard a clanging noise behind me. When I turned around, V was standing there. Tall. Powerful. Every bit the superhero that I needed.

I immediately dropped my backpack and duffel bag and wrapped my arms around him.

"You're shaking. What's wrong? What happened?"

"Sadie Davis..." I managed to choke out.

"Take a deep breath, okay?" He ran his hand up and down my back, somehow making me feel calm despite Sadie Davis' warning.

"She's going to kill me." I pulled my head back so I could look up at him. That's why I had been running as fast as I could to the only place that I felt safe. I had convinced myself that I only had four days to live. Four days wasn't enough time. It was like I could hear a clock ticking down in my head.

"Who?" asked V. "The other Sadie Davis?"

I nodded. *The real Sadie Davis.*

"No one is going to hurt you ever again. I promise."

"You shouldn't make promises that you can't keep."

"I can keep it. Let's get inside, okay?" He reached around me and pressed the code into the keypad. The window made a whirling noise as it slowly rose. He let go of my waist, grabbed my backpack and duffel, and stepped into his lair.

For some reason I stood frozen on the fire escape.

He put his hand out for me. "I promise I'll keep you safe, Sadie."

I didn't believe his words. But I did believe that he'd try. Besides, I couldn't face this alone. I put my hand in his and stepped through the window. He intertwined his fingers in mine and silently escorted me to his bedroom.

"Athena, lights on." The lights immediately turned on. He dropped my hand and placed my backpack and duffel on the bottom of the bed. "There are a few things you might need in the bathroom. Just let me know if there is anything else."

I nodded.

He didn't say anything about being glad I was going to spend the night again. It was as if he knew I'd be staying all along and it wasn't a surprise to him at all. He sat down on the edge of the bed, looking slightly uncomfortable even though it was his room. He leaned forward, placing his elbows on his knees, and clasped his hands together. "Tell me what happened," he said.

Even though he didn't specify, I knew he wasn't referring to changing my mind about my sleeping arrangements. "I saw her yesterday and..."

"Why didn't you tell me?" he asked, cutting me off.

"There was a lot going on with Eli, if you recall. And I completely forgot about it until I saw her again. Yesterday she put her hand up like she was telling me to stop. It was odd because I wasn't trying to approach her. But today she did the same thing and then lowered her thumb. She's counting down the days until something happens. I have this awful feeling that I'm running out of time. Like you said today. We're living on borrowed time."

"I was referring to our time together. Not your life. Nothing is going to happen to you."

Why did he keep saying that? He didn't know the future. I swallowed hard.

"We'll figure it out together. The others should be showing up any minute."

"Don't you think I'm right?" I asked.

"It's a leap. We don't have any reason to believe she wants to hurt you."

"She's working for Don."

"Liza should have a better understanding of her motivations by now. She's been researching her all day. I should give you a few minutes to settle in." He looked down at his hands. Despite his words, he didn't move from the bed.

"V?"

He lifted his head and locked eyes with me. And for the first time I was able to read him. At least, I thought I could. He looked sad. I swallowed hard. Because I was pretty sure I knew why he was sad. He thought I was right. He thought I only had four days to live, even though he said my conclusion was a leap.

He grabbed the top of his hoodie and pulled it down slightly to cover his eyes. He cleared his throat and stood up. I watched him walk out of the room before I could say anything else.

I didn't need any time to settle in. It wasn't like I was going to unpack my bags. This wasn't a permanent situation. Either we'd figure it out in four days or I'd be dead anyway. Despite what V thought, there was no need to analyze Sadie Davis' motivations. I could see it in her eyes. The hollowness. Don had the same look in his eyes. They were killers. They sucked the joy and life out of everyone they met. *Just like me.*

"Eli Serrano is at the entrance," Athena's computerized voice said through the speaker system.

I quickly walked out of the room. It would be better if Eli didn't know I was sleeping here. Having V and him in the same room was awkward enough. I didn't need to add to the hostility.

"Access granted," V said and the window whirled open.

I wasn't sure why, but ever since finding out that Eli was 26, I could see it. He didn't carry himself the same way the other boys did in my classes. He stood up a little straighter and had more of an air of authority around him. Maybe that was why I was so easily attracted to him. His confidence was a little contagious. It made me believe in myself too.

Eli smiled as he made his way over to me. "How were the rest of your classes?"

"I had a hard time focusing."

"Why?"

"Because I was thinking about time. And the fact that I'm running out of it." *Now more than ever.*

"You don't have to go through with it."

"Go through with what?" V asked.

I turned toward him. For the first time, I realized that he carried himself in the same way that Eli did. Everything about him oozed confidence. He must be older than me too. Why wouldn't he just show me his face? Or give me a name more than just one letter?

"Go through with what?" V repeated.

I wasn't sure how he'd react to me wanting to kill Don, so I was relieved when Athena's voice interrupted us.

"Liza Roth is at the entrance."

"Access granted," V said. He took a step toward me. I knew he wanted to know what Eli was referring to. He wasn't just going to forget about it. Especially since I was acting so guilty.

"What the holy hell is all this?" Liza asked.

Thank you for another distraction. We all turned toward her.

"Welcome to my headquarters," V said.

She walked past us, completely ignoring V, and stepped up onto the raised platform where all his computers were. She immediately touched one of the buttons on the first monitor she approached.

"Access denied," said Athena.

Liza jumped and then turned around with a goofy smile on her face. It looked like she had just walked into her favorite dream. "You have a virtual assistant? That's freaking awesome. What's its name?"

"Her name is Athena," V said.

"What else does she do?"

"Everything I need her to. Athena, light up the base."

The floor Liza was standing on suddenly lit up blue.

Liza glanced down and pushed her glasses up the bridge of her nose. "What processor does she use? Can I take a look at her back end?"

Eli laughed.

Liza glared at him. "Eli Serrano from Grand Junction, Colorado. You graduated top of your class at the police academy and decided to work as a detective instead of a beat cop like your father." She hopped off the elevated platform and the lights on the floor automatically turned off. "You clearly have stalker tendencies and a penchant for danger. I'm Liza." She held out her hand for him. "And I wasn't referring to Athena's ass."

I was glad he had laughed at the back end comment and not me. Even though I was pretty sure I already knew what she thought of me, I didn't want everyone else to hear it.

Eli reluctantly shook her hand. "I don't have stalker tendencies."

She turned away from him instead of responding. "As the only one here without a death wish, I want to make myself perfectly clear. I work in the shadows. If even one word of me being part of...whatever this is...gets out, I'm done. And if I'm going to work efficiently, I'll need access to all of that." She pointed to the computers behind her.

"Done," V said.

She smiled. "And you need to stop hacking into my surveillance system. If you want, I'll set you up with your own. But I don't like being spied on. Especially when you don't know how to cover your trail. You're going to get us all killed."

V nodded.

"Okay then." She sat down in one of the chairs at the glass table. "If we're all going to be working together, I think we need complete transparency. So we should probably address the main question on everyone's mind before we begin, don't you think? V," she said without waiting for anyone to agree with her. "Who are you really and why are you doing this?"

CHAPTER 22
Monday

V clenched his left hand into a fist. I wasn't sure if anyone else noticed, but it was all I could seem to focus on. I could almost feel the hostility in the air. It made it hard to breathe.

"That wasn't part of the deal," V said.

"How are we supposed to uncover the truth if all the details aren't laid out?" Liza asked.

"This has nothing to do with me."

"If that were true, we wouldn't all be here right now. In your apartment."

"She has a point," Eli said.

V shook his head. "Liza, we already negotiated. I'll add access to my computers and Athena. And I'll stop hacking you. Nothing else."

"But what if..."

"He doesn't have to tell us," I said, cutting her off. "I really appreciate that you're all here to help me. But if this is just going to be us fighting, I don't want any part of it." I wouldn't willingly walk into a situation that made me feel like I was burning. I couldn't think straight like this. It would be better to work on my own.

"Obviously she doesn't care who you are," Liza said. "She was living with the leader of the Helspet Mafia and didn't even realize it. She's clearly mentally unstable."

"Excuse me?" What was her problem? Who came into someone's home and started throwing out insults like this?

"All I'm saying is that he's asking a lot from us when he doesn't even trust us with his identity."

"That's not what you just said. You called me crazy." *What a bitch.*

"To make a point. Don't be so sensitive."

We all jumped when V slammed his fist against the glass table. I hadn't even seen him walk over there. He folded his arms across his chest. "Liza, we could really use your help. I've already told you that. But if you're not going to let this go, I'm going to have to ask you to leave."

She glanced over at the computers with a dreamy look on her face. "Fine." She shrugged her shoulders. "Consider it dropped."

V nodded. "If everyone would take a seat."

The rest of us joined Liza around the table. I sat down across from Liza and Eli quickly stole the seat beside me, almost running into V. Eli draped his arm on the back of my chair without touching me.

The hostility was back in the air almost immediately as V took the seat across from Eli and glared at him.

This wasn't going well at all. I wanted answers. Not whatever the hell this was.

V cleared his throat. "Liza, what have you found out about Sadie Davis?"

"Not as much as I would have liked. She's ex military. More importantly, she's a highly trained sniper. Hopefully that doesn't come into play."

My stomach seemed to churn at her words. So that was how I was going to die. When I least expected it.

"There is a development on our end," V said. "Sadie ran into her yesterday. She put her hand up," V raised his hand, his five fingers spread apart. "She thought she was telling her to stop. But today when they ran into each other again, she only had four fingers raised."

"Is she counting down to something?" Eli asked.

"It sure seems like it." I shifted slightly in my chair. "We have four days to figure out what."

"Four," Liza said. "Huh."

We all turned toward her.

"What if she was telling you to stop yesterday. But today, she could have been saying something else. I mean, V called this thing the meeting of The Four. What if it's about us?"

A chill ran down my spine. We all looked back and forth between each other.

"We won't be able to figure out what she's saying until we pinpoint what her purpose here is," V said. "I think we should have Sadie walk through her whole story. We must be missing something."

I tucked a loose strand of hair behind my ear. I wasn't used to talking about my past. It was like this small piece of me I kept locked away, close to my heart. I put my hand in the middle of my chest, expecting to feel my pendant, but instead just being reminded of all that I had lost. "When I was eight my parents died in a car crash." I locked my hands together and put them on the table. "I moved in with my grandmother. She died a little less than a year later." I stared down at my hands. "I bounced around in foster care a lot. Until Don." I swallowed hard. "I don't know what you want me to say."

I felt Eli's arms move off the chair behind me and wrap around my shoulders. "We already know all of this. I don't think making her talk about it is helping anything."

Thank you.

"Well, I have plenty of amendments to that detailed story Summer just weaved," Liza said with a laugh and pulled out a notebook from her bag. "Someone created a false report saying that Summer and her grandmother both died of carbon monoxide poisoning. I traced the cyber footprint to sometime earlier this year. Which means whoever did it was trying to make it look like you disappeared and resurfaced with a stolen identity. It looks like you changed the records, falsified reports, and stole someone's identity. It's enough to put you away for a long time. The adoption papers I uncovered, on the other hand, were actually legit. You were legally adopted by Don Roberts when you left foster care."

She held up her hand like she was waiting for me to protest. I hadn't planned on saying anything, though.

"But, now we know that he changed your name and adopted you as Sadie Davis so that everyone else would think Summer Brooks was missing. He was never enrolled as a foster parent. So whoever took you to him wasn't a part of the system either. Do you remember who it was?"

I bit the inside of my lip. "I was just a kid. I don't..." I tried to pull back the memory of when I first met Don. My mind was drawing a blank. All I could remember is that I thought he had a friendly smile. I had thought my luck had finally changed. Just the thought made me want to throw up. I shook my head. "I don't remember."

Liza sighed. "Okay, so we don't have a lead there. All we have about the missing persons case is the claim that Rebecca Young filed. Did you know her, Summer?"

"Yes. She was my neighbor."

"You lived at several addresses with your parents. Which address was she a neighbor at?"

"The last one."

Liza jotted something down in her notebook. "Okay, so Rebecca Young was the only person looking for you. Is that something we should look into? Maybe..."

"No." I was surprised by how authoritative my voice sounded. "Can we please just leave her and her family out of it? I don't want to pull anyone else into this mess."

"I haven't left a cyber footprint since I was five. I think it's worth looking into. But right now, we're talking about what we already know." She pulled out a file from her bag and opened it. "Back to where your story left off. Summer lived with Don Roberts for almost six years. During that time she was physically assaulted on multiple occasions, leaving her with dozens of broken bones, yet only one known trip to the emergency room. She was also sexually assaulted..."

"Liza please stop," I said.

Liza ignored me. "And she suffered irreparable damage to..."

"Liza stop."

"...Her pelvis."

The air seemed to leave my lungs.

Eli's arm fell from around my shoulders. "What does that mean exactly?" He grabbed one of the papers from Liza's file and looked at the report she had written up.

"It means I can't have children," I said. It was probably the first time I had ever spoken those words out loud. Hearing it made it seem so final. I placed my hand on my stomach, remembering everything Don had taken from me. "I'll be right back." My chair squeaked behind me as I abruptly stood up. "I just need to use the restroom." I walked away before anyone said anything to me.

I locked the door behind me, placed both hands on the vanity, and stared at my reflection in the mirror. And for a brief moment I saw it. I saw the look that was in Don's eyes. In the real Sadie Davis' eyes. *Death*. I lifted my hands and took a step back. I was becoming them. He was turning me into my worst nightmare.

I ran my fingers through my hair and turned away from the mirror. He had killed my hopes and dreams. He had killed my reason to live. Maybe continuing down this path was what he wanted. I suddenly felt exhausted. Like all the fight in me had just seeped out of my bones.

Tonight wasn't going as planned. I didn't expect my most intimate details to be revealed. No one at the table needed to know about my likelihood of reproduction. Or lack thereof. Liza had crossed the line. How could she have not seen that revealing that would hurt me? I took a deep breath to try to calm myself down.

None of that mattered. Especially if we didn't figure out what the real Sadie Davis was going to do in four days. We had more to talk about. Me locking myself in the bathroom wasn't helping anyone. Without taking another glance in the mirror, I walked back out into the hall.

I froze when I saw a picture being projected onto the wall in front of the glass table. I pressed my lips together.

It was of Miles' family. *And me.* His mom and dad were standing with their arms wrapped around each other's backs, huge smiles on their faces. Miles and I were standing in front of his parents and his father's hand was on his son's shoulder. There was an awkward gap between me and Miles. When I was little, I had always wanted that space to disappear. But what I hadn't realized was that the space between us never existed. I thought about Miles' story about meeting me. And how different it was from what I thought had happened. It was clear as day in the picture though. Because Miles wasn't staring at the camera. He was staring at me.

I quickly wiped away a tear that had fallen down my cheek. "I asked you not to look into the Young family."

The three of them turned toward me. I guess they hadn't heard me exit the bathroom.

"When were you going to tell us that your RA was Rebecca Young's son?" Eli asked.

"I..." my voice trailed off. "I didn't think it was important. It was a long time ago. He doesn't know that I'm Summer."

"You don't know that for sure."

"Yes I do. He would never lie to me." I let that thought sink in. All I had been doing to Miles since I was nine years old was lying to him. Telling him I was fine. Telling him I didn't mind foster care. Telling him no one was hurting me.

"People change, Summer."

I knew that better than anyone. Because I wasn't Summer anymore. I looked back up at the picture on the wall. *He loved me. And I let him down.*

"If she doesn't think her identity has been compromised, then it's not an issue," V said.

"You may have been watching her, but so have I." Eli stood up. "This Miles guy wants her. You should see the way he looks at her, like a fucking piece of meat."

"He doesn't." How dare he talk about him that way? I walked back over to the table. "You don't know him. He's not like that."

"Miles Young has probably slept with half the women on campus," Eli said. "He's a womanizer."

I couldn't' exactly argue with him. It was the same thing that Kins had said. Apparently Miles was a total player. But I hadn't seen any of that. It seemed like he only had eyes for me. "He's changed then."

"He's just playing you," Eli said. He directed his attention back to V. "Look, she turns heads. We both know that. Miles has been trying to date her since the semester began. We can't have anyone else knowing about this. All I'm saying is that it's safer for her if everyone thinks she has a boyfriend..."

"We already talked about this," V said.

When had he had secret conversations with Liza and Eli? It was like he had bartered with both of them to be part of this weird group. What had they agreed on?

"I'm the best option," Eli continued. "We need her to be left alone. If she walks around with me that'll happen."

Liza was nodding along with every word that came out of Eli's mouth. "I agree with Eli."

"She can talk to whoever she wants to as long as she keeps her distance," V said.

"Not if it puts her and the rest of us in danger." Eli put his hand down on the table and leaned forward. "We're asking her to end one friendship, it's not a big deal."

"Does anyone care what I think?" I asked.

They all turned toward me.

And I realized I didn't exactly know how to phrase what I wanted to say. I had feelings for Eli. Yes, sleeping with him was an accident, but if anything it made those feelings stronger. V and I had chemistry that I had a hard time ignoring. It was as if our pain drew us together. I didn't want this to end up with both of them hating me. "Miles is the last part of me that makes sense. He was my best friend growing up."

"And now?" V said.

I bit the inside of my lip. *I've been in love with him since I was eight years old.* "I just don't want him to get hurt."

V turned back toward Eli. "Fine. Pretend to be her boyfriend in public to keep her safe. Let's leave the make-believe at the door, though, shall we?"

For a few minutes, it seemed like V had been on my side. But then like a flip of a switch, he had just written off my relationship with Miles too. Everything they said was right. Being with Miles put him in danger. Maybe just talking to him did. I had to give him up, yet all I wanted to do was watch the meteor shower in his arms.

CHAPTER 23
Monday

"That brings us to our next topic," Liza said. She pressed a button on her phone and the picture of Miles disappeared. "We need to figure out who the mysterious Mr. Crawford is."

I wrapped my arms around myself and rejoined them at the table. Maybe analyzing my life was easy for them, but it wasn't for me. And just thinking about alienating Miles made me feel so cold. I had accidentally done that before. I wasn't going to do it again. Not when I finally knew the truth about what had happened. He hadn't abandoned me at all. In reality, he and his mom were the only ones who even cared whether or not I was still breathing.

"Earth to Summer," Liza said and waved her hand in front of my face.

"What?" Apparently I had missed something.

"How did you say you got in touch with Mr. Crawford in the first place?"

"I didn't. He approached me on the way to my shift at the local diner back home one day. He said he had been sent by the foster care system to check up on me. He claimed that they had recently been notified of the abuse."

"And you believed him? Don't those people usually come to the house to check in with kids?"

"I thought maybe because of the abuse he didn't want Don to be present." I knew it sounded stupid now. But in the moment, it felt like someone was finally on my side.

"Plus, if he worked for the foster care system, why didn't you think it was odd that he was also handling your time at the witness protection program? Clearly all red flags."

"I was scared. The day before Mr. Crawford came, Don had tried to kill me. I didn't think..."

"No, you didn't think at all." Liza pushed her glasses up her nose. "Well, he's definitely not a member of either the foster care system or the witness protection program. And we don't have any photos because he never set foot in Don's house. Or else Eli may have actually been of some use."

Eli leaned back in his chair. "Tear me apart all you want. But cut her some slack, Liza. You know what she's been through."

"I just don't understand what kind of person blindly follows a strange man when they've been previously assaulted," Liza said. "That's insane."

"He promised that I'd be safe," I said quietly. The now familiar chill seemed to run down my spine and I looked over at V. He hadn't said a word since the discussion of Mr. Crawford had begun. And he had said those exact words to me about an hour ago, promising me something he couldn't really ensure. It couldn't be him though, could it? I had just thought about the fact that V seemed older than the boys my age. But Mr. Crawford was probably in his forties. That was too old, right? V couldn't be older than 40.

V locked eyes with me, as if sensing my question.

"We need more to go off of than hair color, possible age, and height," Liza said. "Think, Summer."

I pressed my lips together. Mr. Crawford had been tall too. Possibly the same height. "V..."

"It's not me," his voice rumbled.

Liza turned to him too. "And that's the kind of thing we could rule out if you'd take off your mask." It looked like she was undressing him with her eyes as she scanned him from head to toe. She was looking at him like a piece of meat more than Miles had ever looked at me that way.

"It's not me," V repeated. "I didn't know who Sadie Davis was until she came to New York."

I thought about the things he seemed to know about me. About how he refused to call me Summer Brooks. He didn't say it because he didn't have to. He didn't know Sadie Davis until she came to this city. But he had known Summer Brooks. He knew me. The real me. I wanted to press the issue but I didn't want to cause another fight. I needed to know who he was. Maybe I had more than just Miles to hold on to from my past. I could really use another friendly face.

V turned his head away from me. "But I did see Mr. Crawford. Sadie and he walked into a coffee shop together across from campus on move in day. And then they left separately. I'd recognize him if I saw him again."

"You were watching me even then?" I asked.

"Yes." He still didn't look back at me.

"When you went to my bank, then, it wasn't just a co-incidence?" I already knew the answer. I had known it all along.

"I was looking for information."

"And?"

"And nothing. I got distracted."

"So were you there for the bank robbers or something else?"

"I wanted to trace the bank transfer to your account. The men robbing the place was a perk. But they didn't have a connection to Don like I had hoped. And really they just ruined my shot at figuring out more information."

"I've already looked into the deposits," Liza said. "Her parents did leave her a trust fund and had really high life insurance policies. And she got her grandmother's inheritance too. It all came straight from their accounts, no middle man that I could find."

"So maybe Mr. Crawford's just a good Samaritan," Eli said. "Maybe he was a banker or something and found out her inheritance was about to unfreeze because she was turning 18."

Liza shook her head. "And found her how? With a new name and a new address, the police couldn't even locate her."

"So it was someone who knew about my kidnapping?" I wrapped my arms back around myself. "I don't believe that. He wasn't like Don or any of his hit men. He was kind." *I didn't feel the flames when I was beside him.*

"You just said yourself that you were scared. Maybe you just saw what you wanted to believe."

"You're looking in the wrong place. He was just undercover or something. Like Eli." I pointed to him. "Couldn't you do some digging? Look through your channels or whatever?"

"He's not a cop," Eli said. "I already ran it in the database. Unless he was using a fake name, which is highly possible."

"See. Fake name," I said. "He's probably a cop too. I mean...why else would he help me?"

"She has a point," Eli said. "There's no reason why one of Don's men would help her and risk putting themselves against the rest of the mafia. It doesn't add up, Liza."

"Fine. I'll look into some other things and see what I can find. But like I said, he doesn't work for either office he claimed to, at least with the last name Crawford. And I can't do much without a picture. I'm assuming you didn't snap one when you were spying on them in the coffee shop?" she said to V.

He shook his head. "You've hacked my phone enough times to know that I didn't."

She laughed. It was the first time I had heard her laugh all night.

"Fair enough," Liza said.

"I'm glad you think that's funny." V folded his arms across his chest.

"I can help you fine tune some of your security if you'd like."

"You're welcome to everything here. I can show you Athena too," V said.

"Great." Liza's cheeks turned slightly red as she pushed her glasses up her nose. "Is now a good time?"

He nodded. "Unless there's anything else we need to go over? Liza and I can do a little more digging about the mysterious Sadie Davis countdown and Mr. Crawford."

I was pretty sure I had just witnessed how Liza asked someone out on a date. V didn't seem to believe me when I told him Liza had a crush on him. But it was completely obvious to me and he had just unknowingly agreed to a date with her. Or maybe he did it knowingly. I was surprised when a small twinge of jealousy seared through me. *What is wrong with me?* V had already told me that we could just enjoy our borrowed time together. And I had already decided that I was putting the brakes on that. Either way, I didn't want to stick around to watch Liza flirting with him the rest of the night.

"Sounds good," Eli said. "We should probably get going anyway. I have an early class tomorrow." He stood up. "You ready to go, Summer?"

"I'm actually staying here."

Eli laughed. "Come on, I'll walk you home."

"No, I mean, I brought all my stuff. I'm staying here for the next few days. Just until we figure out what's going on with Sadie Davis." I didn't want this to turn into a fight. It wasn't that I didn't feel safe when I was with Eli or anything like that. I bit the inside of my lip. Or was that exactly the reason why I preferred staying here?

"You can just spend the night at my place. It's not a big deal."

"She's not leaving," V said. "We'll see you tomorrow, same time."

It looked like Eli was going to argue, but he immediately closed his mouth before any words came out.

I let go of the breath that I had been holding.

Eli leaned down and whispered in my ear. "Call me if you feel at all uncomfortable. I know that you trust this guy, but we don't know who he is. Just say the words and I'll be back." He placed a soft kiss against my cheek.

And for the first time, I didn't feel the flames. I wasn't sure if it was because I finally knew who he really was or because my feelings had shifted. For some reason, though, I wasn't at all sure that it was a good thing.

"Goodnight everyone," Eli said with a wave.

"Night!" Liza said cheerily. "So, um, about the processors..." her voice trailed off as she stared at V. She ran her fingers through her hair and they got caught in the tangles halfway down and she had to awkwardly pull her hand out.

Smooth.

V turned to me. I wasn't sure if he was going to invite me to do more research with them, but I cut him off before he got a chance to say what was on his mind.

"Is it alright if I head up to the roof?"

He eyed me curiously. "Why?"

"I just...want some fresh air."

"You're welcome to join us," he said.

"Psh." Liza waved her arm. "It's just boring stuff. And we can handle the rest of the research. Right, V? Have fun on the roof!" she quickly added before V could respond.

I stood up before V could try to get me to stay, partially wondering if he even wanted me to. I shook my head to try to rid that jealous feeling that was creeping into my mind. Earlier today I had told him he should date Liza. Maybe he was following my own stupid advice.

"Have a good evening, Sadie," Athena said as I approached the exit. The window slowly rose in front of me.

"Um, thanks, you too," I said awkwardly and looked up at the speaker above my head. That was the first time she had ever been nice to me. Maybe she just took some time to adjust to people. I turned around to see if maybe V had told Athena to say that.

My heart stopped beating for a moment. V was staring directly at me. Liza was talking beside him, but he definitely wasn't engaging in the conversation. It felt like my insides were melting. I quickly turned around and climbed out the window.

CHAPTER 24
Monday

The air felt heavy tonight, almost as if it was going to rain. But the sky was perfectly clear above me. Maybe the weight on my chest was the feeling of impending doom. I couldn't seem to silence the ticking clock in my head.

A tear slid down the side of my face and dropped into my hair. The few stars that were visible in the city sky blurred above me. For the first time in a long time, I finally felt like I wasn't alone. At least, there were people surrounding me who had my best interests in mind. But I kept pushing them away. Somehow that made me feel even more isolated than when I really was alone.

I lifted up my phone and stared down at Miles' name that I had just input into my contact list. I hadn't come up here for air. I had wanted to watch the meteor shower. But the stupid city lights blocked out everything. I wiped more of my tears away.

For years I had stared at the stars, wondering where Miles was. Missing him. Loving him. Cursing his name. And now he was right here. And I needed him. God, I so desperately needed him. I put the cell phone down.

I couldn't go against what everyone else that was trying to help me wanted. I felt like for the first time since I was a kid, everyone could really see me. I placed my hand on my stomach and stared up at the dark sky. The problem was that there were parts of me that I didn't want anyone to see. I was angry at Liza for sharing information to Eli and V that they didn't need to know. She had no right. She clearly didn't care about my feelings. So why should I care about hers?

I lifted up my phone again and typed out a message to Miles. "I can barely see the stars tonight." It was innocent enough. I wasn't flirting with him. I just needed to know he was out there looking at the same thing as me. For the longest time I hadn't gotten that validation. I needed it tonight. Before I could talk myself out of it, I pressed send.

If he really was a player like everyone thought, he probably wouldn't know it was me. He had probably just picked up some other girl to go watch the meteor shower with him. I jumped when my phone buzzed. I lifted it up and slid my finger across the screen.

"You're just not looking hard enough."

His words made my tears fall even faster. It wasn't the first time he had said those words to me. I remembered being back in his tree house, bickering over which stars made up certain constellations. He was the one that had always helped me see. He taught me to appreciate the smallest constellations. I wiped my tears away and tried to focus on the darkness above. The first time we had watched a meteor shower together, I swore I thought the stars were shooting out of the sky. He explained the difference to me with a whole bunch of terms I didn't understand. A part of me still believed it was the stars fleeing their spot in the sky. Escaping. Doing the one thing I could never seem to do.

I sat up as I saw the first meteor shoot across the night sky, just barely visible. A smile spread across my face as I grabbed my phone. "I just saw one," I typed out and pressed send.

"Told you so," he responded a few seconds later.

I rolled my eyes. He seemed more like his younger self via text message. I wasn't sure why. Probably because I wasn't distracted by his chiseled jaw line. I bit the inside of my lip and lay back down. I continued to stare at the screen of my phone instead of back up at the sky. It wasn't the stars that made me feel close to him right now. Or a lost pendant against my neck. I had the real him. I could say anything I wanted to him. But the years had silenced me. What could I say to a complete stranger who used to be my best friend, when all I wanted to do was apologize and tell him I forgave him too. I wanted us to start over. I wanted another chance to not let him down.

My phone buzzed in my hands before I could think of what to say.

"Are you happy?"

His words made me freeze. I closed my eyes for just a second, remembering when he had asked me that same question on the roof of my grandmother's house. Something seemed to tighten in my chest. I was able to say I was happy back then because I had him in my life. I still had my grandmother. I still had this undeniable sense of hope.

Because I hadn't met Don yet. I hadn't been beaten. I hadn't lost a baby. I hadn't given up.

I couldn't tell Miles the truth about who I was. But that didn't mean I needed to lie about my answer. I opened my eyes and typed the two letters that I was pretty sure I had forgotten how to use. "No." I pressed send. I was tired of telling everyone I was okay. I was tired of the lies. This was me reaching out.

Right after he had asked me if I was happy on my grandmother's roof, we had shared our first and only kiss. A kiss was probably an exaggeration. It was really just a peck. But we had kept our lips locked together for a few seconds. I remembered thinking I would never stop smiling.

I lifted the corners of my mouth and smiled at the sky. It terrified me that the sensation of smiling felt foreign to the muscles in my face. Like I had to strain in order to do it. And I couldn't help but think that if I had been stronger, I'd still have everything I had lost. Just the thought made my chest hurt.

My phone buzzed again. I looked down at his text: "Me either."

Was that him reaching out to me? Was he telling me that I could make him happy? The air suddenly felt heavy again. I thought about his version of what had happened when I entered foster care. He had talked about being an angry kid. I had been so preoccupied by my own pain, that I had never even bothered to ask if he was happy before. "I'm sorry if I ever let you down," I typed out and pressed send.

"You couldn't possibly."

I sat up and drew my knees to my chest, resting my chin on the top of my knee. I didn't know what to say back to him. If he knew who I was, he wouldn't have said that. Because all I had done since I was nine years old was disappoint him.

Another text came through from Miles. "Meet me on the corner of 6th and Pine in 20 minutes. There's this ice cream shop I think you might like that's open late."

I stared down at the words. I wanted to run to him. I wanted my life to be like a movie where everyone had a happy ending. The credits would start to roll right after I jumped back into Miles' arms. I shook my head. There was a reason I stopped watching Disney movies after my parents died. "I can't," I wrote back.

"You were happy that night in Central Park, right?"

"I was drunk."

"That wasn't why and you know it. Twenty minutes."

He had reached out to me just like I wanted. "I can't. I'm sorry, Miles." And I had stomped on his effort.

"I'll be waiting."

I placed my phone down beside me. *Stop waiting for me.* I buried my face in my knees and let my tears roll down my shins. Miles Young was the happy ending I would never get. I had four days. That was it. He had a whole lifetime to forget about me. I had ruined my life. I just hoped I hadn't ruined his too.

I wasn't sure how much time had passed when I started to hear a clanging noise growing closer to me. I knew the vigilante was climbing the emergency escape stairs up to the roof. But I really didn't want to see him. I quickly wiped my tears away just as he stepped onto the roof.

He walked over to me and stopped when he was directly in front of me. I blinked as I stared up at him. He put his hand out for me.

I shook my head.

He kept his hand out, waiting for me to grab it.

"I'm watching the meteor shower. I don't want to go in." I sounded like a petulant child.

"Okay," his voice rumbled as he put his hand into his pocket.

"How was your date with Liza?"

"That's why you're up here? You're jealous?" He didn't smile or laugh. Really, he showed no emotion at all. It shouldn't have surprised me. I knew what we were. A moment in time.

I sighed. "I'm not jealous." Maybe a small part of me was, but what did it matter? "You can do whatever you want."

He slowly knelt down in front of me and placed his hands on my knees.

I swallowed hard.

"I want you." He spread my thighs with his hands and leaned forward until his lips brushed against mine. "I need you." This time when our lips touched, it wasn't gentle. His hunger was back.

I put my hand at the base of his neck, pulling him closer. I needed him too. He so easily took away the pain in my chest. I knew that I was out of my mind. But I also knew that whatever this was could get me through another day.

CHAPTER 25
Tuesday

Something was seriously wrong with me. I had issues, but the vigilante did too. That's why it felt right. But that wasn't a good reason to run into his arms. Especially when I clearly had feelings for Miles too.

I bit the end of my pen as I stared at the words the professor was writing on the board. I should have been paying attention, but everything the professor said seemed to pass over my head. What was I even doing in this class? Despite what Liza thought, Sadie Davis wasn't talking about the four members of our group. She was counting down the days. I was running out of time to figure out what it all meant.

I shoved my notebook into my backpack and slipped out the back door of the large lecture hall. The professor didn't even turn around. *No one's going to miss me.* I immediately shook away the thought.

The leaves were just starting to change color. I took a huge breath of fresh air. The bright green of campus was slowly fading away. *Just like I'm fading away. Stop.*

Eli was supposed to meet me after class to walk me back to V's, but I couldn't make my feet stay still. There was no time to wait around. I needed to move, to feel the burn of my muscles. Three days wasn't enough time to learn how to defend myself. But it wasn't going to stop me from trying. Hopefully V would be up for a training session.

I started walking toward V's apartment when I saw her. Sadie Davis was sitting on a bench reading a book, like she was just another college student on campus. It was like she knew that I was going to walk by here after class. Did that mean she knew where V lived?

Unlike the other times I had seen her, this time I didn't freeze. I actually started walking faster. This could be my one chance to speak to her. I needed to understand why she was doing this. And what exactly she was doing.

As if sensing my presence, she closed the book and looked up at me. The expression on her face made it seem like she was surprised to see that I was coming toward her. She immediately held up three fingers. There was no smile this time. She looked like she was panicking because I wasn't stopping.

Hoards of students suddenly started to pour onto the walking paths between us, blocking her from my line of sight.

By the time I reached the bench, she was gone. But the book she had been reading was still there. I lifted up the tattered copy of Heart of Darkness by Joseph Conrad. I had read it for an English assignment in high school. It had no connection whatsoever to what Sadie Davis was doing here. It was about a group of men sailing the Congo. The book itself did have a connection, though.

I loved reading growing up. It was like I was able to escape from my life through the pages of a book. But I had hated this one. It didn't feel like an escape at all. I could barely make my way through it. And it wasn't just because I didn't enjoy the story. I opened it up and saw the blood smeared across the title page.

I remembered blocking the bottle with my hand. Bleeding until I felt dizzy. Slowly pulling the shards out one by one. Wiping my palm against the pages of the book and hiding the evidence in my backpack. Thinking the bandages and the blood was enough to put him away. Being laughed at for having stories running in my head.

After Don found out I went to the police, I ended up with a broken arm, a welt on the side of my head, and a distrust of law enforcement. He beat me with the book I tried to get him arrested with. I hated that book. I hated him. But I learned to keep my mouth shut and I stopped believing in a better life. In a lot of ways, this book had been the end of my hope.

It wasn't just the memory that this book served either. My heart truly was filled with darkness, just like the title said. Don knew that. He had put the darkness there with his own two brutal hands.

I glanced at the bottom of the page where a note was scrawled. "This would have been more fun if you hadn't already stopped living, Sadie." My name was in quotes again, just like the notes I had gotten before Don had gone dark. He was back. This was his handwriting. And it wasn't Sadie Davis that I should be fearing. It was him.

***

"What other proof do you need?" I said and slammed my hand down onto the book.

Liza just stared at me. "Don could have written that awhile ago. We don't know how long he's been planning this. It doesn't prove anything."

"He's here. Why do none of you believe me?" I looked around the table. Eli and V didn't come to my defense. No one was on my side with this. But I was the one that actually knew Don. None of them did. He was back in the city. I could feel it in my bones.

"Look," Liza said. "If he was back in New York, I would know. I have facial recognition running non-stop on V's computers. He's not here."

"I don't need technology to know that he's close."

Liza leaned back in her chair. "Actually, you do. A hunch doesn't prove anything. He's not here, Summer."

"But..."

"Sadie," V said. "We'll look into it, but Liza is right. We have everything set up so that we'll know as soon as he's back. He couldn't have gotten past that much surveillance."

"And if you'd stop touching that book, we might be able to get some information from it." Liza pulled a pencil out from behind her ear that I hadn't been able to see underneath all of her hair. She pushed the book away from my hand with the eraser end of the pencil.

"It's just my blood. You can't get any new information from that."

"We can run it for fingerprints," Eli said. "Maybe that'll finally point us in the direction of some kind of connection here."

I wanted to slap everyone at this table. "There's no one else involved. Sadie Davis works for Don. She's his messenger. And he's back! And if we don't figure out what they're planning to do I'm going to be dead in three days!" I felt like I was hyperventilating. I couldn't seem to catch my breath.

"Hey," V said. He stood up and put his hand on my arm. "Why don't you go lie down for a bit while we run the book for prints?"

I pulled my arm away from him. "I need some fresh air. I'm going for a walk."

"Let me come with you," Eli said as his chair squeaked across the floor.

"I don't need an escort. There's no danger right? That's what you all think? That I'm crazy?"

"We didn't say that," V said.

You didn't need to. I could see it on all their faces. None of them had my back. None of them believed me. This time when I approached the window it opened without Athena saying anything. It was like she could sense my bad mood.

I wanted to hang out with someone who believed in me. Someone who had always had my back, even when I thought he hadn't. I pulled out my phone and clicked on Miles' name. "6th and Pine you said? I'm going to go check it out now." I pressed send before I could tell myself the millions of reasons why I shouldn't be talking to him. I started walking toward 6th and Pine. Even if he didn't respond, I could still use that ice cream. We had met early for our meeting because I had told everyone I had an important update. Which meant I hadn't grabbed anything to eat. And now I was starving and pissed. Ice cream was the perfect solution.

My phone buzzed before I had even taken a few steps.
"Ice cream for dinner? I'm in. Give me 20 minutes."

I smiled down at the text. For just one night I was going to be normal. I was going to do what I wanted. There was no guarantee that I'd get more time. I knew that I couldn't exactly be myself around Miles. But it wasn't really about that. It was more so that being with him reminded me of who I really was. And if I could have one more hour as Summer Brooks, I'd take it. It might be my last chance.

When I arrived at the ice cream shop, I was happy to see that it was actually ice cream and not some ritzy frozen yogurt joint. I wanted the real thing, not some barely healthier alternative. I peered through the window at the menu posted above the checkout counter. They had every flavor I could possibly think of. I stopped scanning the options when my eyes landed on mint chocolate chip. I smiled, remembering what it was like for Miles to know me.

"You cheated!" I said and grabbed the cards out of his hand.
"I did not."
"Miles, you only have three of a kind instead of four."
"Jokers are wild."
"They are not! You can't just make up rules halfway through."
I folded my arms across my chest.
"Just because I'm better than you at this doesn't mean that I cheated." He picked up the spoon from his empty bowl and leaned over toward my bowl, which was still half full.
"Don't you dare touch my ice cream, Miles Young."

He smiled out of the corner of his mouth. "What'll happen to me if I do, Summer Brooks?" He leaned even closer toward my bowl that was sitting on the floor by my knee.

"Don't you do it."

He put his spoon in my ice cream and took a huge bite.

"You're a cheater and a thief."

He quickly picked up my bowl and stood up.

"Miles!" To me, stealing ice cream was sacrilegious.

"If you want it back, you'll have to come get it." He backed away slowly and took another bite of my ice cream.

I got up off the floor and ran after him. He laughed as I jumped onto his back. He tried to spin me off, but I was clinging to him with all my strength. I reached down, grabbed a sticky fistful of ice cream and smashed it against his cheating, thieving face.

His laughter only grew as he skidded across the linoleum floor. Suddenly he slipped, leaving us in a pile of sticky, tangled limbs.

"What on earth are you kids doing?" Mrs. Young said.

We looked up to see her with her hands on her hips, but there was a smile on her face.

"Summer stole my ice cream," Miles said with a laugh as he pulled away from me.

"I did not, Mrs. Young. He stole mine."

She shook her head, but the smile remained. She opened up the freezer door and pulled out the container of mint chocolate chip ice cream. "Here." She grabbed two new spoons and put them into the container of ice cream and placed it on the floor beside us. "You both need to learn how to share."

The truth was, I didn't mind sharing with Miles. I really just wanted an excuse to be tangled up on the floor with him.

He stuck his tongue out at me. "Fine, if we have to, Mom." He lifted up one of the spoons and held it out to me, almost like a peace *offering. But when I went to reach for it, he wiped it across my cheek, getting a little ice cream off of my face. Then he proceeded to put the spoon into his mouth.*

I gulped. It was the sexiest thing I had ever seen. We always just shared one bowl after that.

"You finally said yes."

I jumped, being pulled out of my memory. I turned to see Miles smiling at me. Seeing him still made me nervous after all these years. "Technically I asked you here. So...you said yes to me."

"Right, right. After standing me up last night I was a little surprised to see your text." He pushed his hair off his forehead.

I shrugged my shoulders. "I like to keep you on your toes."

He smiled out of the corner of his mouth. "That you do."

It felt like my heart was melting. "I hope you didn't wait too long for me last night."

"Only 3 hours."

"What? Really? I'm so, so sorry."

He laughed. "No, maybe fifteen minutes or so. I shot you a few more texts and when you didn't respond, I assumed the worst."

In a few days the worst would probably mean I was dead on the street. I immediately shook away the thought. I wasn't going to think about that tonight. For just a few hours I was going to hang out and be solely focused on the boy who used to eat way more than his fair share of ice cream.

He grabbed the handle of the door to the ice cream shop. "After you." He gestured with his hand.

"Thank you." Maybe he used to be a card cheater and an ice cream thief, but now he was a gentleman. "How has soccer been going?" For some reason, the thought of an awkward silence between us terrified me. We never used to have those. Any stretches of silence between us hadn't been awkward to me at all. They were just filled with thoughts of me wishing he would kiss me. I wondered if he had been thinking the same thing.

He shrugged. "Good. We're undefeated so far. I noticed that you weren't at my last game."

"You couldn't possibly have noticed that. Thousands of people were probably at your last game."

"I noticed."

I pressed my lips together and stared up at the menu that I had already studied.

"Next," the man at the checkout counter called.

"You first," Miles said with a smile.

I walked up to the front of the line. Even though there were dozens of enticing flavors, I knew exactly what I wanted. Not just because of the memory that brought a smile to my face, but because I knew it was Miles' favorite. "One bowl of mint chocolate chip," I said. I glanced over at Miles.

He had lowered his eyebrows slightly as if he was studying me. "Make that two," he said as he pulled out his wallet.

"Oh, no, I can pay for myself."

"I finally got you out on a date. I got this."

"But I..."

"I insist." He put the money down on the counter.

A date. I had been waiting twelve years to go on a real date with Miles. I watched him pay for the ice cream and we stepped to the side to wait for it to be scooped. "So that's what this is...a date?"

"Isn't it?" He smiled as his eyes locked with mine. It still looked like he was studying me.

I blinked, hoping my colored contacts hadn't shifted out of place or something. "That depends on what you classify as a date." I laughed awkwardly.

"Well," he said as he leaned against the counter. "Tonight I was thinking ice cream and a walk in Central Park. And if everything goes well..." his eyes landed on my lips. "We can end it with the best kiss of your life."

CHAPTER 26
Tuesday

My throat made a weird squeaking noise and I quickly turned away from him. It felt like my heart was banging against my ribcage. *The best kiss of my life?* I should have rolled my eyes. Or laughed it off. But I knew he wasn't lying. I had dreamed of him kissing me when I was a little girl. And I had replayed the kiss we did share over and over again as we grew up apart. A new kiss with him would surely shatter that silly peck I held on a pedestal. He was still that same cocky boy, after all. Just older with more experience and a sexier jaw line.

God, what the hell am I thinking? I can't kiss him. But when I looked back over at him, my eyes seemed to travel down to his mouth. And that smile I loved so much. *Why exactly can't I kiss him again?*

The ice cream man set our bowls down on the counter and Miles picked them both up. I tried to focus on the fact that he was still an ice cream thief instead of the fact that I was craving his lips a lot more than I was craving mint chocolate chip. I followed him over to a booth and slid into the seat across from him.

I lifted up my spoon and stared down at my bowl. Usually I dreamed about going back in time. I'd be consumed by the idea of reliving our ice cream fight. I looked up at Miles. But I wasn't sure I wanted that anymore. Sitting across from him now, maybe that was where I was supposed to be. Maybe I could still have a normal life after all of this. I ignored the urge to touch my stomach. Normal might have been a stretch. But what if Miles and I were always meant to be? What if this could be real?

He smiled at me as he took a bite of ice cream. "What are you thinking right now?"

"That I'm happy when we're together."

He put his elbows on the table and leaned forward slightly. "Then why are you trying so hard to keep us apart?" He was looking at me like he genuinely wanted to know. Like he wanted to know my darkest secrets that always seemed to be threatening to tear my happiness to shreds.

"I've heard the rumors. About you being a player."

"Do you always believe everything you hear?"

I took a bite of my ice cream. "No, usually not. But when I've heard it from multiple sources...it makes it seem more likely to be true."

"Sources? Am I under investigation?" He flashed me the smile that made my knees feel weak.

"No. I'm just curious if it's true."

"Well, the short answer would be yes."

"So you only have one night stands?"

"That's one way to put it." He suddenly looked sad. He pushed some of the ice cream around with his spoon.

"How would you put it?"

He looked back up at me. "That's the long answer."

"I think I'd like to hear that one."

"Honestly, I don't see any reason to pretend that something could be more than what it is. Because for my whole life, my heart has belonged to someone else. I couldn't commit to anyone knowing that I wasn't all in. A casual hookup can numb that pain, but that's all it ever was."

I took a bite of ice cream to prevent myself from speaking, because telling him the truth was on the tip of my tongue. I understood what he said. My life apart from him had been terribly lonely. I didn't blame him for trying to numb the pain. Somehow it was better than him having been in love with tons of other girls. I still had his heart. That's what he was saying. Kind of. I had to remind myself that I wasn't Summer Brooks anymore.

I dropped my spoon in my bowl. "Is that what you want with me? Just one night?"

"I'm so tired of living in the past. Especially when the present is so sweet." He leaned forward and wiped his thumb underneath of my lip, removing a tiny trace of ice cream. He proceeded to put the side of his thumb in his mouth.

If I thought a spoon had been sexy in my memories, this was a million times sexier. I crossed my legs under the table. "So you want to commit to me?" I wasn't sure why I was asking him these questions. This was just supposed to be one night of normalcy. But I had a feeling I wasn't going to be able to tear myself away from him so easily.

"I think I've been committed to you since I bumped into you at the Corner Diner."

"Because you thought I was her?"

"No." He reached out his hand and placed it on top of mine. "Because talking to you gave me this weird feeling in the pit of my stomach that I haven't felt in years. Sadie."

He rubbed his thumb along the back of my hand. "You feel it too, or else you wouldn't be here right now. I think we should see where this thing takes us."

A normal girl would find fault in his logic. He had been in love with someone else his whole life. And suddenly he was just willing to throw it all away? But I wasn't a normal girl. I was *the* girl. The one he still loved and the one he wanted to be with now. Really, I was more focused on the fact that my hand fit perfectly in his, just like it had back then. He didn't need to explain anything to me. I was in love with him too. But I couldn't exactly break off my fake relationship with Eli. Especially when the whole purpose of said relationship was to keep Miles away. "Are you done?"

"What?"

I put my spoon in his bowl before he even realized what I was asking. He probably owed me a hundred bowls of ice cream. He couldn't possibly be upset by this.

A smile broke over his face. "Are you seriously stealing my ice cream?"

"What are you going to do about it?" I had this overwhelming urge to be tangled up with him in a sticky mess on the floor again.

He pushed his bowl into the middle of the table and leaned forward slightly. "Actually, I don't mind sharing with you."

I was pretty sure my heart was melting faster than the ice cream. The more we talked, the more we had both started leaning closer. I wondered if he was thinking about the kiss he promised me. Because I sure was.

I thought he might push the fact that I hadn't really responded to his proposal of giving this a shot. But he seemed content with the fact that I was willing to at least share a bowl with him. To us, that's what love was.

"How are your parents?" The words poured out of my mouth before I could stop them. "I mean, you know, what are they like?" I had thought a lot about his mom and dad over the years. In a lot of ways, they were the closest thing I had left to a family. I had been at his house almost as much as my own when I was a kid.

He laughed. "They're doing well. I love my parents. They've been with me through everything, dragging me back and forth to soccer practice. They'll be coming to the homecoming game if you want to meet them."

I swallowed hard. I wanted to take him up on his offer. Honestly, I could really use a hug from Mrs. Young. She had cared that I had gone missing. She had tried to find me. I cleared my throat. "Yeah, maybe. That's kind of a big step isn't it? Meeting the parents."

He laughed. "You've gotten me completely off my game, it's true."

"So on one of your countless dates with random women, what would you be doing right now?"

"We'd probably already be in bed."

The way he said it was probably more provocative than the actual words. Or maybe it was just the fact that his eyes on me was making my heart beat uncontrollably. I laughed awkwardly. "I think you promised me a walk in Central Park first."

"We should probably get that out of the way then." He took the last bite of ice cream and winked at me.

I'm pretty sure my jaw actually dropped. "First of all, how rude of you for finishing the ice cream."

"You already finished your bowl." He slid out of the booth.

"But you owe me." Again, words were pouring out of my mouth that made no sense when he didn't know that I was Summer.

"I owe you the kiss that I promised. But beyond that..." his words trailed off as he studied me again. He shook his head, dumped our bowls in the trash, and then put his hand out for me. "And I promise I'm planning on being a perfect gentleman tonight."

I bit my lip so that I wouldn't be compelled to pout. If everyone else could sleep with him, why wasn't I allowed to? I had been waiting the longest. God, I had completely lost it. I put my hand in his and he pulled me to my feet. But instead of stepping back, he pulled me toward him until I was pressed against his chest.

"You're not like those other girls, Sadie," he said and tucked a loose strand of hair behind my ear. "Besides, patience makes everything better, don't you think?"

"You're so full of yourself, Miles Young." I lightly tapped his chest and stepped around him. But he was probably right. He just didn't realize how long I had waited to have him. I looked over my shoulder. He had a playful grin on his face as he followed me out of the ice cream shop. As soon as we were on the sidewalk, he immediately slipped his hand into mine.

I didn't pull away. I didn't tell him the lie that I already had a boyfriend. I wanted to enjoy this one night. The truth was, we just fit. There was no denying it. We were meant to be together. We always had been.

I laughed as he started jogging, pulling me along with him. "Where are we going?"

"I want to show you something."

It didn't matter where we were going. I'd always been willing to follow him to the ends of the earth. But after several minutes I got a cramp in my side. It just proved that what I really should have been doing was training with V. I dismissed the thought. I didn't want to think about V when Miles was right here.

"I need a minute to catch my breath." I stopped, pulling back on his hand.

He smiled as he turned toward me. "Hop on then." He knelt down on one knee in front of me and tapped his back.

I wasn't going to protest. The thought of having my arms wrapped around him was enticement enough. I climbed onto his back and clasped my hands beneath his neck. He stood up, securing his hands around my thighs. I was pretty sure we didn't need a bed. He could have me right here right now.

The neckline of his t-shirt had shifted down slightly and I could feel the softness of his skin beneath the fabric. He laughed and I felt the vibration below his Adam's apple. I dropped my head slightly so that my face was adjacent with the side of his neck and took a deep breath. *Home.*

"What's your favorite constellation?" I asked. I remembered when I went to the observatory, the telescope I had looked into was angled at Sagitta. He had never told me whether it was him that was looking at it.

"I like the small ones. The ones you really have to look for." His head tilted up and I knew he was searching the sky.

I swallowed hard. "But is there a specific one?"

"Sagitta. It's brightest in the fall. But you still need a telescope to see it in the city."

I rested my chin on his shoulder. All those years apart, he had been looking at it too. *It's me.* I was so tempted to whisper those two words in his ear. I had to bite my lip to prevent myself from speaking.

He tilted his head toward me and my nose brushed against his cheek. His laughter vibrated through my hand again. "Close your eyes, Sadie."

"You're not going to do something weird to me, are you?"

"You'll just have to wait and see."

I closed my eyes. I felt him turn toward me again to make sure my eyes were closed. My hands slid further into his shirt. I didn't even care what he thought. There was no way I could stop touching him. One touch was all it took.

He placed a soft kiss against my forearm. The feeling of his lips against my skin made my arm tingle. Clearly he didn't mind what I was doing. I turned my mouth toward the side of his neck. I wanted to taste him. I inched closer.

But before I found the courage to kiss his skin, we stopped. I was disappointed when he let go of my thighs.

"Keep your eyes closed," he said.

I slid down his back and released my hands from him. The next thing I knew he had his hand over my eyes. I felt his body heat behind me.

"Okay. You can look now." He slowly lowered his hand from my eyes.

We were standing on a bridge. The water below us was reflecting the city lights. It almost looked like a reflection of the stars in the sky inside. Thousands and thousands of lights. "It's so beautiful."

"Not as beautiful as you."

I laughed and turned toward him. "Did you seriously bring me here just to set up that line?"

"No, but it was a plus." He smiled out of the corner of his mouth. "They host events at the row house across the lake at night. Usually you can hear music and I had fun dancing with you the other night. It should start any minute."

As if on cue, light violin music could be heard flitting across the water.

"May I have this dance?" He took a step back from me and put his hand out.

I curtseyed and he laughed. I held my breath as I put my hand in his. For one second.

He pulled me close.

For two seconds.

"Sadie." His voice was low and seductive and it made my insides flip over.

For three seconds.

One of his hands drifted to my lower back as the other lightly touched the side of my face.

For four seconds.

"It feels like I've known you all my life," he whispered as he tilted his face down toward mine.

For five seconds.

I tilted my head up until my lips brushed against his. My world was dark and gray. But when his lips touched mine, it was like suddenly everything was in color again. Everything was alright. That was an understatement. Everything was perfect. I stood up on my tiptoes to deepen the kiss. All that pent up passion he had been holding on to for Summer, I could feel it. It reverberated from my head to my toes as we both clung to each other in the darkness.

It took five seconds for me to feel complete for the first time in ten years. And I knew in that moment that I couldn't run from this feeling. Screw everyone else. Screw the danger. I had to tell him the truth. He deserved to know. I pulled back. "I need to tell you something."

A big raindrop landed on my forehead as I looked up at him. That single splash of water was like a wakeup call. My life wasn't meant to be in color. It was dreary and dull. I lived in a nightmare, and this was a dream. And it was time to wake up. Tears started to well in my eyes.

"Tell me." His hand moved to the side of my neck as his eyes searched mine.

The rain started to pick up. "I'm sorry, I have to go."

"Tell me."

"I'm so sorry, Miles." I pulled away from him.

"Sadie don't..." his words faded away as I ran. But I swore I heard him say, "don't leave me." My throat seemed to constrict as I ran. My tears mixed with the rain until I was completely soaked in my own misery. Why did I have to wake up from my dream? I covered my face in my hands and collapsed in the muddy grass, letting the violent sobs rake through me. The last light in my life had just been extinguished. And I was alone in my darkness.

CHAPTER 27
Wednesday

I pulled the covers up to my chin and rolled over once again. Sleep evaded me. Every time I closed my eyes I saw the hurt look on Miles' face. Or the fire he seemed to light inside of me. It was like I had stopped breathing when we were apart. And as soon as he kissed me, my lungs had suddenly inflated.

When I forced my mind to push thoughts of him aside, I'd see Sadie Davis slowly counting down until she reached zero. *This isn't working.* I shoved the covers off of myself and climbed out of bed.

I had gotten back from my date with Miles late, and V's apartment had been empty. Hopefully it still was. I didn't want to talk to V or anyone else. The lights immediately turned on when I stepped out of the bedroom. Maybe now that Athena seemed to like me a little better she'd let me do some research.

I was on my way to the computers when a file on the glass table caught my eye. I opened it up and sat down. It was the results of the fingerprint analysis from my copy of Heart of Darkness.

My fingerprints were on there, which was nothing obvious. I turned the page. The real Sadie Davis' fingerprints were on it. I stared down at the picture of her. Same birthday as me. Matching hair and eye color to my current ones.

Why? I put my forehead in my hand. Why couldn't I piece it together? What possible reason would Don have for making me steal some random woman's identity?

I looked down at her eyes. She looked so sad. And lost. Was that how I looked? I wondered if he was beating her too. Forcing himself on her. That's what caused that look. Suddenly I felt myself feeling bad for the person who was playing games with my head.

Staring at her didn't help anything. It didn't put the pieces together. It made me pity her like everyone pitied me. Really, it just made my chest ache. Because she looked so much like my mother. And it tore me to pieces that she looked so sad. All I could remember was my mom smiling up at my father. Laughing. This wasn't her. It couldn't possibly be her. *But I used to laugh. I used to smile.*

I tried to shake away the thought, but it had settled around me, sending a chill down my spine. *This is not my mother.* I turned to the next page in the file to try to dismiss the nagging suspicion. And...my breath seemed to catch in my throat. *Julie Harris.* I reread the name at least a dozen times. Julie Harris' fingerprints were on the book. I wouldn't have even known my babysitter's last name, but I recognized the picture of her. It looked like it was a picture from a newspaper, announcing her engagement to a man named Jacob. His arm was wrapped around her shoulders as they smiled at the camera.

Jacob. I swallowed hard. I wondered if it was the same Jacob who she had just started dating when I last saw her. The one who bought her the Converses. The one she said she didn't know if she was in love with. I stared at their smiling faces. Clearly they were in love now.

I didn't want to tear my eyes away from the picture. I wanted one person from my past to have ended up happy. But there was another newspaper clipping below this one. I knew in my gut it wouldn't be good. Because why on earth were Julie's fingerprints on my book?

I glanced down at the other clipping. It was a missing persons article. My heart seemed to pound in my chest as I looked at the date. Julie had gone missing three and a half weeks ago. Right around the time I escaped from hell with the help of Mr. Crawford. She had been missing for almost a month. What were the odds that she was still alive?

My mind immediately pictured the bloody bunny slippers. I had been wearing them the last time I saw her. *She's dead.* I put a hand over my mouth stifling my sob. *Oh my God, Julie's dead.* There had been so much blood. I fumbled with my phone as I pulled it out of my pocket. *So much fucking blood.* I needed to talk to V. We needed to try to find her in case it wasn't too late.

As if answering my silent plea, there was a whooshing noise in the apartment. I turned around to see the window slowly rising. V stepped in. When he saw me, he immediately pulled his hood down a little lower.

"You should be sleeping," his voice rumbled.

I grabbed the newspaper clipping and ran over to him. "I know her. Julie Harris was my babysitter growing up. She was the last person who saw me in my bunny slippers. The ones I told you about. The ones that Don sent to me covered in blood." I was almost too terrified to ask him my question. "Is she dead?" My hands were shaking so badly I couldn't get them to stop.

"I don't know."

"V, we have to find her. She's in trouble because of me. Please, we have to do something."

"I've been out all night trying to find her. Or Sadie Davis. Or Don." He pulled off his gloves. "I don't know where any of them are."

"I don't care about Sadie or Don right now. We have got to find Julie. We have to. If she's still alive..." I swallowed hard. Part of me expected him to reassure me. But maybe it was better that he didn't. What was the point of being optimistic when nothing ever seemed to turn out okay?

"We have less than three days to piece this together. We can't..."

"She's an innocent bystander! She has nothing to do with this. We have to save her."

"I'm exhausted, Sadie. I just told you I've been looking for her. I'm sorry."

"Why do you keep calling me Sadie?!" I wasn't sure why I was fighting with him. He had been out all night doing exactly what I was asking him to do. But he hadn't found Julie. And I was upset. And the thought of her being dead made my head pound. "I'm not related to that monster! V we have to do something. We can't let Don kill Julie."

"I can't even think straight right now. I need rest. We both do."

"There isn't time!" I could hear the clock ticking down in my head, racing toward zero.

"Bed. Now." His voice had suddenly gotten stern.

"No." I hated how I always sounded like a child whenever I got in a fight with him.

He sighed and stepped toward me, lifting me up in his arms.

I grimaced. "Let go of me!"

He didn't say a word as he carried me to my bedroom.

"How tired can you be if you can still pick me up? Let me down!" I tried to squirm out of his grip.

He ignored me and tightened his hands on my limbs, making it impossible to move, as he kicked the door open with his foot. He tossed me unceremoniously on the bed.

"I can't sleep right now, V. I can't. Julie's out there somewhere and she needs my help."

"Yes you can. Move over."

"You're not sleeping in here with me."

"Athena, lock the door," he said calmly as he kicked off his shoes.

I heard a clicking noise. "V, seriously, we need to do something."

"Athena, lights off."

The lights immediately turned off and I felt the bed sag.

"I've been sleeping on a couch for the last two nights," he said as his arms wrapped around me, pulling me down onto the bed. "Let's both just try to get a good night's sleep and focus on figuring everything out tomorrow."

"Can't we do that without snuggling?" I was seething. But I was also extremely aware of how strong his arms were around me. And how safe it made me feel. God, he was right. I was exhausted too.

"It's easier for me to sleep knowing that you're safe." His breath was hot on the back of my neck.

"I don't mind sleeping on the couch," I grumbled.

He lightly sighed as his breathing slowed. His hand loosened around my waist and I could tell that he had fallen asleep.

He needed this. Somehow holding me like this made him feel more content. And even though I was furious with him, I needed it too. For years I didn't have any safe form of physical contact with another person. The truth was, only Miles and V made me feel this safe. I closed my eyes tight. And sometimes Eli. When he wasn't angry.

I wouldn't mind sleeping like this on my last few nights of borrowed time.

CHAPTER 28
Wednesday

I slowly opened my eyes and was about to stretch when I froze. V's arm was still wrapped around my torso. I could feel the rise and fall of his chest against my back and the tickle of his out breaths against the base of my neck. The sweet smell of his cologne had completely surrounded me. I couldn't deny the fact that I had slept soundlessly in his arms. Clearly he felt the same or he would have wandered back to the couch once I had fallen asleep. He wanted to hold me. The thought made my chest ache. How could I like this so much when I knew I still had feelings for Miles? Feelings that I had stomped on last night when I pulled away from our kiss.

Suddenly, the realization that V was still asleep replaced the feeling of guilt creeping into my stomach. This was my chance to see who he really was. As slowly as possible, I turned underneath his arm in order to face him.

He groaned and I immediately stopped. I waited a few seconds before completing my roll toward him. His eyes were still closed. I slowly exhaled as I stared at his masked face. His long lashes didn't do much to cover the dark circles underneath his eyes. He was exhausted. My being here had forced him to sleep on the couch the last few nights. And who knew how much sleep he ever really got.

Most of his appearances had been in the middle of the night when he was veiled in a cloak of darkness.

But I didn't want him to be hidden any longer. I needed to see him. I reached out and lightly touched the bottom of his mask. V didn't even flinch. I slowly pushed it up. My fingers brushed against the scruff under his chin. The touch made it feel as though a current shot through me.

As if my touch did the same to him, he grabbed my hand and rolled on top of me, pinning me to the mattress. There was a wild look in his eyes.

"What are you doing?" his voice rumbled.

"I thought..."

"You said you trusted me!" He blinked hard as he stared down at me. It was like he was trying to rid himself of his anger. But no matter how many times he blinked, that wild look remained in his eyes. "Were you lying?"

I don't know anymore. "Trust is a lot easier if it's reciprocated. How can I trust you if you don't trust me?"

"You need to get to class," he said, but he didn't move off of me.

"I can't go to class today. There's no point. I can't focus on anything. We need to find Julie."

"You have to go. It's better if you pretend like everything is normal."

"There's nothing normal about my life. It's just a sequence of one disaster after the next."

He just stared down at me. He loosened his grip on my hands slightly, but still didn't move. "One day you might look back at your life and realize that spending a few days with me wasn't such a disaster."

"I didn't say being here was a disaster. That wasn't..."

He leaned forward and pressed his masked forehead against mine. "You didn't have to."

"V."

He lifted his forehead off mine and stared down at me. He parted his lips like he was about to say something, but immediately closed his mouth again. He climbed off of me.

Without his touch, I was suddenly cold. It felt a lot like our borrowed time had just ended. And even though it already felt like my heart was torn into a million pieces, it still hurt. "You're not a disaster," I said into the silence that had settled around us.

He stopped in the doorway. "Go to class. Pretend to be Eli's girlfriend. I'll see you tonight." He closed the door behind him.

After quickly getting ready, I searched the apartment for V. But he was gone. He was probably out looking for Julie. He was trying to fix my life that I had called a disaster. And I hated that he thought he was a part of that. He wasn't a disaster at all. He was the hero that this city so desperately needed. I just wasn't sure he was the hero I needed. I shook my head. That was the whole problem. A part of me thought that he was what I needed. And I didn't understand what that meant.

***

Kins sat down next to me with a huge smile on her face. The smile almost looked insane, like she had done something diabolical. A knot started forming in my stomach. She had accepted the fact that Eli wasn't the vigilante when I had told her. I thought that we'd agreed for her to drop it. She wasn't still searching, was she?

"Hey, what's up?" I said, dreading the answer.

She leaned on the armrest that separated us. "Double date. Tonight. The Tavern on the Green."

"Sounds fun. Who's going with you and Patrick?"

"What do you mean who's going with me?" She slapped my arm. "You and Eli of course."

No way. "Oh, no," I quickly said. "Shoot. We can't tonight. We already have plans." And technically we did. Eli was supposed to be helping me figure out what the hell Don was planning.

"Eli already agreed. Whatever you two already had planned is officially rescheduled. You're coming with us."

Damn it, Eli. "When did you even have time to ask him?"

"This morning when he was getting dressed." She raised her eyebrows at me.

"God, Kins, what is wrong with you?"

"What? I told you that just because I'm in a relationship it doesn't mean I can't appreciate a fine male specimen. From a distance."

I laughed. "You're ridiculous."

"No, Eli's abs are ridiculous." She smiled at me as I rolled my eyes. "But seriously, tonight is going to be a blast. And you have to dress up. This place is fancy." She gave my Converses a disapproving glance.

"They look cute with a sundress," I said.

"Not really. Oh! We should go shopping after classes today."

"I don't have time to do both." Had I seriously already committed to this double date?

"But..." she stopped protesting when the professor walked in. "We'll talk about it later."

Not a chance.

***

"Seriously, Eli? A double date with Kins and Patrick?"

He smiled at me as he sat down in the desk next to mine. "Good morning to you too. You look really nice today."

I sighed. "We don't have time for a date tonight."

"There's always time to make sure we're keeping up appearances. We all agreed that in public you and I would be dating."

"Eli." My voice sounded desperate. "Kins wants me to go shopping with her for new shoes. I can't handle going shopping and going on a date and any other freaking thing right now. I'm having a hard enough time sitting here like everything's fine."

"Hey." He put his hand on my knee. "If anything, tonight will take your mind off of your troubles. I think we could both use that."

"What, like that party we went to where you completely abandoned me? Because last time I remember us putting pressing matters aside I ended up drunk and alone." But really it hadn't been so bad. I had run into Miles after all.

"I told you that was because of work. I'm sorry..."

"I don't care about your apology." I moved my knee away from his hand. "Tell them we have to cancel."

"Give me one chance."

"I've given you plenty of chances."

"The real me. Summer," he said, lowering is voice. "Please. Just one chance." He put his hand back on my knee.

I looked down at his hand and then back up at his face. "We can't be ourselves on a double date anyway."

"Then we'll cut out early."

I bit the inside of my lip as I stared at him. "I don't think it's a good idea."

"It's just one night."

I shook my head. *Possibly one of my last nights.* "You promise not to ditch me?"

He smiled. "If something comes up, this time I can just take you with me."

I folded my arms across my chest and stared at the front of the room. I hadn't even realized the professor had already started talking. I stared blankly at the board. Class. A date. None of it mattered. I just wanted Julie to be okay. "Okay, fine. But only if V is willing to push back the meeting tonight. And we have to be back for it. On time."

"Deal."

I pulled out my phone to text V. Before I pressed on his name, I realized I had one unread message. It was from Miles. I clicked on it.

"I promise that whatever it is you're not telling me isn't going to scare me away. Please stop running."

Running. That's all I knew. The thought of standing still terrified me. I started bouncing my knee nervously. I could barely even sit here, knowing what was going on in my life, or more accurately, not knowing what was going on. The only thing I was sure of was that I wasn't going to drag anyone down with me. And if that meant pretending for one night that I had a boyfriend so Kins wouldn't get suspicious, or avoiding Miles, that's how it had to be.

Besides, Miles was dead wrong. If he knew what I was planning, it would scare him away. The only thing I was looking forward to was the thought of seeing death in Don's eyes. And not his usual dead stare. I wanted to know what he looked like when he could no longer hurt anyone. When all the life was sucked out of him just like he had sucked out mine. The thought made me veins feel cold.

I deleted Miles' message and typed out one to V requesting that our meeting be pushed back a few hours.

His response came almost immediately. "Whatever you need."

My knee kept bouncing. *Whatever I need? What is that supposed to mean?* He was probably hoping that I'd come home in a better mood than when I left. I almost laughed out loud at the fact that I had called his apartment home. I hadn't had a home since I was nine years old.

I couldn't focus on a word that the professor was saying. My eyes were glued to the phone. I didn't know if he was mad or completely neutral. But I hated where we had left things this morning. "I didn't mean you were a disaster, V," I typed out and pressed send.

I stared down at my phone for the rest of the class. A response never came.

CHAPTER 29
Wednesday

I moved my hand away as soon as Eli reached for it.

He sighed. "Sadie, we're supposed to be in a relationship. That means holding hands after class."

"Relationships mean different things to everyone. And if anyone asks, we're taking it slow." I pushed the door open and took a huge breath of autumn air. I had already agreed to go on the double date with him. There was no reason why I had to hold his hand. What if Miles walked by? I didn't want to hurt him.

I tried to focus on the fact that the air seemed crisp. There were even a few leaves crunching under my feet.

"Is the idea of being with me really so repulsive?" Eli said with a light laugh.

I glanced at him out of the corner of my eye. Even though he had laughed, he looked hurt. "I didn't say that."

"Do you want me to walk you to your dorm or back to V's?"

"Neither." I didn't want to run into Miles at my dorm. And I didn't want to be alone with V right now either.

"So what do you want to do?"

"I want to figure out where Julie is."

"If you want to do surveillance we have to head back to V's." His voice had changed when he said it. Almost like he loathed the idea of needing to go there.

I shook my head. "Don't you have some equipment we can use?"

"It's not as good." He shoved his hands into his pockets. "The local government doesn't rob people to fund high tech secret lairs."

"Right, they just use taxes for that."

He laughed.

And for a moment everything between us seemed normal. "I don't need fancy equipment anyway. I know that none of you believe me. But I can feel him." I stopped and sat down on a bench on the outskirts of campus.

Eli sat down next to me. "I believe that you can feel when something is wrong. But that doesn't mean he's here."

I closed my eyes. "He's here. And if I can feel that, I should be able to figure out where he is. Right?"

"So, you want to sit here and try to feel his presence?"

I laughed and opened my eyes. "You think I'm a lunatic."

"I think that maybe you haven't been getting enough sleep. But I don't think you're crazy. I get the idea that you can feel that something is amiss. I feel it. Everyone in this city feels it." He nodded to a lady across the street. There was a man walking behind her who looked innocent enough. Regardless, the woman had grabbed her purse with both hands and had quickened her pace.

"Even if he isn't here, he left that feeling behind," Eli said. "People are scared."

I looked down at my hands. I had brought that fear here. But I was going to do everything in my power to get rid of it. "I don't want V to know what I'm planning to do."

Eli didn't say a word.

"Please don't tell him," I said and looked up into Eli's eyes.

"If you're worried about him being part of your conspiracy to commit murder, it doesn't matter. He already has enough on his rap sheet to put him away for life at this point. Another murder won't make a difference."

"No, it's not that." The thought of V sitting in jail made my chest ache. Could he really be sent away for life? The only reason he had killed someone was to protect me. *To save me.* "I'm afraid he's going to try to stop me."

Eli leaned back on the bench. "I'm still hoping you'll change your mind."

"I won't ever change my mind about this."

"I get that he robbed you of a normal childhood. But you're still breathing, Sadie. Your heart is still beating. You're strong enough to bury all that pain. You can still move on."

I shook my head. "You saw the reports Liza wrote up about me. You know I can't have a normal life."

"You mean because you can't have children? We can just adopt."

I laughed. "We?"

"Seriously, Summer," he said, lowering his voice so no passersby could hear. "We can get a kid that needs a home. Like you needed a home."

I quickly wiped my tears away that I had unknowingly started to shed. "Maybe."

He smiled. "I'm pretty sure you just admitted you'd like to start a family with me."

"I didn't say that," I said with a laugh.

"It's been a long time since I've seen you smile." He wrapped his arm around my shoulders.

I didn't flinch from his touch. It actually felt comforting. And it was nice to know that someone was still capable of liking me after knowing the truth. Well, part of it. No one knew I had lost a baby. And I wasn't planning on telling anyone that. The truth was, I didn't blame Don entirely for what happened. I blamed myself for not being strong enough. And if I ever said that out loud, I was afraid that my pain would swallow me whole.

"Your future isn't over." He lightly kissed my temple. "It's only just beginning. I just want you to think about it, okay?"

"You're asking a lot of me today." I rested my head on his shoulder.

His arm relaxed around my shoulders, but he didn't say anything. We just sat there, staring at the passing traffic. And for a few moments, I felt normal, like maybe I did have a future. I felt like a college student. I felt like my fake boyfriend was real. My imagination blurred with reality and for just a second, I thought I saw my mom across the street.

I lifted my head. Her red hair. Her blue eyes. The only thing missing was her kind smile. She looked sad, like everything she ever loved had been taken from her. It was as if she missed me as much as I missed her.

"Mom?" I said her name as a whisper. And I realized that it had been ten years since I had spoken that word out loud. It sounded strange in my throat.

"Stay here," Eli said. He stood up and starting sprinting across the street.

The woman looked at Eli and then back to me. Car tires squealed and cars honked as Eli tried to make his way across the street. She held up two fingers before climbing into a waiting taxi cab. The car sped off just as Eli reached the other side of the street.

It was her. It had to be her. I slowly stood up. My mom was alive. How was that possible?

Eli ran back over to me. "Damn it, I almost had her."

"Was that my mom?"

"What?"

"Eli, is my mom alive?"

He put his hands on my shoulders. "V didn't tell you?"

"Tell me what?" It felt like my heart was going to explode.

"There was a small hair follicle on a page in the book. We were able to get a DNA sample of Sadie Davis. The similarities aren't a coincidence. She is related to you."

"My...mom..."

"No, Summer. She's not your mom."

With each word he spoke it felt like he had stabbed a knife in my heart and was slowly twisting it.

I shook my head. "I don't have any family left, though."

"Apparently you do."

"That's not possible." For a few seconds I thought my mother was alive. It almost felt like she was being taken away from me again.

"Liza is looking into it."

"But she looked just like my mom. She looks like me."

"We think that your mom probably had a sister. We don't know for sure."

"She didn't. She would have told me. My grandmother would have told me. There would have been pictures or other proof. She didn't have a sister. It's my mom. Sadie Davis is my mom!"

"Summer, it's not your mom." He said it sternly, like he was trying to shake me out of my hallucination. "Don's just trying to get into your head. He's trying to rattle you. She dyed her hair and is wearing colored contacts to get under your skin. You've seen the real her. She's not your mother," he repeated.

"What if you're wrong? What if it's her? What if she's in trouble?"

"That woman is not on our side."

"But..."

"She's counting down the days to your death!"

His words seemed to ring in my ears. *Death. Death. Death.*

"I thought you all agreed that I wasn't going to die?" I asked. "We've been acting like we're putting together a puzzle, not trying to save my life."

"Sheltering you from the truth isn't helping anyone. Two days, Summer. We have two days to put the pieces together."

I swallowed hard. "You think she's going to kill me? Even if she is related to me?"

"I think she's damn well going to try."

***

I stared down at the last page of the file. As soon as I had read the information about Julie I had freaked out. I hadn't even realized there was another page.

But it didn't make any sense. My mother didn't have a sister. I never once heard of an aunt. And wouldn't my grandmother have talked about her? It was possible that she had a falling out with my family. I tapped my fingers against the glass table.

My grandmother was devastated after my mother died. If she had another kid, wouldn't she have reached out to her even if they were estranged? None of this made any sense. My fingers were making smudge marks on the glass. I quickly wiped them away with the hem of my shirt.

The whirling noise of the window opening made me turn my head.

I slammed the folder shut as V stepped inside. "We need to train," I said.

"Why aren't you in class?" he asked.

I stood up and walked over to him. "You need to teach me how to fight. I only have two days left."

"Sadie Davis is a trained sniper. You can't train for something you can't see."

I swallowed hard. "What...so there's no point?"

"We're going to figure out how to play up the new angle."

"I saw her today. She dyed her hair red and put in blue contacts. She looks just like my mom."

"And now you want to learn how to fight her? That's probably the opposite of what they wanted."

I had all afternoon to think about Sadie Davis. I didn't give a shit that she was related to me. For nine years I had desperately needed a home. And she had ignored my existence. She definitely wasn't my family. I had no family. "That woman is not related to me."

"She shared a large number of genes..."

"Blood has nothing to do with it. She's not on our side. She's on his."

He walked over to me, his eyes scanning my body. "You're not ready, Sadie."

"Of course I'm ready. I need to know how to protect myself. Teach me how to shoot a gun."

"I'm not going to hand a gun to someone who isn't stable." His words were cold.

"Stable? Are you shitting me?"

"You just found out you have a blood relative and you want to learn how to use a gun. You should be trying to figure out a way to talk to her, not practicing to kill her."

"I need to kill her before she kills me."

"That's not true. I told you I'd keep you safe."

"And Eli said you were all lying to me! She's not counting down to some crazy event. She's counting down to my death." I poked him in the center of the chest. "Just like I said." I poked him again. "And you want me to trust you when all you do is lie through your teeth."

He grabbed my hand before I could poke him again and pulled me against his chest.

"You're the unstable one, not me," I said. I was so pissed at him. All I wanted to do was slap the smug look off of his face.

"I'm a reflection of you. And if you don't like it, why do you keep coming back to me?"

"I'm not coming back to you." I pushed him off of me. My chest rose and fell in angry bursts.

"Take off your clothes," his voice rumbled.

"What? I'm not having sex with you. You're out of your mind." *Fuck, why do I want to have sex with him right now?*

"Take them off."

I swallowed hard. "Take them off yourself."

We both stepped forward at the same time and his lips collided with mine. And for the first time all day it felt like I could breathe. I grabbed his strong shoulders as he lifted me up and set me down on the edge of the glass table.

I didn't care that we were going to leave smudges on the table.

I didn't care that I couldn't see him.

I didn't care that I didn't know his real name.

All that mattered was that we were both broken. And somehow doing this made us feel whole for a moment in time. A moment of borrowed time. I was just as unstable as he claimed. And he was right about himself. I saw that reflected in him.

I hitched my legs around his waist and pulled him closer as he tore off my shirt and bra.

"Tell me you don't want this," he groaned into my mouth as his hands found my breasts.

I didn't say a word.

"Tell me you think I'm a disaster." He unbuttoned my jeans.

I just kissed him back.

"Tell me I'm unstable."

God, fuck me already. I pressed my palms down on the table so I could lean into him.

His fingers slid down my sides, stopping at my waist as he pulled me off the table. He turned me around and pressed my naked torso against the cold glass.

"Tell me to stop." He pushed my jeans down my thighs, his hands lingering on my ass.

I moved my legs farther apart.

He grabbed my waist. "Fuck," he groaned as he thrust into me from behind.

The force pushed me forward, making my hipbones dig into the side of the table. That's all it took for me to forget that I was mad at him. I pressed my hands against the table, moving to match his thrusts. It felt amazing. But I hated that I didn't know if I liked it, or if I just didn't know what it was like to experience pleasure without pain.

"Harder," I moaned.

His fingertips dug into my hips. All I could feel was the sensation of his cock rubbing against all of my walls.

"God, V!" I felt myself clenching around him. I didn't care that it was twisted. It felt so fucking right.

He continued to slide his cock in and out of me, riding out my orgasm. As soon as I had come down from my high, he pulled out of me.

I knew he hadn't cum yet. I hadn't felt him. "V?" I panted.

He grabbed my hips and flipped me over so that my back was pressed against the table. He was pumping his hand up and down his length as he stared down at me with a heated gaze. This was his way of proving he was in control of this situation. Of his mind. Of everything I was scared of.

He put his knee against my shin, separating my legs, and stepped between my thighs. His hand slowed for a second and the first stream of hot liquid landed on the center of my chest. Then my stomach. And my chest again. He milked his cock until every last drop was splattered against my flesh.

He pulled his sweatpants back up as he stared down at me. And then he walked away.

"V?"

He continued to walk away.

I pushed myself up until I was resting on my elbows. "Don't leave me like this!" I tried to grab my shirt with my toes without spilling his semen all over the table.

He reappeared just as I made contact with my shirt. He was carrying a towel. I let my leg relax. I just stared at him as he slowly wiped his cum off of my breasts. If this was his proof that he could take care of me, it wasn't quite enough.

"Can I learn how to use a gun now?" I asked.

A small smile spread across his lips. "No." He ran the towel down my stomach.

"You said you were a reflection of me. So if I'm crazy, so are you."

"And I don't use a gun." He nodded over to where his bow was hanging on the side of the target.

"You're going to teach me to use that?"

He laughed. "No."

"V!"

"You don't need to learn how to use anything. Let me protect you."

"I don't want you to protect me. I want to be able to take care of myself."

He wiped the cloth against my stomach once more and then set it down on the side of the table. He leaned forward, placing his hands on the table on either side of me. "Then I'll teach you in two days."

I slid off the table, very aware of the fact that my ass cheeks probably left a mark as they squeaked against the glass. But he didn't move. He kept his hands on the table, caging me in.

"Two days is two days too late," I said.

"After you learn to trust me, I'll teach you how to protect yourself."

"You're asking me to trust you with my life."

"I think you just found that my hands are very capable of taking care of you."

I scowled at him.

"Get dressed. We can start by getting you in better shape."

I'm pretty sure my jaw dropped. "Did you just call me fat?"

He laughed and stepped back, allowing me to pass. "Run faster. Jump higher. That kind of thing."

"Mhm." I snatched my clothes off the ground.

"I didn't say anything about losing weight!" he called after me as I retreated into the bedroom to find some workout clothes.

CHAPTER 30
Wednesday

My shoulders ached as I tried to reach for the zipper on the back of my dress. *Damn it.* But I wasn't upset about the dress. I was upset about the fact that my life was a fucking mess. How could I go on a date with Eli when I was already confused enough? And I didn't have time to be confused about any of it. I was supposed to be focusing on whatever the hell was going to happen in two days.

Telling myself that I needed to eat tonight no matter where I was seemed to settle me down. Eli wanted it to be a real date, but that didn't technically make it real. It was just for appearances. It was to keep Kins safe. Miles safe. *God, Miles.*

I turned to look at my back in the mirror. The zipper was somehow just out of reach no matter how much I twisted and stretched. There was a scar right beneath where the zipper should have ended. I picked out this dress specifically because it didn't show any scars.

I sighed and sat down on the edge of my bed. My eyes gravitated down to my Converses. I could wear different shoes. Eli was coming here to pick me up. He'd be with me at dinner. And then he was going to walk back here with me for the meeting. I'd never be alone. He'd be there with me the whole time to keep me safe.

But reasons regarding Eli weren't why I wanted to take my Converses off. Just seeing them reminded me of Julie. I thought about the picture of her and her fiancé, Jacob. They had looked so happy. And I remembered her getting the Converses from him and showing them off to me. She was so smitten with him. It was almost as if her life was beginning the day mine ended. *And now...*

I tried to dismiss the thought, but I couldn't keep it at bay. *And now she's dead because of me.* I didn't want to believe it was true. It was possible that she was out there, somewhere. It just seemed like we'd be able to find her if that was true. Cases for missing people that weren't found within a month weren't exactly promising. I was an example of that. No, I wasn't dead. But I wasn't Summer Brooks anymore either.

I reached down to untie my shoes but stopped when my fingers touched the laces. Miles liked my shoes. I had consumed a lot of alcohol the night I ran into him in the observatory. But I was pretty sure he had told me that he liked my shoes. Even though they didn't match my dress. Yes, Miles had definitely complemented them. I also remembered that Eli didn't seem to like them. He didn't say so, but he also didn't defend my choice in front of Kins.

I stood up. I wasn't sure if it was because Miles liked them or because Eli didn't that I kept them on. Maybe it was a combination of the two. I also had an eerie feeling that maybe if Julie had still been wearing hers, she wouldn't have gotten kidnapped. That wasn't going to happen to me. I'd die before I was back under Don's thumb.

Before leaving the room, I turned to look in the mirror once more. Normally I'd wear something that hid the pendant around my neck. But I no longer had my most prized possession. I stared at my reflection. There was something different about the person staring back at me. It wasn't the low cut of the dress, or the makeup I was wearing. It wasn't even the fact that I had brown hair and brown eyes instead of my normal red hair and blue eyes. For the first time in nine years, I didn't look scared.

It didn't make any sense. I had just found out that I had a relative I didn't know about who was most likely trying to kill me. I probably only had two days left to live. But there wasn't fear in my eyes. For years, I had no one on my side. Now I had a whole team of people and friends, including three guys who cared about me. *Three.* And it was selfish, but I didn't have any desire to let any of them go. I liked the sense of security it gave me to know I had people watching my back. Because who was I kidding? I couldn't even manage to reach a zipper on my back. How on earth was I planning on protecting myself without them?

And I was pretty sure none of them would love all of me. They just liked the part of me that they saw. Miles was in love with Summer Brooks, a carefree girl with an easy smile. Eli was in love with the tortured part of me, the one who hid in broad daylight and was scared to say a word. And V loved the person I was becoming, a person who'd eventually be strong enough not to need him. Because the truth was, I was unlovable as a whole. I didn't even love myself. I hated looking in the mirror. I hated the person I had become. And I wasn't scared of my current predicament, because the truth was that I was tired of living.

The thought hit me hard as I blinked away my tears. My parents were dead. My grandmother was dead. Julie was most likely dead. And the three people left that cared about me the most would probably all die trying to protect me. So wasn't it just better if I died first? I wiped away the tears under my eyes and turned away from the mirror.

It wasn't that I was giving up. It was simply that there was no hope. We had no leads. We had no idea what Don was planning. Even if I was still breathing in two days, I was still dead inside. And I couldn't even embrace being Sadie Davis anymore because she was already someone else. Coming here wasn't a fresh start. Coming here was the end.

So why did it feel like a beginning whenever I was around Miles, Eli, and V? Maybe it was because I was starved for love. That's why it was so hard to turn any of them away. I was lucky to have met each of them. A part of me could even imagine a future with each of them. I loved Miles because he reminded me of what it felt like to be whole. I loved Eli because he was proof that I could be loved despite being broken. And I loved V because he made me feel optimistic of a future, no matter how unrealistic it was.

But none of those futures could possibly exist. I was incapable of love, despite how torn I felt about each of them. My heart was too full of hate. I was consumed with something that seemed bigger than a feeling. It truly felt like my heart was only still beating because Don was still breathing. And when I ended his life, I'd finally be free.

Before I was out of time, I needed to tell each of them. I needed them to understand that their lives were better off without me in them. It shouldn't be hard. None of them loved all of me. How could they?

I grabbed my purse off the dresser. I'd start by telling Eli tonight after our double date. I knew he wanted a second chance, but what was the point? He should be focusing his efforts on someone who still breathed life.

I walked out of the bedroom. I was hoping V wouldn't be there when I left for my date. Unfortunately he was sitting at the kitchen counter. He looked up as I walked past him. I kept my head down, hoping he'd ignore me.

"Stop," his voice rumbled.

My feet reacted before my brain, immediately stopping at his command. I didn't look back at him as he approached me. His fingers brushed the back of my neck, as he pushed my hair to the side. He slowly zipped up my dress the rest of the way. His touch sent a chill down my spine.

"Why have you been crying?" he asked.

"I haven't."

He grabbed my arm and turned me toward him. "Talk to me."

"It's nothing."

He sighed. "You don't have to go with Eli if you don't want to."

"How do you even know about that?"

"He informed me about the change in schedule. I don't think it's necessary for you to go out of your way to keep up the facade that you two are dating. You don't have to go."

"What does it matter? You said we weren't going to end up together. You've made it clear that all this is between us is just physical."

"That's not what I said." His fingers loosened their grip on my arm.

"Yes it is. You said we were doing this on borrowed time."

"Sadie, please don't push me away right now. Not for him." He lightly touched the bottom of my chin.

"Eli Serrano is at the entrance," Athena's voice said smoothly through the speakers.

I was about to step away, but V grabbed my waist and pulled me against him.

"My heart beats on borrowed time," he whispered, as he pressed his forehead against mine.

I believed he thought that was true. That he thought he loved that small piece of me. Because it would have been easy for me to stay in this moment.

He breathed in my exhales like I was the one that could somehow give him strength, when in reality he was the one that took away my pain.

There was a loud tapping against the window that made me jump. "I'll be back later," I said.

He reluctantly let go of my waist and stepped back. "I meant what I said, Sadie. My heart beats on borrowed time," he repeated, as if the first time he said it hadn't reverberated through my soul.

I didn't turn back to him. If he meant it, he would have called me Summer. If he meant it, he'd love all of me. If he meant it, I probably would have stayed. But it wasn't enough. I needed to feel love for that part of me that was broken. And that part of me that was once whole. I'd never become what V wanted me to be. I didn't have enough time.

The window slowly rose. Eli was standing there in jeans and a blazer with his hair slicked back slightly.

I stepped outside, feeling the last few rays of sunlight on my skin. "You look different."

"This is me." He smiled at me, almost shyly. "I'm Eli Serrano." He put his hand out. "And it's really nice to meet you, Summer."

I turned my head as the window started to whirl closed. V was staring at me with the most piercing gaze. It was almost as if he could see it too, the parts of me that were Summer. And it felt like he hated her. Like he despised her.

My skin felt cold as the window shut. I looked back at Eli. His hand was still outstretched, the smile still on his face. Seeing his smile warmed me somehow. And it wasn't because of the flames lapping at the surface. Eli wasn't bad. He was good. So good. Maybe the fire I felt when our skin touched wasn't because of him at all. Maybe I was the one that was burning.

I reached out my hand. "I already like you, Eli Serrano. I don't want to start over." *We don't have time to start over.* Instead of shaking his hand, I intertwined our fingers, and let our hands fall between us.

His smile grew even wider. "We should probably get going. Our reservation is at 7 and it's a pretty long walk."

I nodded and we walked hand in hand down the fire escape. I didn't feel an ounce of fire in his touch now. There was just this overwhelming sense of comfort. He could protect me. Maybe this didn't have to end in two days. When had my hope dissipated?

I glanced at Eli out of the corner of my eye as we stepped off the fire escape. "You look older."

"I am older than you originally thought," he said with a smile.

"No, I know. I just...I mean, I can see it now. Where did you go to college the first time around?"

He laughed. "The University of Colorado. And then I went to the police academy when I decided I didn't want to go to law school."

"You originally wanted to be a lawyer?"

"I've always wanted to help people. I just wasn't exactly sure how I wanted to do that." His fingers tightened around mine slightly as we crossed the street. The small gesture made me feel protected.

We didn't speak as we entered Central Park. The silence with him wasn't awkward. It wasn't like it was with Miles, when I was worried he'd discover the truth. I felt at peace.

"I believe that you didn't know that Don was hurting me," I finally said, breaking the silence. "I just wanted you to know that. And I'm sorry that..."

"Summer, please don't apologize. It kills me that I didn't know. I swear I would have stopped it if I knew. I was right there. I should have seen it."

I could hear the pain in his voice when he spoke about it. It was almost as if he blamed himself. If I was going to die in two days, I didn't want him to hold on to that pain. "It wasn't your fault, Eli."

He didn't say anything.

"Eli," I said and pulled on his hand to make him stop walking. "I'd say I forgive you, but there is nothing to forgive. But I see it in your face. You have to forgive yourself." I placed my hand on the center of his chest.

His Adam's apple rose and fell as he stared down at me. I could feel his heart racing beneath my palm.

"I could have prevented that pain," he said. "Whenever I look at you, I can see that pain in your eyes. If I had seen it, I could have..."

"You couldn't have done anything. Don would have killed you. You know what he's like. I'm just grateful that you like me despite everything that's happened."

"You think you're broken. But I don't see it that way, Summer." He gently cupped the side of my face in his hand. "And you need to stop beating yourself up over things that weren't you're fault."

My unborn baby dying was my fault. I ignored the sharp pain in my chest and leaned into his hand slightly. I was supposed to be distancing myself from him, but he kept drawing me closer. This didn't feel like an act. This felt real. And I was worried that if I went through with my plan and ended things tonight, the part of me he loved would fade away. I didn't want to disappear.

CHAPTER 31
Wednesday

Eli pulled my seat out for me and I sat down. There were already two glasses of water in front of the seats across from us. Apparently Kins and Patrick had arrived before us, but they were missing now.

A waitress walked over to us. "Welcome to the Tavern on the Green. I'm Lexi and I'll be your waitress this evening. Can I get you both something to drink?"

"Water is fine," Eli and I both said at the same time.

The waitress smiled. "I'll be right back."

"You could have ordered something a little stronger," I said when the waitress walked away.

"But that's a little suspicious for an 18 year old, don't you think?"

I laughed. "Only if Kins and Patrick ever show."

"We were a little late. Maybe they're just looking around the restaurant. This place is amazing, don't you think?"

I looked up at the strings of lights streamed above our heads and turned to view the big tree I had seen when we walked into the outdoor portion of the restaurant. The tree was strung up with lights and the setting sun made the whole scene breathtaking. The lights reminded me of the stars.

IVY SMOAK

I turned back to Eli. "It's really beautiful. Remember the first date we went on, you know, when you took me to Central Park to see the stars?"

He smiled. "I remember."

"I thought it was because I mentioned it was strange that you couldn't see the stars that first night I met you. Was that it? Or was there more to it?" He had been watching me for nearly two years. I had no idea what he already knew about me.

His smile faltered slightly. "Honestly, I always knew what I wanted us to do on our first date. "

"You thought you wanted to go on a date with me before you even knew me?"

"I did know you. I mean, I do know you."

A part of me. "So why'd you want to take me stargazing on our first date?"

"You used to climb out on the roof at night and watch the stars. Sometimes you'd even go on the roof when it was cloudy and bring a book and a flashlight. It was like you just liked being close to the sky."

I liked being close to Miles. "I used to cry on the roof. Didn't you ever see my tears?"

"Some people cry in the face of beauty, whereas I just can't seem to look away."

His gaze made my cheeks flush.

He leaned forward and traced his thumb down my cheek. "You have no idea how often I dreamed of brushing your tears away."

I closed my eyes, relishing the feeling of his touch.

"Hey, lovebirds," Kins said.

I opened my eyes as Eli's hand fell from my cheek.

Kins was smoothing her skirt and Patrick was running his fingers through his hair. Their whole appearance seemed slightly off.

Patrick awkwardly cleared his throat. "Nice to see you again, Sadie," he said as he pulled out Kins' seat for her.

"You too," I said and looked back and forth between them.

Eli lightly nudged me in the ribs. I glanced at him and his eyebrows were raised. His eyes danced with humor.

Oh my God. I turned my attention back to Kins and Patrick. Did they just have sex in the restaurant bathroom? "Where have you two been?" I asked.

"Where have we been?" Kins asked and laughed. "You two were the ones that were late." She picked up her menu.

"Yeah, but... ow!" I grabbed my shin under the table where Kins had just kicked me. It wasn't a light tap either.

"Are you okay?" Patrick said.

"Fine." My voice sounded weird and high-pitched. *Fine except for my poor innocent shin.*

"Anyway," Eli said, "we're sorry we were late." He put his arm around my shoulders. "What are you guys ordering?"

"Probably the bratwurst," Kins said.

"I heard the kielbasa is good," Patrick said.

"Maybe we should just go get hotdogs." Eli laughed and set his menu down.

"Or we could order the calamari?" Why was I so bad at fitting in with their light banter?

"Oh, so close," Kins said. "But not quite phallic enough." She giggled as Patrick kissed her cheek. "Seriously, though, I did hear their food was good here. Oh. My. God." She set her menu down and stared over my shoulder.

No. I immediately held my breath, assuming the worst. *He's here.* For one second.

The small hairs on the back of my neck seemed to rise.

For two seconds.

He can't be here.

For three seconds.

Eli's arm tightened around my shoulders.

For four seconds.

I felt like my lungs were going to explode as panic rose to my throat.

For five seconds.

We both turned around, but there was nothing there. I let go of the breath I had been holding and Eli gently rubbed my back. I knew he had been thinking the same thing.

"What are you talking about, babe?" Patrick said and picked his menu back up.

Kins put her hand on his menu, pushing it back down onto the table. "It's James Hunter," she squealed and pointed to a table behind us.

I looked over my shoulder at a couple seated a few tables away from us. Sure enough, the handsome billionaire was seated with his wife. They were laughing about something. The woman placed her hands on her large pregnant stomach and shook her head animatedly. I wasn't sure why, but I imagined they were discussing names for their unborn child. Something seemed to constrict in my chest. I immediately turned away. No wonder everyone wanted to do their psychology projects about him. His life seemed so perfect.

"God, he's even sexier in person," Kins said. She placed her chin in her hand and blatantly stared at him. "I mean, look at him."

"He's okay," Patrick said. "You should probably stop staring at them, though, it's rude."

"Are you kidding?" Kins slapped his arm. "He's like sex on a stick. I can't not stare at him."

Patrick frowned. "How would you feel if I said his wife was hot?"

Kins scrunched up her nose. "She's pregnant."

"That doesn't mean she isn't hot. And I've seen pictures of her before she got pregnant. She's gorgeous."

Kins slapped his arm harder this time. "Yeah, I wouldn't like it. Stop checking her out."

Patrick smiled to himself as he picked his menu back up. Maybe he thought their conversation was a victory for him. I wondered what he'd think if he knew the way Kins talked about Eli all the time.

Eli tucked a loose strand of hair behind my ear. I glanced over at him. It was like he could sense my discomfort. The small gesture made me smile. It made me feel less broken. He made me feel light even though I knew darkness was creeping into my soul.

"Let's play truth or dare," Kins said.

I shook my head. "You just want someone to dare you to go talk to James Hunter."

Eli and Patrick both laughed.

"I do not," Kins said and picked her menu back up. But she winked at me over the top of it.

I glanced back over my shoulder at the happy couple. And in that moment, I knew for sure that I'd never have that. I could already feel myself disappearing.

***

"Do you ladies want to head back to our place?" Patrick asked as he grabbed Kins' hand.

"Actually, we were going to take a walk. Right, Sadie?" Eli glanced down at me, waiting for me to say yes.

I was having a great time with him. I didn't want tonight to end. He made me feel so normal. "Yeah, if that's alright." I smiled up at him.

"We'll catch you later then," Kins said. "We're just going to go this way." She pointed toward the exit farthest away. The one that would allow her to walk past James Hunter's table. "I'm going to try to get a whiff of his cologne," she whispered as she gave me a swift hug. She did some weird handshake with Eli before Patrick escorted her away from us.

"Do you two have a secret handshake?" I asked.

Eli laughed. "She makes me do it. No reason to be jealous."

"I'm not jealous." But I knew my face probably gave me away. I crossed my arms in front of my chest.

"Are you cold?" he asked as he shrugged off his blazer.

"No, I'm okay. I..." my words died away as he draped his jacket over my shoulders. The truth was, I had been cold. And it was nice that he had noticed. I just wasn't used to asking for anything. I was pretty sure he'd give me the world if he could.

My eyes gravitated toward him as we walked away from the restaurant. He was starting to get a five o'clock shadow. I couldn't believe I hadn't noticed how much older he looked before he told me the truth. He wasn't like the other boys on campus. He was a man. A detective. Someone looking out for me. And I knew he couldn't give me the world. But he could give me something that I needed.

"Will you teach me how to shoot a gun?" I asked.

He stopped walking, and I almost tripped because he was holding my hand.

"Why?" he said when I turned to face him.

I stared into his eyes. "You know why."

"There's still time to figure out another way," he said slowly.

"It's the only way. Please, Eli."

He immediately dropped my gaze. He didn't say anything to me as he hailed down a taxi. Or during the drive. Or even when we walked into the shooting range. He finally broke his silence and turned to me. "Don't say a word. Let me handle this."

I wasn't sure what he had to handle. It wasn't like the place was sold out of guns. I looked around at the storefront as I followed Eli up to a counter in the back. The man behind the counter greeted Eli like they were old friends.

Eli leaned against the counter. "Two today, John."

"So I see." John gave Eli a wink.

I turned away to study the store. I couldn't believe how many guns there were on display. Anyone could just walk in here and buy one.

"I'll just need some ID," John said.

Crap. Not just anyone, then. I couldn't give him my fake ID. I wasn't Sadie Davis. And I didn't know enough about the real Sadie Davis to know if she'd be allowed at a shooting range. I didn't even have my old ID claiming I was Summer Brooks. Not that it mattered. If he ran that, it would say that I was deceased.

"She's a new recruit," Eli said. "All her paperwork is being processed right now. Including her ID. Just set us up with one lane. I'm giving her some lessons."

"You know the rules, Eli. No ID, no entrance." John scratched the side of his chin. It looked like some kind of nervous tick. He scratched the other side too.

Eli laughed. "Her record is clean. Or she never would have been admitted to the police academy."

John turned to me and eyed me up and down before turning back to Eli. "I'm really not supposed to."

"You're acting like I'm doing a sting operation or something." He waved his hand. "It's fine. She's with me."

John shook his head as he pulled out a piece of paper. "At least give me her name. This is a liability nightmare."

"Sadie Davis," Eli said.

"Great." He wrote it down and slid it to Eli. "Sign your name. That way I'll at least have proof that a cop tricked me instead of a regular civilian. And so that you won't turn me in."

"What's got a stick up your butt today? Your wife still giving you trouble?" Eli grabbed the pen.

John laughed. "Don't you know it. The last thing I need right now is to be arrested by my buddy who moonlights as a cop. You owe me one for putting my neck out, man."

I looked away as Eli signed his name next to mine. I didn't want him to get in trouble for trying to help me. Eli had seen me during my worst years. And he wanted to make it so that I wasn't in pain anymore. He just didn't realize that killing Don was the only thing that would numb my pain.

***

I stared down at the gun in my hand. It was heavier than I imagined it would be. I was holding the thing that would give me justice. It was hard to pay attention to Eli's instructions when I realized just how heavy justice felt in my hands. Or was it revenge that weighed so heavily on my shoulders? I tried to keep the thought below the surface as Eli repositioned the large earmuffs on my ears. He nodded toward the target.

I turned around and lifted the gun. My arms shook slightly, but I wasn't sure if it was because of the weight on my sore muscles or something more. Everything was muted and time seemed to slow down. Even the safety glasses I was wearing altered reality. None of this felt real. I stared at the target, an outline of a man. And I pictured Don. I pictured the smile on his face that he got whenever he took away mine. I wasn't sure how long I stood staring at the target before I felt Eli's body behind me.

He steadied my hands with his and lifted the gun slightly. His fingers expertly removed the safety while I stared at the target. With his help, I pressed the trigger for the first time. With his help, I didn't fall backwards from the recoil of the gun. With his help, I shot the target right in the chest. With his help, I felt stronger than ever. I turned around. Eli's hands still lingered on my arms. It somehow grounded me.

He took the gun from me and set it on the tray nearby. "Let me do it," Eli said. "Let me pull the trigger."

I was supposed to be saying goodbye to Eli tonight. He had witnessed the worst part of me. And that part of me was growing. Soon it might be all that I had left. So, no, I wasn't going to let him go. If I did, that part of me might fade. And I needed it. I needed the darkness in order to end my pain.

"It has to be me," I whispered against his lips. Every second he seemed to move a fraction of an inch closer to me. "I don't want his blood on your hands."

He placed his hand on the back of my neck, drawing me even closer. "I'd rather it be on mine than yours." He stopped moving, as if he was waiting for me to make a choice.

I had made my choice the first time Don had touched me. But there was a new choice I could make. I could let Eli in. I could let him love that part of me that he knew. And I could revel in it. I could cherish it. I stood on my tiptoes and let my lips brush against his.

He immediately deepened the kiss. I had been right earlier. I did love him. I loved that he could love me despite how broken I was.

Maybe love was just an excuse to get hurt. Maybe I was just trying to die from all the pain in my life. When his lips were on mine, though, it felt an awful lot like living.

But I had a terrible lingering thought as his hand slid down my back. What if I liked being hurt? What if that feeling was all I'd ever truly know? I tried to focus on the kiss, hoping that the warmth of his body against mine could take away the chill creeping down my spine.

CHAPTER 32
Wednesday

"Finally," V said as Eli and I walked into the door. "We've been waiting for you guys."

Liza continued typing on her computer without even looking up. "We were doing just fine without them, I think."

"Where have you been?" V said, ignoring Liza.

I didn't want V to know about the shooting range. "The restaurant. It just took a little longer than we thought it would."

"Yeah, the service was ridiculously slow for such a fancy place," Eli added.

V shook his head and turned away from us.

"Thank you," I mouthed silently at Eli.

He smiled and shrugged his shoulders. We both made our way over to the glass table. I cringed as I sat down next to Eli. Everything in V's apartment was spotless. But V hadn't managed to clean off the smudges my body had made against the table earlier. I could feel my face flushing. Had he done that on purpose? Did anyone else notice that there was an outline of my ass on the edge of the table? I glanced up at him and noticed the frown on his lips. I immediately looked back down.

"Glad you had fun on your fake date," Liza said. "Meanwhile, we've been doing all the real work. And you won't believe what we found." She finally looked up from her computer.

"What did you find?" I asked. It was good that someone else wanted to change the subject too.

"Well after a lot of digging, V and I figured out who Sadie Davis is," Liza said and lightly touched her hand on V's arm. She kept her hand there a beat too long.

I tried to focus on her words instead of her actions. Besides, I had just kissed Eli. I couldn't be jealous of a simple lingering touch. "So who is she?" I asked.

"Her real name is Jane Davis."

"Okay, so she isn't related to me then. Wagner was my mother's maiden name. Not Davis."

Liza shook her head. "No, your mother did have an older sister. The DNA proves it. And so do the records. Jane Davis is three years older to be exact."

I looked down at my hands. I ran my thumb along my index finger, remembering what it was like to feel the trigger. "Then where has she been the past 18 years?"

"That's the strange part," Liza said. "She's been...dead."

I looked back up at Liza.

"Her records show that she died when she was 16 years old."

"Okay," I said slowly. "But obviously that's not true. She's still alive."

"Right." Liza glanced at V and then back at me.

"We're still figuring out the specifics," V said. "We'll tell you when we finalize the data."

They didn't want me to know. My heart started to race. It was bad. If it wasn't bad they'd tell me. "Who is Sadie Davis if it's not me and it's not her?"

Liza cleared her throat. "Well, that's what we were wondering. Obviously she stole the name too. Technically you stole a stolen identity."

Liza stared at me as if she was expecting me to laugh. Was that supposed to be a joke? God, it wasn't funny. It felt like my heart was slamming against my ribcage.

"Tell me." I shifted forward in my chair. "Please just tell me."

"Jane Davis supposedly died in an accident when she was 16. But her body was never found. She completely disappeared. She didn't resurface until she enrolled in the army right after your mother died. With her new name. We think she was probably being held against her will somewhere and she joined the military once she got away for protection."

"Why do you think that?"

"Because of your mother's statement about the accident. Or rather, lack of one."

A chill ran down my spine. "My mom was there?"

Liza nodded. "Your mother was only 13 years old when it happened. She was clearly terrified. The statement shows that. Apparently they had been walking in the woods alone. Your mother said someone approached them. A male in his late teens. He tried to assault your mother. But Jane stepped in and attempted to fight him off. She told your mother to run. And as she was running she heard Jane's scream. The man was never seen again. Nor was Jane."

"Why did they say she was dead instead of missing?"

"They had been walking near a cliff. It was beside a river. They found Jane's shoe pretty far down the cliff. And some of her blood on the rocks. They thought the body washed away."

I went to reach for my pendant, but just felt the emptiness. It always gave me strength. I pressed my hand against my chest instead, trying to somehow ground myself despite the fact that it felt like I was sinking. I had been young, but even I could see the shift in my grandmother's demeanor. She hadn't really been able to lift herself back up after my mother died. Her smiles seemed rare. Her scolding became more constant. She was devastated. And the devastation was so much worse than I had imagined. Because she hadn't just lost one child. She had lost two.

I felt Eli gently rub my back, pulling me out of my thoughts. I pressed my hand a little harder against my chest. "So everyone thought Jane died trying to protect my mom?"

"Yeah. And that's not even the weirdest part," Liza said. "The name..."

"We really don't know everything yet, Sadie," V cut in. "I'd like to finalize everything before we fill you in."

"Whatever you have, you need to tell both of us," Eli said. "Keeping her in the dark isn't helping anything."

V glared at him.

"Please just tell me." I hated how desperate I sounded, like I was barely holding on. My heart couldn't take waiting another second. It felt like it was going to explode in my chest.

"The report also said your mother recognized the man," Liza said. "Apparently she had seen him around town before. She said she almost felt like he had been watching her. We think he probably followed her into the woods to...well, you know." Liza awkwardly cleared her throat.

"She was only 13 years old." I realized the irony of what I said as soon as the words fell from my lips. I had only been 12 when Don started hurting me. I swallowed hard. *Touching me.*

"The cops thought he may have been stalking your mom. Apparently it was clear to them that Jane didn't recognize the man, where as your mom seemed to. But your mom swore she didn't know the man's name. After the accident, your grandmother was so paranoid that he'd come after your mom again, she changed their names and moved away."

"So they became Wagners?"

"Right."

"So...Sadie Davis?"

Liza glanced at V and then back at me. "Sadie Davis was your mom's real name. But I guess she would have been Sadie Brooks after marrying your dad."

I felt sick to my stomach. Neither one of those names had meant anything to me a month ago. Now I was sitting here with the same name as my mom, a name I never knew belonged to her.

"Which brings us to Mr. Crawford," V said. "Whoever he is, he clearly wanted you to know the truth or he wouldn't have gone to such lengths to get you that new ID and everything."

I just sat there, staring at him.

He took that as a sign that I wanted to hear more. "But that doesn't necessarily mean the mysterious Mr. Crawford is on our side," V said. "He could have had reasons of his own to tell you."

I felt numb. I could barely even focus on V's words. Jane had risked her life to save my mom. And now she was trying to kill me? She was my only living relative. She was my last family. It didn't even make any sense. *Unless...* The queasy feeling returned as a terrible thought settled in my stomach. "Who was the man in the woods?"

"Your mom swore she didn't know his name," Liza said. "All that was in the report was this sketch of his face." She pulled it out and placed it on the table in front of me.

I put my hand over my mouth. *Don.* I could have been wrong. He was clearly younger. It was just a sketch. But those eyes. The death in them. I let the tears stream down my face.

"Shit," Eli said. He shifted closer to me and wrapped his arm around my back.

I immediately placed my head against his chest. I needed the comfort. For just one second, I needed to pretend that none of this was real.

"We agreed to leave the make-believe at the door," V said, his voice an octave lower than usual.

"Jesus, you psychopath," Eli said, continuing to hold me against his chest. "She's crying."

"And I'm asking you to get your hands off of her," V growled.

"Did you ever think that what you and her have is what's make-believe?"

"I'm giving you two seconds to..."

"Cut it out!" Liza yelled. "While you guys are busy having a fight over doomsday, I'm the only one trying to figure out just how long we have. We don't exactly have a lot of time to waste here."

I pulled away from Eli, wiping away my remaining tears. Liza was right. Crying over the past didn't change anything. We were running out of time. I could hear the clock ticking down in my head. "Did you just call me doomsday?" I asked.

"Mhm." Liza looked down at her notes. "We really need to know whether or not it's like a three-two-one-go deal, or just a three-two-one boom right away."

I hadn't even considered that the one would be the last day. I thought when Sadie Davis showed me one finger, I'd still have one whole day to figure it out. "I think the first one."

"It's more diabolical to jump the gun, don't you think?"

Everyone was silent.

"So that's it?" I asked. "I'm going to die tomorrow?"

"You're not going to die," Eli and V said at the same time.

I looked at Liza. For some reason her silence was louder than their words. All she seemed capable of was the truth, or at least, whatever she deemed the truth. "What do you think, Liza?"

She shrugged her shoulders. "We still don't know who Mr. Crawford is. We're not 100 percent certain what happened in the woods, but I'm pretty sure that Don had some kind of weird sexual infatuation with your mother. Who you happen to look a lot alike. And with the dye job that your aunt just got, he's probably fornicating with her too. Maybe consensual though. She looks a little off her rocker. I wouldn't even be surprised if the name change was her idea."

"This isn't helping anyone, Liza," V said.

She pushed her glasses up the bridge of her nose, ignoring him. "Regardless, I'd have to run some calculations to get a more precise number, but I think the odds that you're going to die tomorrow are roughly 87 percent. And obviously the odds are even higher the following day because if you don't die tomorrow you're even more likely to die the day after that. Since death really appears to be the only logical conclusion to her threats. So that has to be like a 99.8 percent chance of you dying on Friday with a slight possibility of skewed data if there were any errors in the research V did. Because all my research was logically sound and I didn't have time to double check his work."

I swallowed hard. The information was jarring. But I appreciated her bluntness. There was no reason to sugar coat anything when I was living on hours. "So I'm probably going to die tomorrow. And if not tomorrow, definitely Friday?"

"Most definitely, yes."

"That isn't true," V said. "She's pulling numbers out of her ass. And we don't even know if it was Don in the woods. That could be a picture of any teenager. She's making leaps she can't justify."

"I never pull anything out of my ass, thank you very much. No one has ever even touched me there. Not that I'm opposed to it, it's just never happened is all." Liza cleared her throat.

God. I looked down at my hands. The uneasy feeling in my stomach was gone. My heart palpitations were gone. All the fight in me had just drained away. "Well, thank you all for trying to help me. I really appreciate it..."

"Summer, we're not going to let anything happen to you," Eli said.

I stood up from my chair. "I'm tired. I think I'm going to call it a night." But I wasn't really tired. At least, not physically. Maybe I was tired of living, but I hated the idea of even thinking that. Really I was just lying. I needed to do something. Before it was too late. Before I ran out of time.

"Awesome," Liza said and closed her laptop. "So, are we all done here?"

V slammed his hand against the table. "No, we're not done! Sadie, you don't just get to give up when things get hard. That's not how this works. You can't quit right now. We're so close."

"I'm going to die before I ever fully understand any of this. And I can't die before I let the people I care about most know the truth. I just need to write..."

"You can't leave a paper trail," Liza quickly said. "Are you trying to get us all killed?"

"Fine. Liza, I appreciate your help. I'm glad you always told me the truth when no one else did. And that you gave us a perspective that this group so desperately needed.

Because I'm just one person in this sea of people and no one...no one gives a shit about me."

"Summer..." Eli started.

"And Eli. I get that you think you know me. You think I'm some tortured girl that needs to be saved. I love that you want to save me. But honestly, I don't need to be saved. All I want is to be that kid again. A person that you never knew. But Don stole that from me and I'm never going to get it back. I'll never be the person I want to be because Summer Brooks is dead. She's gone. And I hate the tortured part of me the most. I hate that you fell in love with the worst side of me. I hate that it's tainted by pain." I wiped the tears off my cheeks. "But I so appreciate you. You deserve so much better than a small piece of me."

He parted his lips like he wanted to say something, but nothing came out.

"And you," I said and pointed at V. "I love you too."

"Sadie." He started walking toward me.

"But you don't want my love. You can't accept it because you don't love yourself. And I get that better than anyone. Because you're a reflection of me, right? I hate looking in the mirror. I hate what I've become. Stop."

He was standing right in front of me.

"You fell in love with the idea of me becoming something great. Becoming something better than whatever the hell I'm existing as now. You said you saw a light in me. But it's only darkness. I loved your hope. But it's wasted on me. Don't you see that? You fell in love with a piece of me that will never come to fruition."

V put his hands on my shoulders.

I ignored the feeling of my pain being taken away. I wanted the pain tonight. I pushed his hands away. "You don't get to decide how I deal with my own fate. None of you do." I took a few steps away from him, breathing easier the farther away I got. "So thank you for helping me." I opened up the door to my room. "I meant what I said. But you don't get to tell me how to spend my last night." I stepped into my room. "You don't get to tell me to keep living when none of you know my full story. You have no idea how hard it is to breathe. You have no idea how many nights I'd fall asleep and pray I wouldn't wake up. You don't know me."

None of them said a word.

I closed the door and locked it. "Athena, lights on," I whispered.

She didn't reply.

I pressed my back against the door and slid down until my butt hit the floor. "Athena, lights on," I said through my sobs.

Nothing.

I didn't question her decision to not speak to me. I was mad at myself too. Or maybe she just realized that my soul was so dark that I wouldn't be able to see the light.

CHAPTER 33
Wednesday

I stared down at the words I had written. I could barely see them through the small amount of light streaming underneath the door. There was no right way to describe what had happened. No right way to make it better. I had already hurt him and I had no idea how to fix it.

I crumpled up the piece of paper and tossed it into the trash before pulling my knees up to my chest. Eli was going to be fine. V was going to be fine. They had both only known me for a short period of time. But Miles? That was different. I couldn't put words to it.

Or maybe that wasn't the problem. Maybe I had too many words. I picked my notebook back up and started writing again.

Miles,

I fell in love with you the first time I ever saw you. It didn't even feel like a choice. I honestly couldn't help falling in love with you. And a part of me has always believed it was because we were written in the stars.

That night in your tree house when you took my hand, I thought it was the best night of my life. But life is such a fleeting thing. You can have your whole life in front of you one second, and then it can be taken away in a flash. But I always had you. I needed you after my parents died and you were my one constant.

Until suddenly you weren't. For years, I felt so alone. You hurt me. So I know I hurt you too. And for that, I'm so sorry. I'm sorry I disappeared. I'm sorry you couldn't find me. But it wasn't my choice. I never wanted to disappear. I never stopped wanting to be found. I never stopped needing you, Miles. That was the whole problem. I needed you more than ever and it felt like you didn't need me.

My love for you mixed with hate. I still loved you, but I fucking hated you too. I hated you for abandoning me. I hated you for forgetting about what we were. But I understand now. I'm sorry about the years apart. I'm sorry if you ever felt cut as deep as I did. And I'm sorry if your life stopped like mine.

I lived with a monster. And I became one too. I was torn between wanting you to find me and wanting you to never see what I had become. The truth is, I'm not the girl you remember. The years changed me more than you could ever know. And I don't want you to know what happened. I don't want you to dig. I don't want you to get hurt more than I've already hurt you. Summer Brooks is dead. It's important that you understand that.

But you've always seen me. You saw through my disguise right away at the diner. I had never heard anything as sweet as my name on your lips. And I'm sorry I couldn't tell you. I got mixed up in something bigger than you and me.

I just need you to know that I don't forgive you. Because you never did anything wrong, so you don't need my forgiveness. And you deserve everything I could never give you. Live your life for me. Just because I don't get any more heartbeats doesn't mean your heart has to stop beating too. Live the life I couldn't.

And if a part of you still remembers me when you look at the stars, let it be the smallest part. Let it be the smallest constellation in the sky on a late night in September. And let it slowly fade away as the seasons change.

I looked down at the letter. I didn't know how to sign it. I wasn't Summer Brooks. And I wasn't Sadie Davis. I lifted my pen back up and wrote Sagitta at the bottom. It made sense. My heart wasn't racing. I wasn't jittery. I didn't feel like fighting. But there was one resounding feeling. It felt like my whole body was on fire. And all the stars in the sky were blazing. I'd become a distant memory. Maybe I'd live forever in Miles' mind as a ball of flames in the sky. There was something comforting about the fact that I'd never really extinguish.

A knock on the door made me jump. I quickly tore the sheet out of my notebook, stuffed the paper in an envelope, and slid it into my backpack.

"Can I come in?" V said from the other side.

He didn't sound angry anymore. But I didn't want to see him. I felt like I had already said my goodbyes. I kept my mouth shut, hoping he'd think I was asleep.

He sighed and his feet shuffled. The light diminished in the room as he sat down on the other side of the door. "You can't give up, Sadie." He whispered it, like he really believed I was sleeping. "I need more time."

I bit the inside of my lip. *More time for what?* He wasn't the one who was going to die tomorrow or the next day. He wasn't the one running out of time.

"You're stronger than you realize," he whispered. "You're made of steel, remember?"

I heard something slide across the wooden floor. Even without the small amount of light filtering into the room, I would have known what it was as soon as I reached out and touched it. *My pendant.* My fingers tightened around it. Why did he have my pendant? I quickly stood up and opened the door.

V fell backwards into the room. He groaned but then a smile spread onto his face. "I knew you were awake."

"V, why did you have this?" I held out the pendant by the chain.

He sat back up and just stared at me.

"V."

"It was on your neck that night when I found that man assaulting you. Your shirt was torn. It was clearly visible."

"So you stole it from me?"

"I took it so that no one would recognize you. So that no one else would put the pieces together."

I swallowed hard. "You mean Miles?" I remembered being at the hospital. I was worried he'd be able to see the pendant through my hospital gown. For some reason, I found myself sinking down onto the floor beside V.

"Anyone, Sadie. Wearing that was putting you in unnecessary risk."

"How do you know that? How do you know what this means to me?"

"I didn't. It looked old. I assumed it was from your past..."

"Stop lying to me. Eli was watching me before I got here. Were you watching me too?" I didn't even wait for a response. "How long have you been watching me?!"

"I didn't..."

I pushed his shoulder. "How long have you been watching me, V?"

"It wasn't like that. I've read your files. I found you here."

"Why were you looking for me? What am I to you?"

"Everything!" His voice echoed around in the small room. "Everything," he said a little gentler.

It wasn't the first time he had said something like that to me. "This is everything to me," I said, holding up my hand. "Why did you keep it from me?"

A strained laugh fell from his lips. "That means everything to you? Really? You could have fooled me."

"What is that supposed to mean?"

"It's a trinket. It has no value. It's nothing. I'm a living, breathing person, Sadie. You put more value on that piece of shit than you do on me."

"That isn't true."

"You just said it was everything. Everything. It's a fucking object, Sadie."

"It's not the object itself. It's the meaning behind it." I could feel the tears starting to well in my eyes. What did he want me to say?

"And what is that? What is the meaning that is so important to you?"

My lip was trembling. "I don't understand what you want from me."

"I want you to tell me the truth!" His voice cracked. "We weren't supposed to run out of time." He was breaking in front of me. "It wasn't supposed to be like this. We need more time."

I was watching him fall apart and there was only one thing I could do. He was always there to catch me when I fell. I needed to be there for him too. I leaned forward and wrapped my arms around him.

His body was stiff, but he slowly relaxed into me as he rested his chin on my shoulder.

The strangest feeling washed over me. It somehow felt like we had come so far even though we hadn't known each other that long. I let him pull me onto his lap and hold me even tighter.

"Just tell me you won't let go," he whispered into my ear. "Tell me you're not giving up."

I was done lying. I would never tell someone I was okay when I wasn't again. White lies were sometimes the most painful to tell. So instead of answering his question, I pulled his head away from my shoulder and held both sides of his face in my hands. "When I'm wearing it, it feels like I'm not alone. That's why it's important."

"Who gave it to you?"

"Miles." The m in his name used to tickle my lips when I was young. I felt it now. Like a small trace of my past creeping up to me. I pressed my lips together.

He nodded, making my hands fall from his face. "So when you wear it you feel close to Miles?"

"When I was little that was all it was. A way to be close to my friend. But as the years wore on and I lost touch with him, it became something more than that. It makes me feel close to my parents. And my grandmother. It reminds me of my past. It reminds me of what it was like to be happy."

He sighed and his warm breath hit my face. "We need more time." He pressed his forehead against mine. "We're so close."

"I think that's the problem with time. You don't realize how fast it goes by until you're about to run out of it."

CHAPTER 34
Thursday

I woke up alone in my bed. The last thing I remembered from the previous night was being in V's arms. On the floor. He must have put me on the bed after I fell asleep.

I took a deep breath. I had an aunt I never knew about. My babysitter from when I was a little kid was missing. And Don was out there, still trying his best to ruin my life. Or end it. I shoved the covers off of myself.

Today could be it. My whole life could culminate in this one moment. My stomach growled. Eating would be a good start. I couldn't brush aside the eerie feeling that this might be my last meal as I made my way out of the room.

"Good, you're up," V said.

I turned toward him. He was sitting at the table rummaging through papers that were scattered everywhere.

"What are you doing?" I asked.

"We're playing up the new angle."

"The angle of Sadie Davis being my aunt? I hate to break it to you, but it's not a new angle. She's been my aunt the whole time I've been alive. She's just decided not to be a part of my life. That's not going to change today."

"Well, we think it might. Especially if you hit a nerve. If we can get the two of you close enough to talk, you can ask her about what happened that day in the woods. You can get her talking about where she disappeared to. We might be able to piece together some things with a little more information."

I walked over to him. "Maybe we should just have a really fun day. Like, I don't know...sky diving or something."

V looked up from his notes. "No."

"You're going to deny a dying girl's last wish?"

"You're not dying."

I sighed. It was odd that he was the one in denial and not me. "V..."

"And I can think of a million better things to do than that," he said and stood up. "Your breakfast is in the oven. Eat it and then we'll go set our trap." He pushed the papers into a sloppy pile. "We're meeting everyone in half an hour."

"I don't get a say in this at all?"

"If it was your last day, you would. But it's not, Sadie. Not even close." He grabbed the papers off the table. "And besides, we're a group. We decided with a majority vote that this was the best course of action."

"You didn't even ask me."

"Three to one vote. Half an hour, Sadie." He walked away from me, disappearing into the room I had never been in.

Talking to my aunt wasn't going to save me. The only thing that would save me was putting a bullet in Don's skull.

***

"This isn't going to work," I said.

Eli's fingers tightened around mine. "It's worth a shot."

"I don't have anything to say to her."

"What if Don was holding her against her will for all those years everyone thought she was dead? If she lived with him, she might know his weaknesses."

"Weaknesses?" I almost laughed. Don didn't have any weaknesses. "I lived with him for a long time and couldn't tell you a single one. If that's the information you're looking for, you're not going to get it."

"But you were just a kid. You could have missed something."

"I grew up pretty fast, Eli."

"I know. I'm sorry." He gave my hand a gentle squeeze. A beeping noise sounded through the hallway and Eli touched something on the side of his watch. "Class is going to let out in a few minutes. Hopefully she'll be early and we can do this fast before anyone sees."

I let him guide me through the hall of the building where I'd normally have class. I hadn't attended. This was all for show. Sadie Davis always seemed to know where I was. And she was always waiting for me to spot her in the crowd before she disappeared. It wouldn't be the first time she had appeared after one of my classes.

As we stepped outside, Eli dropped my hand. He went left and I went right. I had turned right out of this building dozens of times before. I glanced around. Sadie Davis wasn't in my line of sight. I squinted up at the building where V was supposed to be. There was a glint of his arrow in the sun, but anyone else would have missed it. I only recognized it because I knew he was there.

This is a terrible idea. I quickened my pace. The sooner I got to my mark, the sooner this whole thing would be over. Sadie Davis appearing made me stop in my tracks. She looked frazzled today, like she had gotten fashion advice from Liza. Her hair was unruly and her shirt was hanging off one shoulder.

A smile spread on her face as she lifted up one finger. Liza's words from last night came back to me. Was it three-two-one-go? Or was this it? The way she was smiling made it seem like this was the grand finale. I thought everything was supposed to slow down when you were about to die. But it felt like everything was speeding up. I saw Eli running up behind her.

"Can we talk?" I said, taking another step forward.

She shook her head and then turned around. She stopped when she saw Eli running toward her and turned back to me. Her eyes grew wide, like a caged animals'.

"I just want to talk," I said. "Please. I know who you are."

She ran to the side, off the path and screamed when an arrow landed in the grass in front of her feet. "You don't know what you're doing," she mumbled as she stepped backwards.

"You're my only family," I said. "Please, why are you doing this?"

"You don't know what you're doing," Sadie Davis repeated. "You don't know what you're doing." She sounded like a broken record as she backed up and collided right into Liza's hand.

Sadie Davis' body started convulsing and she fell to the ground, still shaking.

"Oh my God was that exhilarating," Liza said. She was holding out the taser she had just used on Sadie Davis. It looked like she was studying it.

I probably would have laughed if I wasn't in shock. None of that had been part of the plan. Where had Liza gotten a taser?

"What the hell, Liza?" Eli said as he sprinted up to them. "You were supposed to distract her until I got close enough to put her under, not tase her." He knelt down next to Sadie's body. "Where did you even get that thing?" He pulled a vial out of his pocket and placed it against the side of Sadie's neck. Her body immediately stopped shaking. She appeared to be unconscious.

"You walk around with a gun and V walks around with a bow and arrow," Liza said. "I thought I should have protection too."

"We have to get her out of here." Eli leaned down to lift up Sadie Davis' unconscious body.

"Class is about to let out," Liza said. "You have to make it look more natural. How about a piggy back ride?"

"Just fucking help me, Liza."

The two of them lifted up Sadie Davis and got her to look semi natural on Eli's back.

"You coming?" Liza said.

I just stood there. They had just unceremoniously kidnapped the person threatening me. Did that mean I was okay? Was I going to make it out of all of this alive? The hairs on the back of my neck prickled and I looked over my shoulder. Why did it still feel like someone was watching me?

"Don't you want to meet your aunt?" Liza asked, pulling me out of my thoughts. "What are you waiting for?"

I quickly caught up to them. There was no way I wanted to be left alone in the open like this. Just because Sadie Davis was unconscious didn't mean I was in the clear. I glanced at the woman on Eli's back. Up close, she didn't look as much like my mom. My mom had never grown old enough for wrinkles. My mom never crawled out of the bed looking like death either. I had to separate the two in my head if we were going to get through questioning. Because despite the differences, I wanted to hug Sadie Davis. I missed my mom every day. Seeing this woman who resembled her hurt my heart. It made me wonder what my mom would have looked like with wrinkles. Or if she had forgotten to comb her hair. Or if she was just still fucking alive.

I clenched my hand into a fist. Right now this woman wasn't my last living relative. She was my key to a puzzle I didn't understand. She was my last hope at getting some answers before the clock stopped.

CHAPTER 35
Thursday

"Let me speak to her alone first," I said.

Everyone was talking at the same time, trying to figure out how best to question Sadie Davis. No one even noticed that I had spoken. I quietly slipped away from them.

Sadie was tied up to some pipes on top of a building nearby V's place. That was one thing we had all agreed on. It was too dangerous to bring her to V's lair. We couldn't risk Don figuring out where it was. Seeing Sadie slumped forward with her wrists bound behind her reminded me of Eli being tied up several days ago. He had been proven innocent. Would she? Had we misjudged her too?

I looked over my shoulder. No one had followed me. No one had even noticed I was gone. I tried to push aside the eerie feeling that I was already slipping away as I walked toward Sadie. It didn't look like she was quite as out of it anymore. I sat down on the concrete a few feet away from her.

"Sadie?" I whispered, but she didn't respond. Maybe because that wasn't really her name. I studied the worry-line in the middle of her forehead and the crow's feet by her eyes. I tried to focus on what made her different from my mother. "Jane?" I said.

She blinked her eyes and slowly looked up at me. Her taunting smile was gone. She looked utterly terrified. I wasn't sure if it was because she was tied up or because she saw a little bit of herself in me too. She looked away from me and more panic rose to her face when she realized just how high up we were. No one would hear her scream. Just like no one had heard my screams when I lived with Don.

"You look just like my mom," I said. I had never been this close to her before. I had the undeniable urge to hug her. A stranger. A monster. *Stop.*

She shook her head. "No. Your mother looked like me. I was the older one." She pulled against the restraints. "Untie me."

I ignored her icy words. "What happened in the woods, Jane?"

"How do you even know I'm related to your mom? It's not like they kept a picture of me on the mantle."

"You're right. They didn't. But we ran a strand of your hair for DNA. It fell on the copy of Heart of Darkness you gave me."

"Well, it doesn't matter now." Her eyes frantically darted around, taking in our surroundings. "You have to untie me before it's too late."

"Tell me what happened and I will."

"Your mother ruined my life, that's what happened!"

"How?" I feared I knew how. Don had been following her. Jane had stepped in to protect her. That's what the reports made it seem like. That Jane had died saving my mom. But really she had been taken by the devil himself.

"Your mother always got everything she wanted because everyone loved her. And she loved being the center of attention. She couldn't get enough of it. She smiled too much. Her skirts were too short and her shirts too low. She was a naive, dumb girl."

"She was only 13."

"Of course you'd say that. You were only eight when she died. You never saw how self centered and egotistical she was!"

Her words made tears pool in my eyes. "People change, Jane. She was a wonderful mother. She was selfless, she always put me first."

Jane laughed. "She and my mom gave up on me. They thought I died and they just moved away and disappeared. I needed them and they ran away. That's not selfless."

No, it wasn't. But I understood the desire to run. Part of me wanted to run right now. I didn't want to know these things about my mom. I liked the memory of her I kept in a bubble. That bubble was about to pop. I took a deep breath. I needed to butter her up so she'd tell me what I wanted to know. "So you tried to save my mom in the woods? That was very selfless of you." And it was. It's possible that I never would have been born without Jane's sacrifice. I owed her my life. I owed her for the extra years my mom got to live.

"Saved your mom?" Jane laughed. "No."

"What do you mean? You fought him off. You..."

"I told him the truth. That your mother was a tease. That she would never give him what he wanted. That she wasn't woman enough for him. That she was just a dumb girl with a pretty face. She ran away because I made her cry. By telling her the truth that no one else would. That no one would ever see more to her than her beauty."

"That's not what the reports said."

"Of course not. Why would your mother tell them the truth that she didn't even want to hear?"

"I don't understand," I said. "They said there was blood. They found one of your shoes on the rocks."

"I hated being second. No one ever saw me. And that man in the woods was so handsome. When I saw him promising the world to her if they ran away together, it made my blood boil. She didn't have anything to run away from. I was the one that needed a fresh start. From her."

"What do you mean saw? Weren't you and my mom on a walk together?"

Jane laughed. "We never did anything together. I hated her. I always hated her. And when I saw that handsome guy that was too old for her, I intervened. I told him the truth. I told him everything he needed to know about my so called perfect sister. And even after everything I said, he ran after her. He was so blinded by infatuation that he couldn't even see it. That there was nothing behind her pretty face but a sad, pathetic girl."

There were a lot of things I could have focused on in that conversation. But there was one piece of information in the forefront that made my heart stop. "My mom knew him?"

"Knew him? She was dating his best friend. And honestly I wouldn't have been surprised if she had been screwing around with him behind her boyfriend's back. It's not like she was a good person."

What? That didn't make any sense. "It was Don in the woods, right? Don Roberts?"

"Yes. And he was so perfect. And so handsome."

Her words made me want to vomit.

"And when he came walking back through the woods, I knew she had told him no. He was wiping tears off his perfectly structured cheekbones. She broke his heart. Just like she did with everyone."

Don Roberts never cried. Don Roberts had no emotion but rage.

"So I promised him the world if he'd take me out of that dump of a town. I promised him everything he'd ever want if he took me with him."

"You chose to go with him?"

"I begged him to take me." A tear rolled down her cheek. "We staged a scene to make it look like I'd died. So that no one would look for me. So that I'd be free. I thought he was my knight in shining armor. But your mom tricked me. She ruined my life!"

"My mom didn't ruin your life, Jane. You ruined your own."

"I was only 16. I made a mistake. By taking her place, I saved your mother."

"No, you made a choice. You can't blame her for that."

"She ruined my life!" she repeated. "But you know that right? You know what kind of man he is? How he gets off on others' pain? How he wants you even more when you scream?"

I winced. "You knew he had me? You knew what he was capable of and you didn't do anything?"

"Do anything?" She smiled. "I thought it was fitting. It was justice for what your mom did to me."

"Justice? Are you joking?" Every word out of her mouth made my blood boil.

"It should have been her. And when I finally escaped, he kidnapped you to replace me. He wanted someone who looked just like me, and we do have a striking resemblance, don't you think? Maybe striking is a bad choice of words. But we look very similar."

I swallowed hard. "I don't think that's true."

"Well, it is."

"No," I said. "I don't think he wanted me because I looked like you. I think he wanted me because I looked like my mother."

"You don't know what you're talking about."

"Isn't that the only reason he agreed to take you with him? Because you looked like her?"

"Your mother looked like me. Not the other way around. I was born first! Why does everyone always overlook that very important fact?"

"But he was in love with her. Not you."

"You need to untie me. You don't know what you're doing."

"Who was my mother dating?"

"It doesn't matter. It's too late."

"Who was Don's best friend?"

She smiled. "You two have met. But he lied to you. He wasn't who he said he was. That's the thing about men. You can't trust them. None of them. And they only care about looks. Just take your father for instance. He never even knew your mother's real name. He never suspected a damn thing. He never even knew she was still in love with someone else. He was too stupid to..."

My hands were around her throat. I wasn't even sure how it happened. But there they were. I knew what it was like to be on the other side of this. And I was almost positive she had been in this position before. But I tightened my fingers anyway.

"Sadie, let go of her!" V yelled from behind me.

I tightened my fingers. This woman wasn't my relative. She hated my mother. She hated my father. She hated me.

"Summer, stop." Eli's voice echoed around me.

Hearing my real name made me immediately let go. I clasped my hands together. I wasn't a monster. I wasn't him. What was I doing?

Jane heaved and coughed.

I stared at her and I felt no sympathy. *I am a monster. I'm becoming him.* "My mother loved my father," I said. It was one of the only truths I knew. I needed to hold on to that. I was digging my fingernails into my palms so hard I thought I might have pierced the skin. "That was true love."

"True love? What are you, five? Stupid girl, just like your mom. She was still in love with her boyfriend from all those years ago. William Crawford."

Mr. Crawford? "No." My voice sounded small. "You should have seen the way she looked at my dad." It was one of the only things I could remember. The two of them dancing. Her laughing and smiling at him. I could never seem to remember her smiling at me. But I could picture that so clearly. They loved each other.

"She probably looked at him without any guilt because she was a terrible person. Haven't you been listening to anything I've said? God, I wouldn't even be surprised if William was your actual father. That's probably why he's helping you."

It felt like all the air left my lungs. "My father is David Brooks," I said as firmly as I could. But my mind was on Mr. Crawford. He was probably in his mid-forties, somewhere around the age my parents would have been. And he definitely wasn't who he said he was. But I had a father. I had the best father in the whole world. "My father is David Brooks," I said more firmly.

"Wrong tense, Summer. Your father *was* David Brooks. And your mother was a slut!"

It happened so fast it took me a moment to register the fact that V's fist slammed into Jane's jaw. I swore I heard a cracking noise.

She spit out some blood and stared at him.

"Don is going to kill your niece," V snarled. "Are you going to help us or not?"

"She's her mother's daughter and I want nothing to do with her," Jane said.

"You're her family."

"I have no family," she said.

"You have to help us." V's voice sounded desperate, like he was holding on to one last hope.

"It's too late. It's already written in her blood. You can't do anything about it. Her life is going to end tomorrow."

"In her blood? She's talking in riddles. We should probably tase her again," Liza said from behind us.

Jane laughed. "And it's not just her. You're all going to die. Don's going to take over this city and destroy it. Like he destroyed me. Like he destroyed you," she said and looked at me. "Like he destroyed your mom."

"What do you mean by that?" I asked. "Did Don kill my mom?"

She laughed. "What do you think?"

I suddenly realized I had a million questions to ask.

"Is Julie Harris still alive?"

She laughed. "What do you think?" she said again.

"Just tell me!"

"Finally," she said, breathing a sigh of relief. "Time's up."

I looked down at my chest. A red light was shining right in the center of it. With a quick glance I verified that each of my team members had a matching red dot on their chests as well.

"No one move," Eli said calmly.

"Now untie me," Jane said. "I've done my part. I'm finally free."

None of us moved.

"You," she said and nodded at Eli. "Untie me. Now. Or they'll shoot."

Eli slowly approached and reached behind her back.

"So that's it?" I said. "This is how we all die?"

"Oh no." Sadie Davis laughed. "No, not at all. That's going to end with quite the boom. And like I said before, it's not until tomorrow. Perfectly fitting. It is the anniversary of your parents' car accident, right?" She stood up as soon as Eli finished untying her. "Now if you'll all excuse me, I could really use a vacation." She walked past us toward the exit door on the roof. "Don't move an inch and you'll be allowed to live for one more day. If not, the game's over now."

"He's going to kill me!" I called after her. "You can stay and help us. You can get revenge for everything he's ever done to you."

"I want him to kill you. Don't you see, Summer? We made a deal. It's the only way I'll ever be free." She opened up the door and disappeared through it.

"No one move," Eli said calmly.

"This is why I wanted to stay in the shadows," Liza said. "If this doesn't kill us, I'm going to kill all of you!"

"Are you okay?" V said.

I hadn't realized how close he was to me. I didn't risk moving my head. "No."

"She faked her own death when she was 16. She's a liar, Sadie," V said. "You can't believe anything she said to you."

"It didn't seem like she was lying." And it didn't. Yes, she was clearly jealous of my mother. And a little insane. But she thought Mr. Crawford was my father. She thought my mom never loved my dad. She thought Julie was dead. She thought Don had killed my parents.

"I've pinpointed the four snipers," Eli said. "They're in four different buildings. 12 o'clock, 4 o'clock, 7 o'clock, and 8 o'clock. When they drop their targets, we each need to run to a building and find them."

"Like hell," Liza said. "My taser does not put up a fight against a sniper rifle. I'm going back to V's and I'm not leaving until the boom is over tomorrow or whatever that crazy person just said."

"One of them might have more answers."

"More answers? What other answers do we need than that?" Liza asked. "I'm not trying to die."

"Liza's right," I said. "It's over. That was our last chance..."

My words were drowned out by a loud booming noise. I glanced around, terrified that one of my friends had been shot. But we were all okay. The red lights on our chests all disappeared. We were in the clear. So what the hell was that noise?

"Over there," Liza said and pointed behind me.

I turned and saw smoke billowing over the edge of the building. I ran to the railing and looked down at the fiery explosion on the street. It look like a car bomb had been set off or something. There were flames everywhere.

"Get back!" Eli yelled. He grabbed my wrist and pulled me down just as another explosion went off. He kept his arms wrapped around me. "It was just a matter of time before the gas tank exploded too. Are you okay?"

My heart was beating out of my chest. "Was that Jane? Is she dead?"

"I don't know. We need to get you back to V's where it's safe."

I didn't protest as we all went back to V's. I didn't protest when they said Liza and I could stay there while they went out to see if they could locate the snipers or figure out if Jane was in the accident. I just stood there. Could Don really have killed my parents? Could Mr. Crawford be my biological father? Was Julie really dead? And I kept hearing a clock ticking down in my head. Tick tock. Tick tock. Tick tock.

"So you didn't think it was a good idea to mention that this whole countdown was leading up to the anniversary of your parents' deaths?" Liza said.

I didn't bother turning around to face her. "I didn't remember the day," I whispered.

"How could you not remember? You go around acting like it was the end of your life. If it was really that big of a deal how could you just forget?"

"I didn't forget." *I'd never forget that night.*

"Obviously you did or we would have known all along that tomorrow was your last day and..."

"I blocked it out, okay!?" I whipped around. "Don't you have something to do besides berate me?"

"What? Go follow a lead? We have nothing, Summer."

"Jane said that William Crawford was best friends with Don Roberts. Can't we use that to figure out who he actually is and find him? Maybe he is on our side. Maybe he can help us."

"Right, let me just pull up my best friend database," she said and rolled her eyes. "That information is useless. They were friends twenty years ago. It means nothing. What we need is a DNA sample to help us." She looked at me.

"You think he's my father?"

"I don't know. We could run it for a partial match. Jane said something about it being too late and that it was written in your blood. Maybe she's talking about the fact that you're related to Mr. Crawford."

It was crazy how much information you could get from a small sample of DNA. I lightly touched my wrist. My foundation had just been rocked. Not that I truly believed everything Jane had said. My mother was good. She was kind. But Jane's words stung. What if my mother wasn't who I thought she was? What if my father wasn't my father at all? "Can you really get that information from my blood?"

"It's not as good as a fingerprint for what I want to do, but it's something," Liza said.

"Oh my God." A light seemed to just go off in my head. "Holy shit." I started to walk past her. I felt so stupid. After getting the DNA sample from Heart of Darkness I should have put it together days ago.

"What?" she said as she watched me. "What's going on?"

I went into my bedroom and opened up my duffel bag. The copy of Harry Potter and the Sorcerer's Stone was sitting there. I walked back out and held it up. "Mr. Crawford put this book in my suitcase. He had to have touched it."

"Okay. And you're touching it now..."

"Sorry." I dropped it on the table in front of her. "But there's also a sticky note." I grabbed a pen and lifted the cover page, turning to the front page where my father had inscribed it. Mr. Crawford's post-it note was stuck on top of the inscription. I tried not to think about the fact that he had covered up my father's words with his own. "You can run it for prints."

"Have you touched that too?"

"Yeah, but so did he. And he touched the book too. Surely you can get a print."

"I'll definitely try. But, Summer, that's not going to tell us if you're related to Mr. Crawford."

I nodded. "I don't want to know." If I was going to die tomorrow, I'd die knowing who my parents were. My memory was all I had left. I didn't want to tarnish that.

"We might still need a blood sample if this doesn't work."

"Okay. Work on the print first. I'll be back soon."

"Where are you going?" she asked.

"Do you really care?" My words sounded harsh, but it was true. Liza and I were working toward a common goal, but we weren't friends. I was pretty sure she hated me.

She shrugged her shoulders. "V will want to know when he gets back."

Right. And you don't want to let him down. My next words weren't going to help with that, though. "I'm going to go talk to Miles."

"You can't do that. We all agreed..."

"It's my last night," I said firmly. "I'm not going to tell him anything. I just need to see him." I thought about the letter sitting in my backpack. I didn't know exactly what I was going to do yet, but I did need to see him. One last time. "It's not like I'm going to die tonight," I said and laughed awkwardly.

"Well, we won't know for sure until I run this." She turned back to the book. "Jane could have been lying about everything."

Maybe. But the lump in my throat really made it seem like Jane was telling the truth.

CHAPTER 36
Thursday

I touched my Sagitta pendant in my pocket. I had kept it there since V had given it back to me. For some reason I couldn't bring myself to put it back around my neck. It was almost like V handing it to me had taken away part of what made it special. It was a gift from Miles to me. I had put a chain on it and worn it around my neck because that's where it belonged. Next to where my heart beat.

And now it was almost done beating. My fingers tightened around the pendant. So why couldn't I put it back on? Was it because I didn't know if it belonged there anymore? I had feelings for V and Eli. But if I was being honest with myself, it wasn't the same way I felt about Miles. I didn't feel bad about that, though. I couldn't. What was the point of regretting my feelings when my whole life was a series of regrets? I didn't have the strength to feel any worse.

But I did feel guilty for a different reason. Miles deserved to know the truth. By this time tomorrow he would. By this time tomorrow it would also be too late. I let go of the pendant and let it settle back in my pocket. Tomorrow Miles would know and my guilt wouldn't be so heavy. I'd be able to put the necklace back on and I'd be wearing it when my heart stopped beating. No matter what. It belonged next to my heart.

It was possible that my parents' whole relationship was a lie. Which meant the only thing I knew for sure was that Miles loved me. And I loved him. That was it. Jane was wrong. True love did exist. My new appearance hadn't changed anything. We were drawn to each other just like we had been when we were kids.

I looked up at my dorm building. I still didn't know what I was going to do. It wouldn't be easy to slide the letter under his door and walk away, but it might be for the best. Luckily, I had time to decide because I had written a letter to Kins too, thanking her for being such a good roommate. I waved my access card against the scanner and the doors clicked open.

Recently I had taken the stairs. But tonight I felt weak. I wasn't sure if I could climb that many stories. So I hit the button for the elevator. I was relieved to see that no one else was in it when the doors dinged open.

I stepped off the elevator and the hallway was empty. It was past 9 o'clock on a Thursday. Students were probably out getting wasted, doing normal college things. I made my way down the hall and stopped outside of my room. There was no reason to knock. Kins wasn't there. She spent all her time with Patrick. I knew what young love was like. It was supposed to be all-encompassing. I leaned down and slid my letter to her under the door.

The hallway was still empty as I approached Miles' door. I looked down at the letter in my hand. I loved him. I couldn't tell him who I was right now. But I could show him. A letter wasn't enough. I definitely needed to show him. I needed him to know. I knocked on his door.

But there was no answer.

I knocked again. *Please, Miles. I need you.*

But he wasn't there.

I looked back down at the letter in my hands. Maybe this was how it was supposed to be. I thought about his hand in mine in his tree house. And his lips brushing against mine on my grandmother's roof. And our kiss in Central Park. I wiped a tear from beneath my eyes. *No.* None of this was how it was supposed to be. We were supposed to live happily ever after.

I leaned down and slid the letter under his door. It seemed harsh to end it with a letter. But our letters were what had torn us apart in the first place. I wished I had never stopped writing to him. I wished I had never let my heart fill with hate. I knocked one more time even though I knew it was useless. I pressed my palm against the door and then I walked away.

At first I felt numb. But then it felt like I couldn't breathe. I touched the pendant in my pocket, but it didn't calm me down. I was falling. And no one was there to catch me. I took a huge gulp of air. I needed the stars. I fucking hated this city. I needed to scream at the top of my lungs. I needed to touch the sky.

I opened up the door to the stairs. I knew I wouldn't be able to get up on the roof like Miles had that night. He had a key. But I needed to try. I couldn't breathe. I was running out of heartbeats. I was running out of breaths. I was running out of reasons to keep living.

When I reached the top I jiggled the handle of the door. It was locked. *No.* I pounded my hand against the door. *Someone help me. Please.* I pounded my hand against the door again. I was going to run out of time in this dingy stairwell.

But then there was a clicking noise and the door opened. And he was there. And the fresh air filled my lungs. Or maybe it was just the sight of him that made me feel like I could breathe again. "Miles."

He smiled out of the corner of his mouth. "Sadie."

I stepped onto the roof and stared at him. For some reason, I thought I was imagining him. It wouldn't be the first time. I used to dream of him all the time. But this wasn't a dream. His presence calmed me like only he could. His body radiated warmth. He smelled like home. He was everything to me. I swallowed hard. I thought I needed the stars, but that wasn't true. I needed him. And that damn smile.

I grabbed the front of his t-shirt, stood on my tiptoes, and kissed him. I think that maybe my heart started beating when I met him. He might be the only thing that kept it going all these years. And kissing him jumpstarted it again. I needed him to understand that. A letter wasn't enough. It would never be enough.

And I knew he felt it too. He moved forward, pressing my back against the door, sandwiching me in place. He made the ticking in my head slow. But it was still there. I was still running out of time. I needed more.

I ran my fingers down the front of his shirt to the waistline of his pants.

"Sadie," he groaned. "The last time we kissed, you freaked out and ran away."

I undid the button of his jeans and slowly unzipped them.

"We should slow down." He grabbed my hand and lifted it away from him.

But that wasn't going to stop me. "I don't want to slow down, Miles. I want you."

"You can't just keep showing up and pretending everything is okay." His Adam's apple slowly rose and fell as he stared down at me.

"I'm not pretending." I swallowed hard. He already felt my distance. He could feel my lies. Could he feel me slipping away?

"Jesus, you're crying."

Before I could reach down to wipe my tears, he pulled back and lightly brushed my tears away with his thumbs. There was something so intimate about the action. It made my tears run faster.

"Talk to me," he said. "Tell me what's wrong."

"Nothing's wrong. I..."

"Sadie." He lowered his eyebrows slightly. "Talk to me. Please. Let me in."

I wanted to. I wanted to be able to tell him everything. He deserved that. "I don't want to talk," I said instead. I wanted to show him how I felt. I tilted my hips slightly so I'd rub against his erection. He said he wanted to go slow, but he was rock hard. He wanted this too.

"Fuck." He grabbed both sides of my face, but didn't pull away from me. "I told you that you weren't like other girls. This isn't about sex for me. Please tell me why you're crying. Please talk to me. I care about you." He wiped my tears away with his thumbs again.

Before I could stop myself, I said the one thing I could say without telling him the whole truth. "I'm in love with you, Miles. I've been in love with you ever since I met you. And no matter how hard I try, I can't stay away from you. It's like I'm magnetized to you." I realized I was holding a fistful of his shirt, keeping him in place. A part of me was terrified that he was going to run away. I needed him to stay for just a few minutes so that I could keep breathing. "It's like you said. It's easier to breathe when we're together."

"Sadie..."

"It's okay." I felt my heart sinking. I quickly shook my head. I didn't really expect him to say it back. He had already told me he still loved Summer Brooks. He didn't know it was me. He couldn't know. But I wanted to know what it felt like to be loved. I couldn't remember. I wanted to remember before I died. "You don't have to say it back. I just...that's why I was crying. Because my feelings for you are all consuming. And for one night I just want to know what it feels like to be loved back. Maybe you could pretend that it's you and me written in the stars? For just one night?"

"Haven't you been listening to me?" He smiled out of the corner of his mouth. "I don't need to pretend with you, Sadie Davis."

I imagined him saying Summer Brooks as I breathed in his exhales.

"I've never pretended with you," he said against my lips.

"Then show me what it feels like to be alive." I grabbed the back of his head and kissed him again. My whole world was suddenly in color once more. I clung to him because I needed him to remind me what it felt like to love. To live. To remember a time when we made sense. When I was in his arms, I was complete. There was no ticking clock. There was no sense of doom. I was at peace. Screw what anyone else thought. True love did exist. This was our own twisted love story. And I wasn't going to let it end before discovering everything it could have been.

I swore I heard him groan when my hands wandered beneath his shirt, exploring his chiseled abs. And I know I moaned when his palms slid against my skin, pushing my shirt up. I tilted my head back as he kissed the side of my neck. This was how it was always meant to be. Him and me beneath the stars.

He pushed my shirt up past my ribs and I lifted my arms in the air as he slowly peeled the fabric away. He made short work of my bra too. I knew he was experienced. But to me, it almost felt like he knew we were running out of time too. And that this was our last chance to be together.

"God you're beautiful." He grabbed my ass and lifted my legs around his waist. I breathed in his familiar scent. The only smell in the world that made me feel content. I let the smell consume me as he lowered me onto the cold roof of the building.

"We can go back to my room if..."

"No." I grabbed both sides of his face. "I've never been so close to touching the sky."

He didn't tell me I was crazy. He didn't say he didn't know how to fly. Instead, he leaned down and kissed the inside of my ankle.

God.

He left a trail of soft kisses up the inside of shin and thigh. And then he moved to my other ankle and made his torturous ascent.

"Miles," I panted, catching both sides of his face when he reached the top of my thigh. His eyes landed on my breasts.

My chest rose and fell because of him. I didn't have to say that. He felt it too, right? He had to. It had always been us. His fingers slowly unzipped my jean shorts. I lifted my hips so he could lower my shorts and thong down my thighs. Slowly. So fucking slowly.

"Miles, please."

He placed his hands on the insides of my thighs, slowly spreading them apart. His thumbs traced gentle circles at the apex of my thighs. "I feel like I've been waiting to taste you my whole life."

I knew what he meant. He just didn't realize how true what he said was. I closed my eyes when he thrust his tongue deep inside of me. And I saw the stars brighter than I ever did with my eyes open. He devoured me like he was starving. Like I was the only thing that could possibly sustain him. Maybe I was. Because he certainly was the only thing that could sustain me.

My hips rose to meet him, but he pushed me back down with his strong hands, holding me in place. He rubbed his nose against my clit and the most perfect feeling overcame me.

"Miles!" My eyes fluttered open and I stared at the stars as I shattered into a million pieces. I squinted and saw Sagitta. I saw our constellation. And I knew what it was like to fly. I knew what it was like for my body to be worshipped. I knew what it was like to be truly loved. If I died right now, I'd die happy.

But then my eyes met his. And just from his gaze I knew it was going to get even better. I watched him wipe his mouth with the back of his hand as he knelt before me. He grabbed his t-shirt by the nape of its collar and started to pull it off over his head.

He had the body of soccer player. Lean, toned muscles. Skin tanned from the sun. When he removed his shirt completely, I'm pretty sure I stopped breathing. There it was. The tattoo that Kins so desperately wanted to see. The one that couldn't be seen in any of his pictures. But it wasn't for her or for anyone else's eyes. I reached out and ran my index finger along the small arrow tattooed on his left peck. *Sagitta.* It was for me. Because he wanted me close to his heart. Just like I had worn my pendant close to my heart all these years. We belonged next to each other's heartbeats.

I pressed my palm against his tattoo. I could feel his heart beating against my hand. I had been waiting my whole life for this moment. The past didn't matter. The future didn't matter. It was just this moment. This one perfect moment we had carved out in time. "Make love to me, Miles," I whispered.

He leaned forward, placing his hands on the ground on either side of my face. He kissed my forehead and the tip of my nose before brushing his lips against mine. He kept one hand by my head as the other trailed down my body. Down my collarbone, over my right breast, down my torso, until he found my hip. "You're perfect."

I'm not. If only you knew.

"You." He kissed the bottom of my chin. "Are." He kissed my clavicle. "Perfect," he repeated, as if he could read my thoughts.

I quickly blinked away the tears in my eyes. He always had been able to read my thoughts. And he knew I needed him too. Because he thrust inside of me harder than I expected.

There was no hesitancy. No questions. We belonged together. That was clear as day. And God did he feel amazing. There was no better feeling in the world than coming together with your destiny. We always had been written in the stars.

He slowed his pace, and it somehow filled me even more.

Jesus. I arched my back, giving him full access to my body. His lips encircled my nipple and he gently bit down.

I wasn't going to be able to take this for long. I hadn't even come down from my high from earlier and I was already about to let go again. Nothing had ever felt this amazing. Nothing had ever felt this right.

"Don't you ever think this is pretend," he whispered in my ear. "Don't you ever stop believing in what we have. Don't you ever diminish this to something else."

In his own way, I think he was asking me to not let go of hope. But how could he know that I was? And how did he know that he was the only thing making me hold on?

My fingertips dug into the skin on his shoulders. "I love you Miles Young," I whispered into the darkness. *I've always loved you.*

He didn't say it back. And I was glad he didn't. Part of me thought it might feel like a betrayal to hear it out loud.

But I felt it. I knew he loved me too. I felt it with each kiss on my skin. With each thrust of his cock. With each groan that fell from his lips. It was better that it was left unspoken. Hearing something and experiencing it were very different. I'd take the experience any day.

"Come for me," he said and kissed the side of my neck. "I need to feel you."

"Not yet. Please not yet." This couldn't be over. This was my last chance at living.

"This isn't the end, Sadie." He pulled back slightly and smiled down at me. That smile I loved so much. "It's only just the beginning."

I felt the twitch of his cock and I immediately let go. I clenched around him and I savored the feeling of how warm he felt inside of me. I flew high.

But then I crashed low. So fucking low. Because he was wrong. This wasn't the beginning, it was the end. We began when I was six and he was eight. And we ended now. Tonight. Under the stars. I reached up and pushed his hair off his forehead like I always wished I could do.

He groaned as he rolled over, pulling me on top of him.

I looked down at the tattoo on his chest. *Forgive me*, I silently pleaded. I kissed his tattoo. I kissed every inch of him I could reach. I tried to kiss away his years of pain. He was broken because of me. I just hoped one night of my love was enough to heal him. I hoped that he'd keep breathing even when I stopped.

He ran his fingers through my hair. "That was amazing. You're amazing."

I'm not. I ran my index finger along the arrow on his heart. "Thank you for tonight, Miles. But I should go."

He lowered his eyebrows. "Thank you? What is that supposed to mean?"

I climbed off his lap and started to pull on my clothes that were scattered about the roof. "Thank you for showing me what it was like to truly live." *Every day you showed me that. But tonight...tonight you made me fly.* I grabbed the doorknob.

"Don't leave. Stop running." He stood up and yanked his pants on, like he was going to come after me.

"I have to go."

"You can't leave me." There was so much emotion in his voice. It's what I had thought he said when I ran away from him after our kiss in Central Park. I thought I had imagined it. But he had just said it again. It was almost like he knew what was going to happen once I walked away. He knew our time was over. I stared at him. His jeans were still unzipped. His hair was sticking up from the way I had grabbed it. His shirt was still on the ground. He was perfect. My eyes gravitated down to his tattoo. So perfect.

When my eyes met his, I almost gave in. I could feel his pain. I'm sure the look in his eyes was a reflection of my own. Tears brimming at the surface. Tired bags underneath. He looked exhausted. And broken. I hadn't been able to heal him. I had probably made it worse. Coming here had been selfish.

Jane's words about my mother came back to me. Maybe I was more like my mom than I thought. Maybe we were both evil. But Miles would never turn into a monster like Don had. Miles could never be bad. His heart was too pure. His love was too strong to be conquered by hate the way mine had been. *Don't let me break you. Don't let me ruin you. I'm sorry. I'm sorry. I'm sorry.*

"I left you a note under your door," I said. "It explains everything. Please wait until tomorrow morning to open it. I'm so, so sorry, Miles. But I do love you. And I'm so grateful for every moment we ever had together."

"Sadie!" He called after me as the door closed.

I knew he said Sadie. I knew it. So why had it sounded like Summer? I started to run down the stairs. I remembered him calling after me as I ran away from his tree house the night my parents had died. The most perfect moment had turned into one of the worst. But this time I was prepared. I knew what was going to happen as I ran away from him.

I knew that I was breathing my last breaths as my feet hit the pavement. My lungs were filling for the last time. Tomorrow he'd know the truth about who I was. And tomorrow I'd be gone. He had given me the gift of being Summer one last time. He had always been my only reason to keep living.

I kept running. And running. And running. Closer and closer to the end.

CHAPTER 37
Friday

I touched the pendant around my neck. I had put it back on next to my heart. Where it belonged. Thinking about Miles made it hard to breathe. He would have opened the letter by now. He'd know I was Summer. He'd be hurting. I wondered if his hand would be on his chest too. I wondered if he had the same habits as me. Holding on to something that wasn't there.

I looked back down at the reports about William Crawford that Liza had generated. There wasn't that much information about him. He moved a lot. He had lived near my grandmother's house for awhile. He had lived near my last home with my parents. He had always been nearby before my parents died. So why was that?

Jane's answer was an obvious one. Because he was having an affair with my mom. That didn't necessarily mean he was my father though. And it wasn't the only logical conclusion. Maybe he was stalking my mom. Maybe he was crazy like Don. Or maybe he was just an old friend. *God.* I put my face in my hands. How could my mom have cheated on my dad? How could she?

"Do you want us to run the blood test?" Liza asked.

Her voice made me jump. I had lashed out at everyone this morning. They had been keeping their distance. "No, that's okay." I looked back down at the papers.

"We could really use some more information. If he's your father..."

"I have a father," I said firmly.

"We need help. If you die..." her voice trailed off. "It doesn't end there, Summer. Don's going to ruin this city. This is my home. I want to help stop him. Mr. Crawford might be able to help us. He's not in the city or my facial recognition software would have found him. We need more information."

If I die. It wasn't a matter of if. It was when. The ticking was driving me crazy. It was like it was reverberating through my whole body. Each inhale I took could be my last one. I sighed and put my arm out.

"Thank you." Liza sat down in the chair beside mine. Apparently she had assumed my answer because she already had a needle in her hand. I turned away. I knew the needle would sting. But I had certainly felt worse.

What I didn't expect was to hear Liza shriek in my ear.

I turned to see the needle snapped off, sticking out of my arm.

"What the hell, Liza?" I said. "I thought you knew what you were doing?" I grabbed the needle but her hand wrapped around mine, stopping me.

"Don't touch it. V!" Liza called. "V!" She slapped my hand off the needle.

He came running out of the room he kept locked. "What's wrong? Is she okay? Are you okay?" He knelt down by my side.

"I'm fine. Liza's just terrible with needles."

He looked up at the needle sticking out of my arm.

"I'm not terrible at it," she said defensively. "But I hit something."

"What do you mean hit something?" V stood up and looked at the needle.

"I don't know," Liza said. "There's something hard under her skin. It snapped the needle in half."

"It's written in blood," I said slowly. "That's what Jane said. That there was nothing we could do because it was written in blood. It's in my blood!"

"You think Don put something under your skin?" It looked like Liza wanted to throw up.

"He also wrote, "Your Move," in blood on my arm. Right near where this needle is."

"That's disgusting." Liza put her hand over her mouth.

"How did you not find this when I asked you to search her wrist earlier?" V asked.

"What are you talking about?" Liza said. "You never asked me to check her wrist."

"Yes I did. Well, I told Sadie. Don't you remember, Sadie? After I helped you get away from those guys at the hotel? I told you to get Liza to check your wrist."

"I thought you meant because I hurt my arm, V. Because of slamming against the building. But I was fine. I didn't tell Liza about it."

"Jesus." He ran his hands down his masked face. "We have to get it out. The Helspet Mafia is known for wearing tracking devices so that backup can always find them. I'm surprised they're not knocking down the door right now."

"But it's not her wrist," Liza said. "It's her forearm. And if it was a tracking device, you're right, they'd be here by now."

V was already walking toward the kitchen. He pulled a drawer open, slamming it against its hinges.

"What's going on?" Eli asked. He had just emerged from the room V kept locked.

I didn't have time to focus on what mysterious things they were doing behind that door. "What's in my arm then?"

V lifted up a knife. "A tracking device."

"V." My heart was racing too fast. The ticking was taking over my mind. "But Liza just said..."

"What else could it be? It's just a tracking device. Now let's get it out." He tore off one of his gloves and tossed it at me. "Bite down on that. Liza boil some water for me. There's a sewing kit in a drawer in the bathroom. Sterilize one of the needles."

"Whoa." Eli stepped in front of V. "What the hell are you doing, man?"

"We're pretty sure there's a tracking device in Sadie's arm. We need to cut it out."

Fuck. This was going to hurt a lot more than a needle. I lifted up the glove and put it in my mouth.

Eli knelt down beside me and slipped his hand into mine. "Hey, look at me."

I locked eyes with him.

"It's okay, Summer. I'm right here. V's going to get it out and..."

I screamed into the glove. Tears streamed down my cheek. I remembered the knife cutting into my stomach. I remembered the feeling of metal inside of me.

Eli grabbed my chin and turned my face back to his. "Just a few more seconds. Take a deep breath."

And then the pain felt muted. I looked down and V was already stitching up the small cut in my arm.

"See. Just a tracking device." He lightly patted my back and tossed the small piece of bloody metal down onto the glass table. "Are you okay?" He turned my face away from Eli and removed the glove from my mouth. He gently ran his fingers through my hair.

I slowly nodded. I was fine. I was used to pain. But for some reason my tears didn't stop. The tracking device was written in my blood. It was supposed to be the answer. But it was nothing. It was just how Jane always knew where I'd be. It was why it always felt like someone was watching me.

V lifted up my arm and wrapped some gauze around it. Eli stayed crouched beside me, gently rubbing my knee. They weren't fighting. They were just supporting me. I felt a little dizzy when I saw the blood seeping through the bandage.

"Um...you guys?" Liza said. "It's...well, it's...vibrating."

We all turned toward the small device. And then it moved, leaving a small trail of blood on the table behind it. And a few seconds later it moved again.

The ticking. I had felt it pulsing inside of me.

"It's a bomb," V said. "It would explain why they couldn't find a bomb in that car explosion yesterday. Maybe it was inside of Jane."

"I don't think there are any bombs that small," Liza said. "It's so tiny. Right?"

Eli picked it up. "Shit." He popped something off the top of it. "Shit, shit, shit!" His eyes darted around the apartment.

"Is it a bomb?" Liza yelled. "Throw it out the window!"

"I can't throw it out the window. There's innocent civilians out there!"

"I'm an innocent civilian!" she yelled. "Throw it out the damn window!"

"Everyone get to the bunker," V said calmly and grabbed the device out of Eli's hand. "Now."

Eli grabbed me by the hand and pulled me to the room that V always kept locked. I would have protested, but I froze when I stepped inside. It was at least twice as big as the bedroom. And the walls were covered in photos. Lines of yarn connected pictures with dates. And they weren't just recent pictures. I stared at the smiling face of an eight year old with no worries or fears. My smiling face.

My eyes shifted to my parents. Miles. Miles' family. Don. Mr. Crawford. Julie and her fiancé, Jacob. Jane. My grandmother. Kins. Patrick. Liza. Eli. The pictures of Liza and Eli were crossed out, like they had been eliminated from suspicion. V had been watching me since I was a kid. It didn't start here. It went back further than I even knew.

The door slammed shut behind us.

"Where did you put it?" Liza asked.

"The freezer," V said.

"That's not going to work! It couldn't possibly contain the blast. If it's the same bomb that blew up that car, it's going to blow up the whole apartment!"

"We're safe in here."

"Not if the floor collapses!"

"This room is secure," Athena's smooth voice said over the speaker system. "Please turn your attention to channel five while I assess the threat level."

The room was eerily silent as V picked up a remote and turned on the TV in the corner.

A reporter was on the screen, announcing the nightly news. "We just received word of some breaking news," the reporter said and placed his index finger on the side of his ear like he was listening to something. "Police believe that the fatal car crash that occurred on Broad Street yesterday was no accident. An unidentified woman was killed in the crash and several others remain in the hospital under critical condition. The lead suspect is wanted for homicide and other charges and is suspected to be armed and highly dangerous."

An image of me with my brown hair and brown eyes showed up on the screen. The picture from my fake driver's license.

"The suspect's name is Sadie Davis," the reporter continued. " Again, she is suspected to be armed and highly dangerous, so police advise that you do not engage. Any information of her whereabouts or information regarding the crash should be reported to the hotline number below immediately. Now, back to our regularly scheduled news. A new candidate for mayor has joined the race," he said in an upbeat voice. An image of Don appeared on the screen.

"Oh my God," I said. "That's not possible. He has a criminal record. How is that possible?" I thought about when I went to report everything to the police. They didn't believe me. They said Don Roberts didn't have a rap sheet.

"His slogan is already hitting the streets of NYC with buzz," the reporter said. "He's asking the people of our city to join together, saying it's 'your move', NYC."

Your move. I thought about the message written in blood on my arm. It was a nod to me. He was doing this because of me.

"Well, now can we change your identity like I wanted to do in the first place?" Liza asked. "We should probably start by cutting this," she said and lifted up a strand of my hair. "A new color too. And a new name. And drop the brown contact lenses, they're not fooling anyone. They slide too much when you cry."

"Liza, shut the hell up," Eli said. "Summer, are you okay?"

"Am I okay?" What kind of question was that? "Of course I'm not okay. How is he doing it? How is he controlling everyone? What are we missing?" This couldn't be happening. Liza was worried he was going to destroy this city as a thug. What was going to happen when he was the mayor and he controlled everything? *Fire.* I could already see the flames he'd unleash.

"Threat level 10 out of 10," Athena said over the speakers. "Brace for impact."

V grabbed me and pulled me into his chest. "I don't love a piece of you," he whispered in my ear. "I love all of you. And I'm sorry I didn't tell you that sooner. I love you, Summer Brooks. I love you."

A booming noise echoed around the room and I wrapped my arms around V's back. I waited for the floor to collapse like Liza said. I waited for the room to melt. But nothing happened.

He loved me? I had broken all of their trust by telling Miles the truth. And I didn't know what they'd do once they found out. I had just set in motion a way to ruin my support system. To destroy my team. I had bet against us. I had believed that I was going to die. And now everything was broken. V had told me he loved me because for a second he let his fears take over. He didn't mean it. He couldn't mean it. I was in love with Miles. So why was I still clinging to V like he was my only source of life?

I immediately stepped back from him.

Eli's phone started ringing. He pulled it out of his pocket and looked down at the screen. "They know I'm working your case, Summer. They want me to bring you in." He locked eyes with me.

"Maybe you should," I said. They were all better off without me. "We tried to figure it out on our own. And it just escalated to a whole new level. Don has everyone after me. And meanwhile he's running for mayor? What the hell is going on? None of us are safe. You should take me in. Do it. Please, just do it." I held out my wrists to him.

"Stop," V said and pushed my wrists back down. "No one is turning you in. We'll figure this out just like we planned to do. This is just a minor setback."

"Minor? Athena, open the door," I said. The door swung open and a blast of heat hit us. I was staring out at the side of the building next to V's. The whole wall had been destroyed. *Shit.* Everything was destroyed. The floor had collapsed, just like Liza had said. People were screaming outside. Papers fluttered around in the chaos. It was all gone. "That bomb was inside of me," I said. "It could have killed all of us. Don wanted it to kill all of us. You have to turn me in."

"And it didn't," Eli said. "We're not turning you in. They think you killed Jane. They're not going to try to help you. They're going to finish you the way Don wants." Eli dropped his phone on the ground and stomped on it with his foot. "We're not going to let that happen. We need to disappear. All of us."

I shook my head. "You can't. It's suicide."

"Agreed. You can count me out," Liza said.

"You're a part of this, whether you want to be or not," Eli said. "It's too late, Liza."

Everyone was quiet.

All the hurt. I swallowed hard. All the lies. I wasn't made of steel, because I felt like my body was burning to ash along with V's apartment. I breathed in and let the feeling of fire expand in my body.

I felt V's hand slip into mine. Eli placed his hand on my shoulder.

"Fine," Liza said from behind me. "Luckily Athena's hardware was in here. We'll need a new headquarters."

The smell of smoke filled my lungs. And I realized just how much I loved the feeling of fire. Flames were empowering. I was going to burn everything in my path until this ended. Maybe Jane was right. Maybe my mom was a villain. Maybe I was a villain. My flames had already lit my friends afire. They'd burn. They'd burn because of me.

I held my breath, letting the warm feeling of flames lap against my lungs. For one second.

Jane thought it would end with me. But I was still here. I was still breathing.

For two seconds.

I stared out at the chaos.

For three seconds.

There was only one way to stop a fire. You had to cut it off from oxygen. Don needed to stop breathing. That was the only answer I could see.

For four seconds.

I needed to stop running. I needed to face him head on. Just like he said, it was my move.

For five seconds.

I closed my eyes, and all I could see were flames.

LETTERS FROM MILES

Want to read more about what Miles was up to while
Summer was in foster care?

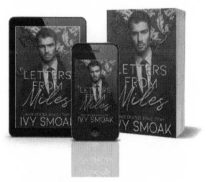

Letters from Miles contains the letters he sent Summer over
the years they were apart. The letters that she never received…

To get your free copy of *Letters From Miles*, go to:

www.ivysmoak.com/forged-in-flames-amz

CARVED IN ICE

It's time to unmask V!

Find out his secret identity in book 3 of the Made of Steel
Series, *Carved in Ice*…available now!

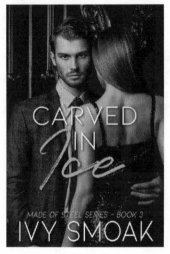

A NOTE FROM IVY

Summer Brooks. My heart hurts. There isn't much else to say. I'm a complete mess. My fiancé told me I couldn't work on the rest of this series until after our wedding. It's like this darkness has settled over me while I wrote this story. I'm too invested, if that's even possible.

But guess what? You're one of the lucky readers that discovered my books after I got hitched. So book 3 is ready for you right now!

And it's finally time to figure out who V is! I promise this time. He's about to be unmasked for real for real. And I think you're going to be surprised about who's under there. Ah I'm so excited!

Ivy Smoak

Ivy Smoak
Wilmington, DE
www.ivysmoak.com

ABOUT THE AUTHOR

Ivy Smoak is the international bestselling author of the *Made of Steel Series* and *The Hunted Series*. When she's not writing, you can find her binge watching too many TV shows, taking long walks, playing outside, and generally refusing to act like an adult. She lives with her husband in Delaware.

Twitter: @IvySmoakAuthor
Facebook: IvySmoakAuthor
Goodreads: IvySmoak

Recommend *Forged in Flames* for your next book club!

Book club questions available at:
www.ivysmoak.com/bookclub